He was tall, ... d
he wa... ...

"Hello, my name's Jericho Becton. Have we met before? You look very familiar."

Talisa smiled and shook her head, her gaze sweeping over the man's face. From the other side of the reception her friends were calling her name. Their voices momentarily pulled her attention away, but in a heartbeat, her glance returned to the man standing in front of her.

She stammered searching for her words as she stood lost in the sensation of her small hand resting in the warmth of his large palm.

"I...I was just...thinking the same thing," she finally managed to say. All of a sudden, the room seemed to spin in a slow circle around her.

"You don't look like you are having a good time," Jericho said.

"Have you been watching me?" Talisa asked coyly, her excitement now shining brightly from her dark eyes. Her hand was still held hostage in his firm grasp.

"I couldn't help myself," Jericho answered, his voice dropping to a seductive whisper.

Books by Deborah Fletcher Mello

Kimani Romance

In the Light of Love

Kimani Press Arabesque

Take Me to Heart
A Love for all Time
The Right Side of Love
Forever and a Day
Love in the Lineup

DEBORAH FLETCHER MELLO

is the author of five Kimani Arabesque romance novels. Her first novel, *Take Me to Heart,* earned her a 2004 Romance Slam Jam nomination for Best Author. In 2005 she received Book of the Year and Favorite Heroine nominations for her novel *The Right Side of Love.*

For Deborah, writing is akin to breathing and she firmly believes that if she could not write she would cease to exist. Weaving a story that leaves her audience feeling full and complete, as if they've just enjoyed an incredible meal, is an ultimate thrill for her. Born and raised in Connecticut, she now calls Hillsborough, North Carolina, home, where she resides with her husband, son and two dogs.

Deborah
Fletcher Mello

IN THE
LIGHT
LOVE
of

KIMANI
ROMANCE

To the children of Uganda,
You have not been forgotten,
And you are remembered with much love.

 KIMANI PRESS™

ISBN-13: 978-0-373-86006-7
ISBN-10:   0-373-86006-4

IN THE LIGHT OF LOVE

www.kimanipress.com

Printed in U.S.A.

Dear Reader,

I have an emotional attachment to my stories. Each has been fueled by an experience that has stayed with me, haunted me, encouraged me and motivated me to capture the moment as eloquently in words as was humanly possible.

In the Light of Love was one of the stories that I wanted to tell, needed to tell and fought to write with the emotion and passion of the experience itself. I hope that you enjoy it. I hope that it inspires you to reach out to someone in need, to question what you might not know and to find the light that burns especially for you.

Many thanks to all of you for your continued support. Please visit me at my Web site (www.deborahmello.com) and continue to send me your comments.

With much love,

Deborah Fletcher Mello

Chapter 1

The first wave of intravenous medication had quickly dulled the blinding pain that had cut through her abdomen only moments before. Talisa London could breathe again and she gulped oxygen, fearful that it might be denied.

From some distant place above her, a male voice was eerily calming, the deep tone even and controlled as the man explained the impending procedure, assuring her it would be quick, and over before she knew it. As she felt her body being lifted from the gurney onto the operating table, panic swept over her. A large, brown hand that patted her gently against her bare shoulder instantly soothed the fright-filled emotion.

"You're doing very well," Dr. Jericho Becton whispered softly, warm breath blowing against her ear. "Everything's going to be just fine." His voice was melodic, a soothing bass tone that eased right through her.

Focusing her attention upward, Talisa's eyes met his, her stare floating up to his intense gaze. His eyes reminded her of the ocean, the irises a deep, blue-green liquid balm. The black lashes were forest thick; long, luscious, enviable strands. The warmth he exuded was consuming and she could feel herself swimming in his gaze, the sensation like a warm wet blanket wrapping around her. There was something ultra-soothing about his stare and when he smiled, she willed herself to smile back. An anesthesiologist placed a mask over her nose and mouth, instructing her to breathe deeply.

"That's a good girl, deep breaths," Dr. Becton said, echoing his associate, the warmth of his hand still pressed against her shoulder.

Talisa stared upward, her smile widening. "You're very sweet," she said, mumbling into the mask. "And you have beautiful eyes. I think I could love you," she chimed, her eyelids fluttering open and then closed. As drug-induced sleep tiptoed in to possess her, Talisa heard the man laugh, a faint "thank you" echoing into her dreams.

"Talisa? Are you sleeping, baby?"

Talisa opened her eyelids to find her mother staring down at her. She blinked quickly, wiping at her face with the length of her fingers. Lifting herself up against the bed pillows, she yawned widely. "No, ma'am. I think I just dozed off for a quick moment."

Mary London smiled at her daughter. "You was asleep. I woke you up. Sorry 'bout that, but it's time for your medicine. That doctor said you had to take your medicine every four hours." The woman glanced down to the Timex watch on her wrist. "It's past time."

Talisa nodded, extending her hand for the antibiotic and

pain medication her mother was holding out toward her. As the small pills settled against her tongue, she reached for the cup of chipped ice and cold water the matriarch passed her way.

It had been one week since Talisa had been rushed to Atlanta's Northside Hospital with a ruptured appendix. She could have kicked herself for ignoring the initial pangs of hurt that had teased her only days before. High doses of aspirin had dulled the ache just enough for her to consider it of little importance. A sprained muscle, she'd thought, remembering an aerobics class that had taxed her body's limits. Then, out of the blue, agonizing pain had hit her broadside, crippling her movements and sending her straight to the floor.

She shook her head at the memory. Everything after that moment, from the ambulance ride to the operating room, was nothing but a blur. As Talisa reflected back, one memory swept over her. She smiled, and as she did, her mother gave her a strange look.

"What?" Mary asked, fluffing the pillows behind her daughter's head. "What are you grinning about?"

"I just remembered this man in the operating room who had blue eyes. I think I told him I loved him."

Mary frowned. "There were lots of men in that hospital with blue eyes now. That nice Dr. Pearson has 'em, and that tall boy, the nurse. What was his name?"

"Tim, I think."

"That's it. Tim. He had blue eyes, too. But I know you were not serious about being in love with one of them." The woman frowned, the lines deepening against her dark complexion.

Talisa shook her head, two shoulder-length ponytails swaying back and forth against the sides of her skull.

"No. This man was African-American. He was Daddy's complexion, maybe a little lighter, and he had bright blue eyes."

Mary skewed her face in disbelief. "They was probably them colored contact lenses."

"Did you see him?"

The woman shook her head no. "I would have remembered a black boy with blue eyes. You must have been dreaming from all them drugs."

Talisa shrugged. "Well, if I was, it was a very nice dream."

Her mother sucked her teeth, rolling her eyes skyward. "You don't need to be dreaming about no man. A man ain't nothing but trouble waiting to happen to you. They's devils. All of 'em. Take my word for it." She reached for the television remote, taking a seat in the cushioned wing chair at her daughter's bedside. "It's time for my stories. Erica Kane's in some mess, again. I'll sit here and watch *All My Children* with you, then I need to go get lunch ready."

Talisa laughed, her palm falling against her bandaged belly. She winced slightly, the act of laughing an uneasy feat to accomplish with the multitude of stitches that crossed her stomach.

Mary fanned a hand in her daughter's direction. "Hush, now. I need to hear the television."

Glancing from her mother, to the TV screen and back again, her wide grin continued to fill her face. Settling herself comfortably against the pillows, Talisa closed her eyes and wished for a dream. Wishing the memory of a blue-eyed, black man back to her.

The tall, Caucasian man was pacing the floor anxiously, his distress painting an intricate frown pattern across his face. He ran a thin hand through the short length of salt-and-pepper-toned hair that graced his head, staring intently at the younger man who stood before him.

"This is career suicide, Jericho," Dr. Elijah Becton insisted, shaking his head from side to side. "What are you thinking, son?"

Jericho shrugged, shaking his own head. "I don't agree, Dad. I need to do this."

"What about the practice?"

"The practice will be fine. You will continue to run things just as we've been doing. Besides, I'm not going to be gone forever. It's only going to be for one year."

The elder Becton rolled his eyes. "Why Africa, of all places?"

"Because they need the medical help. Because it's where I need to be for a while."

His father nodded slowly, his own ocean-blue gaze meeting his son's as the two aquatic stares spun one into the other.

The moment was interrupted by a knock on the library door. Both men turned toward the entranceway as the solid oak door was pushed open. Irene Becton stepped into the room, greeting her husband and son with a wide grin.

"Is it safe to enter?" she asked, easing over to stand between the two men.

The senior Becton leaned to kiss his wife's mouth, pressing his lips lightly against hers. Reaching for his hand, the woman clasped his fingers between her own.

"Our son is leaving for Uganda. I tried to talk him out of it but he won't listen."

Irene laughed, reaching to kiss her child's cheek. "Good for you, Jericho. The experience will be good for you."

"For heaven's sake, Irene. He's going to the jungles of Africa!"

The woman shrugged. "Oh, please! Would you have preferred he choose Iraq or Israel, instead? Maybe Bosnia? I'm sure his services are just as needed there."

Elijah tossed up his hands in exasperation. "Whose side are you on?"

"I'm on the side of all those children who will benefit from our son's altruism. You should think about going yourself. Get back to your Peace Corps days."

"I was never in the Peace Corps," the man responded.

"You should have been," she said matter-of-factly, her gaze penetrating his.

Crossing his arms over his chest the man smiled, shaking his head from side to side. "Well, I'm too old to be volunteering in the field now. But I do my part every time I sign one of those large donation checks you keep writing."

Jericho chuckled. "You're never too old to give back, Dad."

Irene winked at her son. "That's right. You tell him, baby boy. So, when do you leave?" she asked, leaning her back against her husband's chest as he wrapped the length of his arms around her.

"I'll be flying out the first week in April," Jericho answered, his gaze dancing from his mother's face to his father's. "I have some time before I have to leave."

The couple nodded, one shifting comfortably against the other. Jericho smiled, warmed by their presence. Irene and Elijah Becton were the pillars in his life, his own personal fan club and cheering squad. Although Jericho understood the adversity the duo had faced being a white male and black female during an era of heightened racial tensions, the two had built a solid relationship on a foundation of mutual respect, passion and pure love. Jericho yearned for what his parents shared—constant companionship with that one person who touched your soul and held the key to your heart. He sighed, and the wistful gesture was not lost on his mother.

"That's good," she said, a smile widening across her ebony face. "I've volunteered you for one of my fund-raisers at the end of the month."

Elijah laughed, giving his wife a quick hug before moving back behind his desk and taking a seat against the leather chair. "You're in for it now, son."

Irene fanned a hand at the man and sucked her teeth. "Ignore your father. This will be fun. My women's group is hosting a bachelor auction and I've put you on the program. You'll need to decide what your date package will be, or of course, I can plan it for you, if you like."

Elijah roared with laughter, wiping at the moisture that rose to his eyes. "Which means she's already planned it for you. I told you, son," he muttered between chuckles. "Didn't I tell you?"

Wide-eyed, Jericho shook his head from side to side. "A bachelor auction? I don't think so, Mom. I can't."

"Yes, you can, and you will. It's for a good cause. We're gifting the money we raise to the hospital for pediatric cancer research. So, you have to do it. Besides, this will give you an opportunity to meet some very nice women."

Jericho sighed, a look of defeat gracing his face. "Yes, ma'am."

"And you need to get your hair cut," his mother said, running her hands through the excessive length of her son's locks.

Jericho bristled. "Never," he said emphatically, shaking

the jet-black strands that fell in a gentle wave against his skull. "I don't have any need to cut my hair, so please don't ask."

Irene rolled her eyes, nodding her head at her husband. "You need to talk to your son."

The man shook his head. "Oh, now he's *my* son. *My* son needs a haircut. *Your* son gets to parade around like a side of beef for the cause. You've got some nerve, woman!"

Jericho's mother laughed. "It's for a good cause and you never know. *Our* son might meet a nice girl, and we might get grandchildren out of the deal."

Chapter 2

The morning staff meeting had gone well, and when Reverend Edward Warren gestured toward Talisa, asking to speak with her privately, she was surprised. It was rare that the minister ever had anything to say to her that he couldn't say in front of them all.

Mrs. Stevie Parrish, the student activities director for the Wesley Foundation and Johanna Bower, the administrative assistant, both watched curiously as Talisa followed Reverend Warren into his office, the man closing the door behind them.

Reverend Warren took a seat in one of the two over-sized recliners that decorated his office, pointing a finger toward the other.

"Make yourself comfortable, Talisa," the man said, smiling at her warmly. "How have you been feeling?"

"I'm doing very well, sir. Fully recovered."

He nodded. "I'm glad to hear it. We were worried about you for a while there."

"Thank you. I appreciate everything you all did to help, and it feels great to be back to work."

The man turned serious as he reached for a manila folder on his desk. "I'm sure you want to know why I wanted to speak with you."

"Yes, sir. I'm a little curious. There's nothing wrong, is there?"

Reverend Warren shook his head. "No, dear. Not at all. Just the opposite, in fact. I have recommended you to lead one of the two student groups we're sending on work team missions this summer. Johanna will be on maternity leave and Stevie already has a group of twenty committed to building homes in Costa Rica. I have ten more seniors who want to work with a medical outreach ministry in Uganda. I would like you to take them. They don't need a lot of hand-holding, but we're obligated to have a member of our staff accompany them."

Talisa pulled herself to the edge of her seat. Excitement shimmered across her face, the ecstatic expression flooding the room.

"I would love to, Reverend Warren. Are you sure?"

"I couldn't be more positive. I think you'll do a wonderful job. I'll let the board know that you're going."

"How long will we be away, sir?"

"Eight weeks. You'll leave right after exams. That's all we have in the budget. The kids are raising the majority of their money and the board will fund the difference, plus pay all of your expenses. But it's going to be a good deal of hard work, Talisa. Not only will you have to complete your work mission, but you'll be expected to do so keeping the spirit of the Lord front and center, and sharing our love of God and the church with the community, as well."

Talisa nodded her head. "Yes, sir."

The man smiled. "You'll do just fine. I have total confidence in you, Talisa. So, do you have any plans for the weekend?"

Talisa blushed. "I'm actually attending a fund-raiser this weekend. It's an auction to raise money for the hospital."

Reverend Warren nodded his head. "Sounds like fun."

Talisa giggled. "I hope so. They're auctioning single men. My father's hoping I'll get lucky and find a husband."

The minister laughed with her. "I should send my daughter. She could use a little help in that direction herself. Well, you enjoy and we'll finalize the details of your trip on Monday."

"Thank you, Reverend Warren. Thank you very much."

Talisa was grinning widely as she exited the office and returned to the small conference room of the United Methodist campus ministry at Georgia Tech. Just as she'd expected, Stevie and Johanna were waiting for her, feigning interest in the paperwork scattered across the surface of the table.

Stevie rose excitedly, rushing to close the door from prying ears as Talisa took a seat at the table. "What's going on?" the woman asked anxiously, dropping back into her own seat.

"Reverend Warren asked me to head the second mission group," Talisa answered, her excitement spilling into the small space.

Stevie clapped her hands as Johanna reached out to hug her. "That's great," her friend said, the other echoing the sentiments. "You'll do just fine. I am so happy for you."

Talisa placed a hand against Johanna's pregnant belly,

patting the haven of new life ever so slightly. "Won't you miss going?" she asked, studying the woman's face.

"Not at all," Johanna said emphatically, her blond ponytail swaying from side to side. "It's time I took a break. I've done a mission trip every year since I was a student here. It'll be a pleasure not to have to worry about inoculations, visas, and all the other stuff you're going to have to bother with. Plus, I love our kids dearly, but they will work your nerves once you get them out of the country."

Talisa laughed. "Now you tell me!"

Stevie shook her head. "I wish we were going together, but you'll do fine. You have David, Paul and Clarissa going with you. They have over ten years of experience between them. They'll be a big help."

"But you won't need much help, Talisa," Johanna said. "You've got great instincts. All you will need to remember is that you are not there to babysit them. They're adults. All they need is for you to occasionally remind them that they represent the church and their school, and that they need to behave like it. Once you get them settled and organized, they're on their own and so are you."

Stevie waved her head in agreement. "When you finish this trip you need to walk away knowing that you fulfilled a calling in your heart, that you served well, and that everyone can be proud of whatever it is you accomplished. You also need to relax, enjoy and have a great time."

Talisa grinned as the two women chattered excitedly around her. She had been working at the student ministry for almost three years, her duties ranging from being a housemother to a homesick freshman, guidance counselor for an anxious senior, maintenance woman, building manager, and everything else in between. The Wesley

Foundation, home of the United Methodist Church's student ministry, had become her second home and she welcomed the opportunities it afforded her to be a part of the campus community.

When she'd initially applied for the position, Reverend Warren had explained their jobs simply. He had explained that they were there to help the students grow in their love for and their commitment to God. At the time, neither knew that the foundation would do that exact thing for Talisa. But from the moment she first stepped into the building and the staff had embraced and welcomed her, Talisa had marveled at how powerful, how healing, how sustaining an environment the place would be for her. She was excited at the prospect of sharing that through their outreach ministry. She was also excited about the opportunity to visit the motherland she only knew through outdated history books, an occasional world news item and the travel brochures she'd periodically picked up at the local travel agency.

Her grin widened as Stevie changed the subject. "How much do you plan to bid tomorrow?" the woman asked, turning the pages of the auction catalog she'd swiped off Talisa's desk.

Talisa laughed again, the sound vibrating between them. "I have no intentions of bidding at all. I'm only going because my friends insist that this is where I need to be for my birthday. That, and my father is hoping someone will take pity on me, marry me, and move me out of his house. I just plan on making a nice donation for the cause, enjoying the hors d'oeuvres, and then I'm going home to a good book and a hot bath."

Johanna stared over Stevie's shoulder as the two

scanned the photographs and read the bios of the auction's participants. "I like this one," she said, pointing to the black-and-white photo of a senior pilot for Southwest Airlines. The man's wide smile filled the image, accentuating his thick eyebrows, dimpled cheeks, and the graying edges of his hairline.

"They all work for me," Stevie said with a deep laugh. "I think he'd be cute for you, Talisa," she finished, pointing to the image of a pro basketball player for the Atlanta Hawks. The young man staring up from the page was a richly toned, blue-black specimen, in a pin-striped suit and wide-brimmed Panama hat, and matching, two-toned, black-and-white shoes. A wide grin filled his very round face and Talisa could almost imagine the number of hearts he'd broken in his lifetime.

She rolled her eyes. "You two are starting to sound like my father. If he tells me one more time how much I need a good man, I'll absolutely bust."

Johanna rubbed her palm against her bulging abdomen. "Personally, a man is the last thing I need. My poor husband is not having any fun with me right now. Every time I look at my swollen ankles, get heartburn or feel a twitch of pain, I take it out on him." She sighed, looking toward Stevie. "I thought you said this pregnancy thing was going to be a piece of cake?"

The older woman laughed. "It was…for me."

"I should never have listened to you. What would you remember? It's been what, thirty-four years since you gave birth to your daughter?"

"About that, give or take a year," Stevie said.

Johanna shook her head. "That's what I get."

Talisa laughed. "You know you're enjoying every

minute of this pregnancy and I'm sure you haven't been that hard on Allan at all. That husband of yours is golden the way he fawns all over you."

Johanna smiled. "Yeah, I guess you're right. Listen to your father. Go find yourself a really good man. Just don't pay too much for him. A bargain is always better than full price any day of the week."

Chapter 3

The morning sun peeked through the blinds of her bedroom, the rising warmth summoning Talisa awake. As she stretched the length of her body against the padded mattress top, she suddenly remembered that her work week had ended well and that she actually had something to do to get the weekend off to a promising start. She smiled.

Although she professed to not be interested in the evening's auction, she was overly excited at the prospect of being in a room with so many eligible, employed, socially promising men. It was an ideal way to celebrate her twenty-fifth birthday—and her best friends had promised her an exceptional birthday party. She stretched again, yawning as she shifted from sleep mode to wide-eyed and awake.

She had already lifted herself from beneath the covers and was returning from the adjoining bathroom when her mother and father knocked on the bedroom door.

"Happy birthday to you...happy birthday to you...happy birthday, Pumpkin Pie...happy birthday to you!" they both sang, one more out of tune than the other.

"Happy birthday, pumpkin," Herman London said, leaning to kiss his only child on the cheek.

Her mother reached for the covers on the unmade bed, instinctively smoothing out the rumpled sheets and blankets.

"Stop, Mom! I can make up my own bed," Talisa said, reaching to pull the covers from her mother's grasp. She rolled her eyes in annoyance.

Mary flipped her hand at her daughter. "I know what you can do. I was just helping out." She smiled widely at the young woman, nodding approval in her daughter's direction.

Herman shook his head from side to side. "So, what do you have planned for the day, baby girl? Anything special?"

Talisa grinned. "Going out with the girls tonight, Daddy."

The man nodded. "Do you need some money?" he asked, reaching for the wallet in his rear pocket.

Talisa shook her head. "No, sir. I'll be fine. Thank you."

"Give her the present, Herman," Mary said, clapping her hands together as she hopped in place. "What are you waiting for, Daddy?"

The man winked, reaching for an envelope in the pocket of his work shirt. "Child ain't even dressed yet and you rushing folks." He passed the envelope to Talisa who looked at them both curiously.

"What's this?" she said, pulling at the sealed container. Her parents stood beside her, beaming in her direction.

"Your daddy and I thought this was the best present for you. Hurry up and open it now!" her mother said excitedly.

Opening the envelope, Talisa's eyes widened as she pulled a set of silver keys and the title to a new car from inside. Her mother had tied a red ribbon around the document that said the vehicle belonged exclusively to her. Talisa stared at the set of keys, her mouth ajar as the engraved Ford logo and inscription stared up at her. "You bought me a car?" she asked hesitantly, looking from one to the other.

Mary's excitement burst out in glee as she pulled her daughter into a warm hug. "Daddy picked out a pretty new car for you. It's blue with gray seats. It's in the driveway. Go look," the woman said in one big breath, gasping for air as she finished.

Her father nodded. "Happy birthday, pumpkin!" he exclaimed for a second time.

Talisa stood shocked, her limbs tied to the floor. "I don't believe this. Daddy, why would you buy me a car? You and Mommy can't afford this!"

Her mother bristled. "Don't tell us what we can afford. Your daddy and I know what we can afford and what we can't." The woman's tone was suddenly hostile.

Her father defused the moment quickly, resting a large hand against his wife's forearm. "Your mama and I been saving up for this since you turned eighteen, Talisa. We've been putting a little away every month. I thought we'd have been able to do it when you graduated college, but that's when I lost my job at the plant. After I started driving buses for the city, we just kept on saving. We wanted you to have something special and since turning twenty-five is a special time, today was as good as any other."

Talisa's hair swayed from side to side as she shook her head. She reached to hug her father and then her mother. "I love you both so much."

"Well, don't just stand there," her mother admonished,

the smile returning to her face. "Get dressed. I gots to go to the store and I want to ride in that nice new car."

Talisa pulled her new car into the parking lot of the Crowne Plaza Atlanta hotel, Mya Taft, one of her closest friends, riding shotgun beside her. The two women were laughing heartily as they exited the vehicle, one just as excited as the other.

"I plan to bid on every tall, Mandingo brother with big feet and an even bigger bankbook," Mya said as they made their way toward the front of the building.

Talisa laughed. "Why does he have to be big?"

"Small men make me nervous. I want a man who eats well, eats often, and isn't afraid to give me a taste when the moment moves me. And you know if his feet are large, then the rest of him won't be a disappointment."

"You are a sick woman," Talisa said with a chuckle as the two women gave each other a high five.

"Where'd you get that dress?" Mya asked as Talisa removed her jacket, admiring the turquoise, floral-printed, silk sundress her friend wore. "'Cause that dress is wearing you, girl!" she exclaimed.

"The new Bloomingdale's in Lenox Square."

"I never find anything at that store. You make me sick."

"Like you don't look good in that size-two slip you have on."

Mya laughed, doing a fashion model strut and spin in the middle of the hotel lobby, flipping the jacket she'd just removed over her shoulder. "Okay. I do look good, don't I?"

Talisa clasped her arm through the other woman's. "We both look good. Now let's just hope these men tonight are worth all the trouble."

As the duo entered the ballroom, stopping first to register at the reception table, they were instantly in awe of the elaborate decorations. Playing with a New Orleans masked ball theme, the decorating committee had outdone themselves. The décor was exotic and sensual. The tables were dressed in white linens with gold and black accented table runners. A large runway had been built room center, the massive structure skirted in a coordinating harlequin print, and miniature white lights sparkled against the high ceilings. With registration, each attendee was given an updated auction catalog and an exquisite Venetian mask on a scrolled wooden handle. An assigned number adorned the back of the mask to be used as the bidding paddle. The gathering of women, varying in shades and sizes, was duly impressed.

Talisa and Mya rushed to their table, greeting the rest of their party who sat waiting for them.

"What took you two so long?" Benita Rivers asked, rising from her seat to give them each a quick hug and kiss on the cheek. Her café au lait complexion was flushed with color that highlighted her reddish-brown afro.

"We were beginning to think your old butt wasn't coming," Leila Brimmer added, gesturing for them to take a seat.

"Who are you calling old?" Talisa said as she settled herself comfortably against the cushioned seat.

"I'm calling you old," her best friend responded teasingly. "Happy birthday, woman!" Leila twirled one of her ebony curls around her index finger. Laugh lines pulled at her thin face, her mahogany complexion shining with glee.

Talisa grinned. "Thank you. And I'm not old. I'm just aging nicely. Like fine wine."

"Like she can talk," Benita interjected. "Who turned twenty-five last month?"

"I'm still twenty-one and I'll deny anything else," the other woman laughed.

Benita rolled her eyes. "Yeah, right. Just like you're still a virgin."

The women laughed again. Talisa's gaze scanned the perimeter of the room, noting the landscape of primped and perfumed women, each dressed to the nines, hair and nails meticulous. "What did we miss?" she asked, taking a mental note of the elderly piano player who sat in the left corner, his fingers skating easily over the piano keys.

Leila shook her head. "Not much. I picked up our tickets for the champagne reception in the VIP suite. We'll get to mingle with the bachelors before this thing gets started. Spend some quality one-on-one time as we decide which ones will be our future husbands."

"We should be so lucky," Mya responded as she peered into a compact mirror pulled from her purse.

Talisa shook her head. "How'd you swing tickets for the reception? I heard it was by invitation only."

Leila shrugged. "The only invitation we needed was the required five-hundred-dollar donation for the tickets."

Talisa spun around in her seat, her mouth falling open in shock. "Five hundred dollars? You spent five hundred dollars for reception tickets?"

Leila laughed. "No. I spent two thousand dollars for reception tickets. We needed four of them," she said, pointing to each of them in turn. "I told you we were going to celebrate your birthday in high style."

"You've lost your mind," Talisa exclaimed. "I can't believe you!"

Her friend laughed again. "Well, let's head on up so you can believe me."

Mya patted at her lipstick. "I hope you don't expect me to pay you back, Leila. You know I'm broke. I don't have a high-powered lawyer's job like you do."

Leila rolled her eyes. "It's a gift, Mya. A gift for all of us. Just make it worth my investment and find yourself a man. Please, do us all that favor."

Talisa laughed. "I declare! For five hundred dollars, they should give us a private reception, an engagement ring, and the two point three kids with a dog."

"Please, don't act poor when we get upstairs, Talisa," Mya admonished. "Just pretend we at least know what money is."

"You mean just pretend we have money we don't," Talisa said, her head waving from side to side.

"It's all tax-deductible and I need as many deductions as I can get," Leila said. "Besides, we're here to support the cause, remember?"

"I'm here to catch me a rich husband." Mya laughed. "You can be here for any reason you want."

Crossing through the lobby, the four women made their way to the elevators on the south side of the building, pushing the button to the upper-level suite reserved for the occasion. Excitement filled the space around them as they traveled the quick distance from one floor to another. Talisa smiled warmly at the three women who stood beside her.

She and Leila had been best friends since kindergarten, when Talisa broke the red crayon in her Crayola box and Leila had offered her own in replacement. They'd been inseparable after that, even following each other to Georgia Tech when they graduated high school. Mya had joined the duo when they'd been in the fourth grade. They'd met her in church two weeks after her parents and twin brothers had moved from Baltimore to Atlanta. Mya had captivated them with her vocal cords, bellowing big hymns out of her tiny body that had made them all stop and take notice. She'd also been the more daring of the trio, enticing them to get into more trouble than any one of them cared to remember. Benita had been Mya's college roommate, evening out their threesome as they'd moved into adulthood.

Leila had graduated college a year early, moving right on to Harvard Law School for her law degree. It had been the first time she and Talisa had been apart, the telephone and e-mail the lifeline between them. Talisa had marveled at her friend's dedication and commitment to her career, still having no idea what she wanted to do with her own life, despite her degree in journalism.

Benita was working her Spelman College marketing degree by running a small advertising agency. Her business was growing rapidly and Talisa envied her ability to build something out of absolutely nothing. Free-spirited Mya was her sister-friend most intent on marrying well, believing that the right union would lift her well above her family's days of food stamps and government housing. Talisa sighed as they giggled beside her, energy flowing from one to the other.

As they stepped inside the tastefully decorated suite, handing their tickets to the woman at the door, their excitement level rose tenfold. Forty good-looking, well-dressed men turned their attention to the entrance as the women stepped inside. Scanning the room from one corner to the other, Talisa felt as if they'd just experienced sensory overload, one human confection more delectable than the other. Every nerve ending in her body was tingling with anticipation and as Mya pushed her way past them, extending her hand toward three men who stood in conversation in front of the bar, Talisa looked to Leila for support. The woman stared back at her and grinned.

"Happy birthday, girlfriend."

Talisa laughed. "I owe you big-time, my friend."

"Just make sure I don't have to wear pink ruffles at your wedding and we'll call it even."

"Ditto for me," Benita said before turning to say hello to a man with a linebacker's build who'd stepped in to greet her.

Talisa suddenly stood alone and nervous as Leila disappeared into the crowd. She followed the clear path toward the buffet table in the center of the room, a smile pasted on her face as she brushed past one good-looking man after another.

"Hello, my name's Charles, Charles Barrow," a voice said from behind her as she reached for a clean plate and a canapé.

Talisa turned to stare up into the dark brown eyes of a heavyset, mocha-colored black man. He reached to shake her hand, then gestured to the green-eyed blond beside him. "And, this is Mark Hayes."

"It's very nice to meet you both," Talisa said, nodding ever so slightly. "My name's Talisa. Talisa London."

"Beautiful name," the man named Mark said, her hand still caught in his as he held on to the handshake a touch longer than necessary.

"Thank you."

"So what brings you here this evening?" Charles asked.

Talisa's grin widened. "It's my birthday. I thought making a donation to a worthy cause would be a great way to celebrate."

The man chuckled. "Ahhh. A woman comfortable with being alone, enjoying her single lifestyle, and not desperate for a man to spend the rest of her life with. A woman here for the larger cause. That's refreshing," he said, a wealth of sarcasm tainting his tone.

Talisa gave him a wry smile. "Yes, it is. It's also nice to be in the company of men who are interested in supporting those in need and not just needing to inflate their overly excessive egos with what they think will be a quick, one-night booty call on someone else's dime."

The man laughed. "Touché," he said.

An awkward silence fell between them as Talisa pushed the food from one side of her plate to the other.

The man named Mark grinned at the obvious dislike his associate and the stunning woman had taken to one another. "Do you participate in these things often?" he asked politely, making a second attempt at conversation.

She shook her head. "No, this is my first time. So why are you two participating?"

Mark shrugged. "I don't know about my partner here, but I'm desperate for a date."

Talisa laughed. "I'm sure it's not that bad for you."

Smiling wryly, the man shook his head. "You wouldn't believe just how bad it is."

"So, what do you do?" Talisa asked, suddenly wishing she'd spent more time studying her auction brochure.

Mark smiled. "We're both anchors on *Good Morning, Atlanta.* Charles does the news and I do the weather. I take it you don't watch much television."

Talisa shook her head, shrugging her shoulders. "Sorry."

Charles winced, his feelings clearly bruised by her lack of knowledge about who he was and what he did. "Figures," he muttered under his breath, more to himself than to either of the two standing beside him.

They all looked toward the door as the lights flashed on

and off. The ticket taker was gesturing for their attention. "Excuse me. If I can have your attention, please." She paused for a quick second, her gaze skating across the faces in the room. "We're about to start the auction in a few minutes. We're going to ask our ladies to please return to the ballroom and take your seats so our guests can have a few minutes to get themselves ready. Thank you."

Talisa smiled as the duo suddenly appeared anxious. She tossed Mr. Charles Barrow a look that let him know clearly that she had no intentions of pursuing any further time in his company. "Well, it was very nice to meet you, Mark," she said, placing the china and half-eaten canapé onto the tray of a passing waiter. "Good luck this evening. Oh," she added as an afterthought, "and you, too, Charlie."

Charles winked. "Same to you, babe."

As Talisa turned toward the door, a tall man standing off in the corner caught her attention. His expression was pensive as he stood alone, knee-deep in thought. From the stern expression, his eyes narrowed to thin slits and his jaw locked hard and tight, the lines chiseled in his face, one could have mistaken his demeanor for brooding. But Talisa sensed that there was something more going on inside the man's mind, something deeply personal and consuming. His face was familiar and she stopped short in her tracks as she stared blatantly in his direction.

The good-looking man suddenly jumped as if startled, his gaze locking tightly with hers. He stared at her boldly, appraising every inch of her with obvious appreciation before lifting his mouth in a deep smile, nodding his head slowly in greeting. The silent exchange of eye contact spoke volumes, whispering promises Talisa suddenly found disconcerting. As a wave of recognition swept over her, nervous energy filled the pit of her stomach. She stood frozen, staring intently as the man slowly crossed the carpeted floor in her direction. Turning a quick gaze to the door, Talisa saw Leila and Mya waiting at the entrance, both staring curiously. Benita still stood chatting with the football player on the other side of the room.

Jericho Becton stopped directly in front of Talisa, smiling warmly. Standing well over six feet tall, he was dressed in an expensive black tuxedo. With his long and lean stature, the formal suit fit him to perfection. His thick hair, the color of black licorice, was pulled into a neat ponytail that hung down his back, stopping just below the line of his shoulder blades. Contrasting nicely against his rich, caramel complexion, his bright white smile washed over her, and Talisa suddenly found herself tongue-tied.

He extended a well-manicured hand. "Hello, my name's Jericho Becton. Have we met before? You look very familiar."

Talisa smiled back and shook her head, her gaze sweeping over the man's face. Her name being called pulled at her attention and she glanced from Jericho to Mya and back again. She stammered, searching for her words, lost in the sensation of her small hand lost in the soft, warm palm of his.

"I…I was just…thinking the same…thing," she finally managed to say, the room seeming to spin in a slow circle around her.

The man nodded, his head slowly bobbing up and down against his broad shoulders. "You didn't look like you were having a good time," Jericho said, his gaze flitting toward the newscaster and back.

Talisa smiled, a sweet bend to her mouth that made Jericho suddenly want to kiss the sugar from her lips. The sudden thought sent a chill throughout his body, a quiver of energy that set his nerve endings on fire.

"You were watching me?" Talisa asked coyly, her own excitement shining brightly from her dark eyes. Her hand was still lost beneath the clasp of his.

"I couldn't help myself," the man answered, his voice dropping into a seductive whisper.

Talisa finally pulled the appendage back, dropping her palm to her abdomen. The deep tone of his voice seemed to swallow her whole, her control lost somewhere in the depths of his intense stare. She inhaled a quick breath, willing the oxygen to calm her nerves.

The woman at the door flicked the lights for a second time, once again directing them back to the ballroom. Jericho nodded, his intoxicating smile still caressing every nerve ending in her body. "Well, it was very nice to meet you, Miss…?"

Talisa's own head bobbed up and down. "London. Talisa London."

Jericho's gaze brushed warmth over her. Talisa felt as if she were on fire beneath his stare. "It's nice to meet you, Miss London. I hope we'll get an opportunity to talk more later."

Talisa continued nodding, then turned on her very high heels to catch up with her friends. Behind her, she could feel Jericho still staring, his ocean-blue eyes calling her back to him.

Back at the table, the four friends were talking over each other, concentrating more on their personal thoughts than each other's conversations. Talisa flipped quickly through the pages of her catalog, searching for one picture in particular. The photographic image of Dr. Jericho Becton smiled up at her as she read the brief biography about the man who'd captured her total attention just minutes before.

"He's a surgeon," she said, leaning to whisper toward Leila. "He was *my* surgeon. He operated on my appendix."

Her friend shook her head. "And he didn't remember you?"

"I don't want him to remember me!" she exclaimed in a low whisper. "Do you know how bad I looked when they brought me into the emergency room? Besides, he wasn't supposed to be there. There was another doctor who was supposed to be covering the emergency room but they couldn't find him. He was the doctor who was filling in."

Leila grinned. "So, do you plan to bid on him?"

Talisa grinned back. "I don't know. Do you think I should?"

Her friend nodded her head up and down excitedly. "It is for a good cause. You could use a man."

Talisa laughed, the warmth of the vibration causing her to shake in her seat.

Mya turned to stare curiously. "What are you two whispering about?" she asked, looking from Talisa to Leila.

"Talisa's trying to decide whether she should go after a doctor or not. What do you think?"

"If she doesn't, I surely will. I've got my eye on John the attorney, Bradley the basketball player, and Stephan the general contractor. Any one of them will do quite nicely."

Benita rolled her eyes. "Do you have that kind of money?"

Mya shrugged. "I've got Visa, MasterCard, and American Express. One, or the other, or all three of them will buy me a man this night."

The group laughed. Their chattering was interrupted by an elegant black woman who approached the microphone

at the podium, gesturing for the few persons standing to
take a seat. Standing prim and proper in a classic-cut, blue
pinstripe suit and a white lace top, she epitomized the
mood of the evening. Talisa imagined her to be as old as
her own mother was, but her obvious wealth enabled her
to wear her age well. This woman lacked the tired stress
lines that graced Talisa's mother's face. The woman's
Hershey's dark chocolate complexion was virtually
blemish free. Wherein Mary London rarely bothered with
manicures and had never had a pedicure, it was obvious
that their hostess for the evening probably never missed her
weekly appointments. With her dark hair pulled back into
a neat French twist, she was sophisticated and beautiful and
Talisa couldn't help herself from wishing that time would
serve her at least half as well. She leaned forward in her
seat and listened intently as the woman clasped her hands
in front of herself and spoke into the microphone.

"Good evening and welcome to our first ever bachelor
auction! My name is Irene Becton and I'm the president
of the Center for Women's Resources. We are absolutely
thrilled to welcome you all here tonight. I'm not going to
bore you with a long speech about why this evening is so
important to the center and the hospital. I know all of you
are here because you want to make a difference in someone
else's life. I'm also sure all those handsome, intelligent,
sexy men who are standing backstage waiting to walk the
runway for you had no influence whatsoever on your
decision to be here." Irene paused and smiled as the
audience laughed heartily.

"So, allow me to say thank you in advance. The donations you make tonight will make a significant impact in
a child's life and your support will make all the difference

in the world. So, with no further delay, I'll turn our program over to our guest auctioneer, local radio personality, Mr. Jarred Nelson. Please, sit back, enjoy, bid, and bid well!"

Talisa watched as the woman made her way to the rear of the stage and disappeared behind the black velvet curtains. She wondered if the woman was any relation to Jericho—they had the same last name. His mother, perhaps. Her thoughts shifted back to the auction as the lights in the room dimmed ever so slightly and the piano player revved up his tune. A spotlight fell on the tall, mocha-toned, gray-haired man who stood in the space Mrs. Becton had just vacated.

The maple-syrup timbre of the man's voice filled the room, sending a chill up the spine of every woman who sat listening as he introduced the first of many men who were scheduled to make an appearance before the evening was over.

Chapter 4

Jericho stood against a rear wall of the large ballroom, his arms crossed evenly over his broad chest. He knew the woman from somewhere, but he couldn't for the life of himself remember where. He'd noticed her the minute she'd walked in, his gaze following her to the buffet table, and watching as she'd engaged in conversation with the two men who'd stood like bookends beside her.

She was full-figured, a perfectly proportioned beauty who would have easily been labeled voluptuous. The dress she wore had hugged her curves like a second skin and he'd felt his body quiver with intrigue as he'd watched her. From where he'd stood, he thought she embodied the image of the woman the Commodores had sung about on that old song, "Brick House." The old rap song by Sir Mix-A-Lot, "Baby Got Back," was just as fitting. Although she was a definite beauty, there was clearly nothing vain about her. Her shoulder-length hair had appeared windblown, soft brown curls billowing around her oval-shaped face. Her makeup was simple at best, just a coat of lipstick across her mouth and a touch of eyeliner beneath her eyes. Not an ounce of foundation touched her clear, copper complexion. And there had been something in her eyes when her gaze had met his that had reduced him to a weak mass, spinning heat from one end of his body to the other. His thoughts were still on the woman he'd just met when his mother came up beside him, slipping her arm beneath his.

"Nervous?" Irene asked, leaning to kiss her son's cheek.

Jericho shrugged, pushing his shoulders skyward. "Not really. Just ready for this to be over."

"You need to relax and have some fun," the woman said smiling. "There are some beautiful, intelligent women out there."

Jericho shrugged again. "Did you get to meet any of the women at the reception?" he asked, his gaze meeting hers evenly.

"No, dear. I was too busy down here. How did it go?"

"There was one woman I met briefly. Her name was Talisa London. She looked very familiar."

Irene's expression was pensive as she mulled the name over in her mind. She shook her head from side to side. "Sorry, baby. It doesn't ring a bell. Could you know this woman from the hospital?"

"I don't know. I recognize her from somewhere though."

His mother nodded. "Well, don't let it bother you. The minute you stop thinking about it the answer will come." She reached to adjust her son's bow tie. "You look quite dashing."

Jericho chuckled. "Thank you."

"Do me proud," she said, giving him a pat on the

back as the event coordinator called him to get in line to await his turn.

Jericho grimaced, heaving a deep sigh as he stepped toward the front curtains.

Behind him, his mother called out his name.

"Yes, ma'am?"

"Good luck, baby."

The emcee had rolled Jericho's name off his tongue with relative ease, the sound of it calling for her attention as Talisa shifted forward in her seat. As Jericho stood at the end of the runway, waiting to walk the length of floor ahead of him, she could feel her heart skip a beat. She clutched the bid paddle tighter in her hands.

"Dr. Jericho Becton, the only son of our gracious host this evening, is a graduate of Duke University's medical school. He completed his surgical internship at Atlanta's Children's Hospital, and is currently in private practice with his father and mentor, Dr. Elijah Becton. Jericho is an avid sportsman. He loves to scuba dive in Bermuda, rock climb in the Grand Canyon, ski the slopes in Aspen, and hike the Georgia Mountains. His ideal woman is just as adventurous, intensely family-oriented, and fiercely independent.

"The lucky bidder will enjoy Dr. Becton's company at the VisionarieSpa here in Atlanta as they get to know each other over luxurious mango body massages and strawberry facials." The man laughed. "Sounds like a lot of dessert before the meal to me," he chuckled before continuing. "Some lucky lady and the good doctor here will end the evening at one of his favorite restaurants, Paschal's, where they'll enjoy home cooking to rival that of my very own mother's. So, brush off those credit cards ladies 'cause our lucky bidder is sure to enjoy a good time with this fine young man. I'm going to start the bidding at one hundred dollars."

Talisa could feel herself beginning to perspire as she stared up at Jericho. Tiny beads of moisture were forming in the valley between her breasts and she fanned herself ever so slightly, fearful that she might break out into a full sweat. The man's gaze sought her out as he sauntered slowly to the end of the runway. When he located her, he smiled seductively in her direction, an easy bend of his lips that deepened the crevice of his dimples and it was as if he'd lit a fire beneath her, causing her to melt like butter against her seat.

Leila grabbed Talisa's hand and pushed it upward, waving the bid paddle in the air.

"I have five hundred dollars, do I hear six?"

"What are you doing?" Talisa said under her breath.

"Winning you that doctor. You can't get him if you don't bid," Leila hissed back.

"I don't have that kind of money, Leila."

"Well, I do, so don't worry about it."

Talisa was prepped to give her friend a tongue-lashing when the emcee gestured in her direction.

"I have six hundred dollars. Will you give me seven? Do I hear seven?"

"Seven!" a tall, redheaded woman called out from the other side of the stage.

Talisa's eyes widened in disbelief as Leila pushed her hand up again. "Eight," her friend called out from behind her.

The room erupted in noise. Jericho grinned excitedly in her direction.

"Eight hundred dollars. I have eight hundred dollars for a day with Dr. Jericho Becton. Do I hear nine? Someone give me nine. I have eight hundred. Eight hundred going once…eight hundred going twice…"

"One thousand dollars," a voice sang out from the back of the room and every head turned to see from where it had come. Women were rising from their seats to catch a glimpse of the woman who'd offered one thousand dollars for time with the beautiful black man who stood before them, an expression of surprise painted across his face.

Talisa watched as the woman made her way closer to the center of the room, her gold-trimmed bid paddle raised high in the air. She was exceptionally tall, a long-legged blonde with pale green eyes and skin the color of whole milk. Before Talisa realized what she was doing, her own paddle was sky-high, her bid rolling off her tongue. "Two thousand dollars."

Behind her Leila laughed. "That a way. Go get your man, girlfriend."

Talisa could feel a sudden wave of embarrassment drop over her. She glanced from Jericho, to the other woman who was eyeing her with obvious annoyance, to her best friend, and back again. Jericho was nodding his head in her direction, a wistful expression gracing his face. The room had gone quiet as everyone watching waited to see what the two women would do.

The auctioneer was waving his gaze anxiously from one to the other. "Do I hear two thousand, five hundred?" he asked, his excitement spilling past his words.

The blond woman nodded, lifting her bid mask high into the air. "Twenty-five hundred," she answered, her voice loud and clear.

Leila poked Talisa in the back, hissing into her ear. "Do not let that woman get your man, Talisa. Bid!" she commanded, her breath hot against her best friend's neck. "I've got you covered. Go ahead and bid!"

Talisa's voice was much less assured as she rose to her feet, waving in the auctioneer's direction. "Three thousand."

Jericho beamed, the glaze in his eyes fueled by Talisa's obvious interest. He pushed his hands deep into the pockets of his silk slacks, the easy gesture meant to hide his obvious nervousness. As he leaned his weight back against one hip, the motion made his six-foot-six stature appear comfortable, the pose accentuating the lines of his firm body. It caused every woman in the room to gasp and Talisa suddenly found herself fighting for oxygen. Jericho's gaze was still locked with hers, his stare piercing right through her heart and when he smiled, the sweet bending of his lips calmed her and Talisa felt herself smiling back.

"Twenty thousand dollars," the blonde called out, tossing Talisa a look that dared her to top so generous an offer. The sudden silence in the room was deafening as all eyes turned to see what she intended to do. The moment was surreal as Talisa's gaze moved from Jericho's face to her opponent's and back again. Talisa blew air past her full lips as if she'd been punched in the stomach, clearly deflated by the turn of events. She dropped her paddle against the table and shook her head as the auctioneer turned to see if she would counter. She suddenly found herself fighting a rush of tears that threatened to spill from her eyes.

"Twenty thousand dollars once…twice…twenty thousand dollars three times…sold to lucky number six-seventy-four!" The man slammed his gavel against the wooden podium top. The women cheered, fueled by the excitement they'd all just witnessed. Through glazed eyes, Talisa watched as her opponent turned to give her a quick nod. Clearly defeated, Talisa smiled a faint smile and shrugged her shoulders, gesturing half a salute in the woman's direction. The blonde turned, sweeping her long hair over her shoulders and gave Jericho a quick wink before heading in the direction of the checkout counter. On the center of the stage, Jericho stood stunned, his eyes still locked on Talisa's face, the line of his smile pulling toward the floor in a deep frown.

Chapter 5

"Can you believe she paid twenty thousand dollars for the man?" Mya exclaimed as they rode home, the bright lights of the hotel dimming in the distance behind them.

Talisa shook her head, then changed the subject, not wanting to be reminded yet again of her loss. "What I can't believe is that you bid on an evening with that anchorman and that you won."

"The way those women were acting I consider myself lucky. For only five hundred dollars my date was a bargain."

"Your date is going to be a nightmare. The man is an ass."

Mya rolled her eyes. "Don't hate."

Talisa shook her head at her friend. "Why am I dropping you off at Kenny's house?" she asked, pulling her car onto Interstate 285. "I would think you'd want to go home to bask in the light of Charles Barrow on the eleven o'clock news."

"Kenny misses me. He called today and invited me to come hang out with him."

Talisa laughed. "I forgot. It's the first of the month. Kenny paying the rent this time?"

Mya laughed with her. "He better. I do not intend to endure bad sex for absolutely nothing. Besides, the last time I broke up with him, he didn't send me anything. He needs to make up for that."

"Just because he's sent you a check the last four times you cut him off doesn't mean he's going to keep doing it. The man may have grown a backbone."

"When that happens I will definitely be through with him. Until then, I plan to bait him along just enough to keep my checkbook out of the red. The relationship works for us. Don't hate the player, just hate the game."

"Personally, I think he's gay. He's just not ready to admit it."

"That's his problem. My bills are mine. If he can't fix anything or keep my car tuned up, then he needs to just keep coming up off the cash. Then he and I will be just fine."

"So what about your anchorman?"

"What about him? I'll play him just like I play all the others. I'm sure he'll be useful for something."

Talisa laughed. "I know this is ugly to say, and Lord forgive me for it, but that's one man I think will deserve any game you run on him and then some." She pulled her car onto a tree-lined street, large old oaks adorned with Spanish moss cascading overhead. At the fifth house on the left, she pulled into the driveway and shifted the engine into Park. "Stay safe, Mya. Please. I don't have time to be worrying about you."

Her friend smiled. "Don't worry about me, girlfriend.

I'm going to be just fine. You need to worry about yourself. When's the last time you had a man? High school or junior high?"

"It hasn't been that bad."

"It might as well be. I suggest you spend more time hanging out with me and less time down at that foundation. You need to devote more time to you and having yourself a good time. Life is too short and that do-gooder stuff you keep doing isn't going to keep you warm at night."

"I love working at Wesley. You know that. And knowing I've done something good for someone else more than warms my heart."

"Sure you do. But trust me, you and that warm heart of yours will love a little Saturday-night Johnson much more."

The two women laughed as Mya kissed her cheek then lifted her petite body out of the passenger seat. Talisa watched as her friend eased her way inside the house, turning to toss her a quick wave as she did. Pulling out of the driveway, Talisa couldn't help but notice as Kenny Davis greeted her friend excitedly, pulling the woman into a deep kiss in front of the home's large bay window. Talisa suddenly thought of Dr. Jericho Becton and wondered what a Saturday night with that man might do for her.

It had been a long time since she'd last had a date. Dating had never been easy for Talisa, feeling more like a chore than an event to look forward to. Talisa had always been more comfortable volunteering her time for some worthy cause than trying to make polite conversation with a man over a meal she was too anxious to eat and enjoy. It didn't help that the few men she had dated had not met her mother's approval, each having some moral flaw or imperfection

Mary London found fault with. Insult to injury was Mary's quickness to point these flaws out with such sheer venom that it caused Talisa to question and doubt her own judgment.

As Talisa maneuvered her car toward home, she heaved a deep sigh, her gaze dancing between the road and her rearview mirror. Reflecting back on the evening's events, she was suddenly appalled by her behavior. What had she been thinking to bid thousands of dollars for a date with some man? Dollars she knew she didn't have no matter what her dear friend had promised her. Talisa shook her head. Jericho Becton had made her lose her mind. Talisa had been so enamored with the prospect of seeing him again that she had allowed the possibilities to sap every ounce of common sense from her head. If her mother ever found out there would never be any peace between them, Talisa thought, imagining the ranting that would ensue if Mary ever gained knowledge of her daughter's actions.

Talisa was suddenly dismayed. Obviously the interest had not been mutual, she thought. After the auction, he had made no effort to find her, hadn't even bothered to seek out her company, if only for a few minutes. The man barely knew her name and didn't have a clue how to reach her. Clearly, she mused as she pulled into the driveway of her home, getting to know her wasn't something Jericho Becton was interested in doing.

The young man's silence had begun to wear on her nerves and Irene Becton said so. "What is your problem, Jericho? You've been pouting since before we left the hotel. And you were downright rude to Shannon Porter."

Her son cut his eyes in her direction, his large palms gripping the steering wheel of his father's latest acquisition, a steel-gray Jaguar XKR sportscar. The vehicle accelerated ever so slightly, the tires spinning over seventy miles per hour in a fifty-five mile per hour zone. The movement was not lost on his mother.

"Slow down before you wreck your father's new car and I have to hear about it. Besides, you don't need to be getting any speeding tickets. Did you drink tonight? Good Lord, that would be all this family needs, you being stopped for a DUI. Slow down right now, Jericho!"

The man pursed his lips, biting his tongue as he pulled the car into a parking space in front of the Corner Bakery Café. Shifting the car into Park, he turned off the engine. Still refusing to meet his mother's gaze, he could feel her stare boring a hole straight through him. "I need a cup of coffee," he muttered under his breath as he stepped out of the vehicle, pretending not to really care if his mother heard him or not.

Irene slammed the car's door as she made her exit and headed into the café behind her son. Taking a seat in an empty booth she watched as he headed into the men's room before returning to take the seat across from her. Jericho focused his attention on a menu, still pretending to ignore her presence.

Irene smiled. "If you were three I'd have smacked that behind of yours already. Now, I'm not going to take but so much more of this foolishness. You're almost thirty-four years old, Jericho. So, act like it. Tell me what has you so upset."

Jericho allowed his gaze to rest on his mother's face. As they both studied each other, he heaved a deep sigh, filling his lungs with air. "I'm sorry," Jericho said, the beginnings of an apology painting his expression. "I'm just irritated that Shannon did what she did. Why didn't you warn me she was coming?"

"Because I didn't know Shannon was coming. But if I had, and if I had told you, you would have refused to participate."

"You're right. I would have. I may still not participate."

Irene shook her head. "Shannon is a sweet girl and she adores you. She comes from an excellent family. We have been friends with her parents since before you two were born. I don't understand why you treat her the way you do."

Jericho rolled his eyes, then gestured for a waitress to come take their orders. A small girl with a large bustline smiled eagerly as she made her way to the table.

"Are you ready to order, sir," she said, her grin as wide as her full face.

"Two coffees, please, one regular and one decaffeinated. And I'll have an apple pastry."

"How about you, ma'am?"

Irene returned the girl's smile. "Just coffee, thank you."

Reaching for the menus the girl promised to be right back, then headed toward the kitchen.

"What happened between you and Shannon?" Irene persisted.

Jericho tossed her a quick glance, then shifted his gaze across the room, avoiding his mother's stare for a second time. He shrugged, driving his shoulders skyward before responding. "Shannon is desperate for a husband and I'm not interested in the job. She seems to be having a difficult time accepting that, though."

Irene sensed that there was much her son wasn't telling her. She nodded her head ever so slightly before responding. "Well, she made a very generous donation to the hospital tonight. You don't have to marry her but you do have to spend a day with her."

Jericho shook his head. "That's what irritates me the

most. Shannon knows full well that I have no interest in spending any time with her. To make matters worse, things were so crazy with her following me around that I didn't get a chance to catch up with Miss London. I really wanted to get her telephone number. Now, I don't know if I'll even be able to track her down. What if she's not from Atlanta?"

"Are you talking about the other young woman bidding against Shannon?"

Jericho nodded, noting how his mother rolled her eyes in response. "What?" he asked, his annoyance resurfacing in his tone.

Irene laughed. "If you want her telephone number all you have to do is ask. You seem to forget that she had to register so that she could bid. I should have her contact information in all that paperwork we packed in the trunk of that car. But, how do you know she'd even want you to have her telephone number?"

Jericho grinned, a sudden rush of hopeful anticipation filling his face. "I just know, Mom. If I'd had half a chance, I'd have given her mine. And thank you. You don't know what this means to me."

His mother waved her head from side to side, reaching to rub her palm against the back of his hand. "I think I do, but if you keep acting up like you were before, you're not going to be very happy with me. You will see the back of my hand on your bottom and then some, and I don't care how old you are."

Chapter 6

Mary London pulled the ringing telephone to her ear. "Hello?"

"Yes, hello. Is Talisa London available, please?"

"Who's calling?"

"Jericho Becton." The man's voice was a deep bass, a rich tonality that would have resonated nicely over the radio.

"Are you a friend of Talisa's?"

"She and I met last week, ma'am, and it's very important that I reach her. I've tried calling her a couple of times before but I don't know if she's been getting my messages."

Mary stood with one hand resting on her hip, the other clutching the telephone receiver. She cleared her throat before continuing. "Well, Talisa's not home at the moment. But I will tell her you called."

"Thank you," Jericho said, following with a heavy sigh.

Mary could hear the disappointment in the man's voice.

The sadness of it echoed loudly in the tone of his voice as he gave the woman his contact information, repeating over again how anxious he was to make contact with Talisa. As Mary dropped the telephone receiver back onto the hook, her husband came through the kitchen door, waving hello as he entered.

"Hey."

"Hey, yourself," Mary responded. "How was your day?"

The man shrugged, not bothering to respond as he took a seat at the kitchen table and reached for the lacings that bound his leather work boots.

"Don't take them boots off in my kitchen," Mary scolded, fanning her hand in the man's direction.

"Why you got to start the minute I come through the door?" her husband responded. He paused, his hands frozen in midair in front of him as he gazed up at her.

"I'm not starting anything. I'm finishing this. Take them boots out of here. I just mopped this floor clean and you come in here ready to kick trash on the floor. I'm not having it."

Rising from his seat, Herman swore, profanity filling the air with his annoyance. That was all it took before the duo was arguing bitterly back and forth, the moment turning uglier with each comment that passed between them.

As she came through the front door, Talisa could hear the two of them bickering loudly. Her mother's voice had risen four octaves, the older woman screaming unintelligibly and her father yelling back just as loud. She shook her head in disgust as she entered the room to stand between the two of them. Her presence was greeted with silence as one parent eyed the other, vile stares racing between them. Her father suddenly turned away from the two women, plopping back down against the thinly padded chair, reaching for his bootlaces.

As Talisa shook a finger at one and then the other, she couldn't help but think she should be used to the ugly that frequently passed between her folks. During the course of their forty-two-year marriage, Herman and Mary London had forever walked a fine line between love and hate for one another. Since Talisa had been three years old she knew she would never understand how two individuals with such an abundance of love for her and everyone else, could totter so precariously from one side of malevolence to the other side of devotion when it came to the relationship they shared with each other.

"Why do you two have to act so ugly? The whole neighborhood can hear you both screaming. Miss Taylor is still standing on her front porch eavesdropping," Talisa said, pointing in the direction of their next door neighbor.

"Betty Taylor can stand wherever she pleases. But she don't ever want to get in my business if she knows what's good for her," Mary proclaimed, spinning her stout body around to reach for the mop. "Just look at what you done to my floor," she hissed in Herman's direction.

The man reached for his boots, standing up straight as he headed out of the room in his bare feet and up the stairs. He muttered under his breath as he made his exit.

"Daddy doesn't need you fussing at him the minute he gets home from work. You know how hard his days are."

"Don't be telling me about your daddy. I've been with that man longer than you've been around. I know about your daddy."

"You just need to give him a break. I bet your blood

pressure is sky-high right now. That's not good for either of you."

Mary shrugged, moving to change the subject. "We're having baked chicken, rice and green beans for supper. I even made some peach cobbler for dessert. Your daddy likes my peach cobbler."

Talisa smiled, leaning to kiss her mother's cheek. "Did I get any calls?"

Mary nodded. "Some boy called here for you. I forgot his number though. Your daddy and his mess threw me right off track. I was just about to get a pen and some paper when he come in here with his evilness."

"Do you even remember the man's name?"

Mary sucked her teeth, tossing her daughter a look that said she should be careful with the tone of her voice. "Jericho. Like in the Bible."

Talisa inhaled swiftly, surprise registering across her face. "Jericho Becton?"

"Yeah, I think that was it."

"And you didn't get a telephone number?"

"I told you what your daddy done. Threw me right off track with his foolishness. That poor boy's number went right out my head. But I'm sure he'll call back. He's called before. He'll call again."

"Before?" Talisa's tone was incredulous. "You mean this wasn't the first time?"

Mary shook her head, reaching for a broom to sweep her floor. "No. He done called two or three times. I just forgot to tell you."

Talisa pursed her lips, rolling her eyes with disbelief. "Thanks," she muttered.

"You're welcome," the woman responded nonchalantly, oblivious to her daughter's annoyance.

Talisa tossed her hands into the air in frustration as she spun out the door. As she headed up the stairs, she passed her father making his way back down. He had changed from his city employee's uniform into a pair of khaki shorts and a white T-shirt. He leaned to kiss her cheek as they stood side by side on the same riser.

"I don't like it when you two fight," Talisa said, leaning her head against her father's shoulder.

"We wasn't fighting. It was just a matter of differences."

"Well, I don't like that either," Talisa responded.

The man laughed, kissing her forehead. "We'll work at it. We'll try to do better. So, when do you leave for Africa?"

Talisa grinned. "In a few weeks. I can't wait."

Her father returned the wide smile. "I'm real proud of you, pumpkin. I hope you know that."

Leaning into her father's hug, Talisa pressed her cheek to the man's broad chest. "Thank you, Daddy. I love you so much."

Herman London winked his eye as he released his grip around her torso. "Daddy loves you, too, baby. Daddy loves you, too."

Sitting side by side in the family living room, Talisa's parents were still trading barbs back and forth, stopping just long enough to watch an old *Cosby Show* rerun, before resuming their bickering during the commercial breaks. Talisa knew it would go on for most of the night, finally calming when one or the other retired for the evening.

Throwing her body across the length of her queen-sized bed, Talisa heaved a deep sigh. Jericho Becton had tried to call her. Not only had he called her, but he had actually tried on three separate occasions to catch up with her, and her mother had let the knowledge of that fact just slip from her mind. Talisa shook her head at the absurdity. For months now she'd been ignoring the woman's forgetfulness, turning a blind eye to the laundry that was left to mildew in the washing machine, or the dinner charred around the edges.

The termination notices from the utility companies had been laughed at as Talisa had rushed to make the payments, insuring services weren't disconnected. "I'd forget my own head if it wasn't attached," her mother would say with a deep chuckle, shaking gray hair from one side of her full face to the other. Talisa and her father would laugh with the woman, both ignoring that there might actually be a problem that they needed to address.

In conjunction with the woman's already volatile temperament, she was becoming increasingly difficult to deal with. Talisa made a mental note to discuss it with her father so that they might consider giving her mother's doctor a call to ask for advice.

Rolling over onto her stomach, Talisa reached into her nightstand drawer for a telephone directory. Flipping quickly through the pages, her disappointment was thick when she found no home listing for Jericho Becton. She found his office number, though, and repeated it in her mind as she agonized about whether or not she should call it. With nothing to lose, she reached for the phone extension and dialed.

A woman with a deep, Southern drawl answered the line. "Doctor's office. May I help you?"

Talisa cleared her throat, trying to will the nervous butterflies from her abdomen. "Yes, please. I'm trying to reach Dr. Jericho Becton."

"I'm sorry, but the office is closed. You've reached the answering service. Is this an emergency?"

"No, it isn't. I just needed to speak with him."

Talisa could hear the woman flipping through a pile of papers before she spoke again. "Dr. Jericho Becton isn't on duty so I'm unable to page him for you. In fact, we're directing all his calls to his father, Dr. Elijah Becton. According to my notes, Dr. Jericho will be out of the country for the next twelve months. His father is handling all his patients. Would you like me to page Dr. Elijah for you?"

Talisa shook her head into the receiver. "No. That's not necessary. I'm sorry to have bothered you."

"Not a bother, dear. If you change your mind, just give us a call back. Any of the operators will be able to reach the doctor for you."

"Thank you." Talisa disconnected the line, wiping at a tear that had edged its way to the corner of her eye. "Just perfect," she muttered under her breath. "Of all the lousy luck…"

Chapter 7

There was nothing left for Jericho to pack. His mother had arrived earlier in the day, navigating his laundry, his shopping, the watering of his plants, and organizing his duffel bag of casual clothing to prepare him for his trip. He smiled as he thought about his mother, the way she easily flitted from one chore to the other, ignoring his pleas for her to let him take care of things on his own. She'd been ignoring him since he'd been knee-high and able to tell her no. She'd chosen instead to do for him as if he were unable to do for himself. The relationship had made for some interesting moments between them when Jericho had grown old enough to challenge her parental authority and assert his independence. Folding his own laundry, preparing his meals, and making his own bed had been more than a task with Irene Becton at the helm.

Jericho reached for the telephone, tempted to dial the

woman's number one last time. Giving it a second thought, he dropped the receiver back onto the hook. He'd already left three messages with the woman who'd answered the telephone. Three times he'd been told that Talisa wasn't home to take his call. Three times Talisa hadn't bothered to call him back. Maybe he had been wrong about what he thought he'd seen in her eyes the night the two of them had met. He inhaled sharply, the memory of her pulling at his breath. The telephone ringing distracted him from his thoughts.

"Hello?"

"Jericho, hello."

The man heaved a deep sigh, pausing noticeably as he recognized the voice on the other end.

"Aren't you going to say hello?"

"What do you want, Shannon?"

"I just called to tell you what a delightful time I had the other day. I was hoping we might be able to do it again."

"I don't think so, Shannon. I was obligated for one afternoon. That's all."

"So, is that what our date was to you? An obligation?" The woman's tone was quickly brimming with tension. Jericho could feel the hostility beginning to spill across the telephone lines.

"It was your twenty grand, Shannon, and you got what you paid for. I was just upholding my end of the contractual agreement."

"I still love you, Jericho. Why are you being so hateful?"

Jericho sneered. "There isn't an ounce of love between us, Shannon. A woman doesn't do what you did to a man she claims to love."

"I made one mistake, Jericho. I deserve another chance."

Jericho scoffed at the thought. "Is that what we're

calling what you did? A mistake?" He shook his head into the receiver. "Don't do this, Shannon. You know that there is never going to be anything else between us. Don't make this difficult."

"I'm trying to make amends, Jericho. I want to show you what you still mean to me." The woman's tone was beseeching as she whispered loudly into the telephone, tears outlining her words.

Jericho refused to be moved by the display of emotion. "I have to hang up, Shannon. I have things to do. Thank you for calling."

"Jericho—" Shannon started before the dial tone filled her ear.

Jericho was annoyed by the rise of anxiety that had suddenly filled the pit of his stomach. As he stood with the telephone still pressed against the palm of his hand, the phone cord pulled from the wall, his body shook uncontrollably.

At the Atlanta airport, Jericho sat waiting for his British Airways flight to Entebbe, Uganda. He had a six-fifteen departure time, so his plane wouldn't land until seven twenty-five the next morning. With an extended twelve-hour layover at London's Heathrow Airport, he wouldn't see Africa until Monday morning, after a second overnight plane flight. He would have more than his fair share of time to while away, thinking about things that did nothing but cause him anxiety.

At that particular moment, Shannon Porter and Talisa London were both on his mind. So deep in thought, he barely noticed the flow of passengers gathering in the hard seats to the right and left of him. When a young child brushed against him, the little boy racing from his mother's side to his father's, the touch against his pant leg caused Jericho to jump with surprise. The child gave him a cautious stare, and then lifted his small hand to wave before scurrying off to peer out the large glass windows to the aircraft parked outside.

Jericho heaved a deep sigh. He had no interest in spending his entire two-day journey to Africa thinking about any woman, especially one who wasn't interested and one he surely didn't want. Unfortunately, the memories of both females seemed intent on haunting his spirit. He sighed again, swiping the back of his hand across his forehead as he finally looked up, taking in the view around him.

A newspaper stand caught his eye and he rose from his seat, shifting his carry-on bag against his shoulder. Pulling a copy of the *Atlanta Journal-Constitution* from a wire rack, he dropped a dollar bill against the counter and headed back toward his seat, not bothering to wait for his change.

As dark as his mood, the paper's headlines were dismal at best, and the drab surroundings of the airport did little to lift Jericho's spirit. He dropped back into a seat, tossing the paper onto the chair beside him. An airline attendant caught his eye and smiled, mouthing hello as she gave him a come-hither look. Jericho gave her a quick bend of his lips, then dropped his gaze back into his lap. He still had over an hour to wait before the airlines would start boarding flight # 0062 and he had no desire to make small talk. He closed his eyes tightly, crossing his arms against his broad chest.

He flashed back to the night of the auction and Talisa's warm smile. The woman had been a breath of fresh air and Jericho had inhaled the essence of her like much needed oxygen. The connection between them had been instantaneous, Jericho had thought, reflecting back on the waves of energy that had spun like a raging fire between them. He had been out of control, his mind lost in the brilliance of their connection. When she had bid, countering each offer, he had taken that as confirmation of his emotions, confident that she, too, was feeling the same things he was.

He bristled at the memory of Shannon's exorbitant bid, the flagrant display of the woman's wealth nothing but an acute irritation. Shannon had always placed far too much emphasis on her father's money, almost to the point of belittling anyone who had less than she did.

Since they'd been in first grade together at Marietta's The Walker School, Shannon had played by rules few others would ever understand. Even at the tender age of six, she'd imagined the world revolved around its axis for her alone and that the sun and moon set and rose as she willed them to. At The Walker School, Jericho's had been the only dark face in the small class of twelve students. The friendship between him and Shannon had been established at birth by virtue of their two fathers both being Yale University alumni and their mothers building an alliance on the demands of their elite social circle. By third grade, Irene Becton had insisted on a school with a more diverse student body and Jericho and Shannon's camaraderie was reduced to weekend gatherings and holiday vacations.

In junior high school, Jericho had become smitten with puppy love and Shannon had found a viable boy toy to manipulate and control. With much instigation from both sets of parents, they had allowed his infatuation and her obsession to define their romantic relationship. Despite both of them dating other people off and on during high school, once in college they'd been easily drawn back into the possibility of forever that their parents had seen for each of their futures. The Porter family had welcomed the prospect of their only daughter marrying a surgeon. Jericho's parents had seen resounding potential in Shannon being an ideal doctor's wife. Shannon had cleverly masked her idiosyncrasy to be self-absorbed from both families, and only Jericho had true knowledge of the woman's propensity for coldhearted antics.

A chill ran through him and he shivered in response. He clasped his arms tighter around his upper body, stealing a glance up at the attendant who was still cutting her eye in his direction, hopeful for his attention.

There had been a part of him that had truly loved Shannon. He'd reconciled her flaws and had learned to turn a blind eye to her deficiencies, focusing as much attention as he could muster on her strengths. His sophomore year in college she'd shown up unannounced at his dorm room door, paying him a surprise visit for his twentieth birthday and the two had become lovers. Shannon Porter had taken his virginity, but the loss of her own was still a mystery to him.

His first taste of heartbreak had come six months later when he'd flown to Vassar College, only to find her in bed with a fellow history major. Shannon had sworn the relationship was nothing special, just a momentary lapse of judgment for a quick minute of sexual release. He'd believed her heartfelt plea for forgiveness, her long lashes batting back the rise of tears. Things between them had improved and he'd actually found himself believing in the possibility of him and Shannon Porter living blissfully in love for the balance of their lives.

His surgical residency had been taxing on the relationship, but they'd endured. Both of their mothers had massaged the strain, rallying support to get them through the bouts of aloneness his intense schedule placed on their time together. But Jericho had seen the signs of their demise, choosing instead to ignore the warning signals that Shannon was clearly not the woman he was meant to spend the rest of his life with. The reality of that fact was made clear the last night the two of them had spent together.

The entire evening had started badly with Shannon in a snit about nothing and unhappy about everything. Dinner had ended with her throwing a tantrum because Jericho had refused to give up his weekend golf plans with his father to fly with her to Aspen, Colorado for an impromptu ski trip. It had been his father's fiftieth birthday and Jericho had been planning the get-together for months. Shannon had refused to understand, wanting him to defer his attention to her instead.

Despite her pouting, Jericho had spent the balance of their evening struggling to make Shannon happy. A spontaneous stop at a local jeweler had netted Shannon a diamond tennis bracelet and cost him a month's salary. After promising to take her away for a one-week holiday in Hawaii for her birthday, Shannon had seemed pacified and back at her apartment she'd feigned contentment. Later that night, as they lay side by side in her bed, he could never have imagined what would happen next.

The clock had barely struck midnight when the bickering began, Shannon once again imploring him to change his weekend plans to be with her. The bickering had increased to an all-out battle with Shannon throwing her possessions from one side of the residence to the other. When she'd lunged at him, slapping his face with the palm of her hand, it had taken every ounce of restraint for Jericho not to hit her back. The arrival of Atlanta's finest, beating their nightsticks against the front door in response to a neighbor's complaint should have been enough, but Shannon had taken their disagreement to a point of no return.

The duo had been separated, him in the living room and she in the bedroom, as the two law enforcement officers listened first to his side of the story and then to hers. Then, to Jericho's dismay, he'd been handcuffed and hauled off to the local police precinct, having to defend himself against an accusation of domestic violence. Shannon Porter had accused him of assault, the tale of her attack complete with sobbing tears and enough dramatic innuendo to place doubt on Jericho's character. Four hours of questioning had finally unearthed the truth and Jericho had been released.

Heartbreak couldn't hold a candle to the pain Jericho had felt. Everything within him had been destroyed. As the sun rose that next morning, so did Jericho's resolve. Shannon Porter became dead to him, nothing more than a faint memory of a bad time in his life. He'd never told his parents or hers what had happened between them. He still didn't know why, just wanting nothing more than to place as much distance between him, her and the memory as he could find. He believed that if he didn't have to discuss it, the easier it would be for him to forget. And now Shannon had the audacity to proclaim her blatant betrayal a mere mistake and her love for him to be real.

The little boy stood at Jericho's knee, watching him curiously. It was only then that Jericho realized his face was damp from his tears. Glancing quickly around to see if anyone else had noticed, he wiped the moisture against the back of his hand and forced himself to smile down at the child.

"What's your name?" he asked, leaning toward the toddler. "My name's Jericho."

The boy laughed, his curly head bobbing against his shoulders as he turned back to his mother, reaching to wrap his arms around the woman's legs. Jericho made a funny face, his eyes bugging out from his head, his tongue reaching down to his chin and the child responded with one of his own. They both laughed and for a quick moment, Jericho allowed the memories of Shannon Porter to stay dead.

Chapter 8

Stepping from the plane, Jericho inhaled deeply, filling his lungs with the scent of Mother Africa. The essence of her homeland was intoxicating and he was delirious with joy at being cradled in the arm of her vastness. As he maneuvered his way through customs and immigration he was greeted warmly by black men whose faces resembled the faces of friends and family back in Atlanta. Outside of the large white building, the warmth of sunshine rained down upon him, cascading heat through his body. The scent of flora planted in stone containers lined the airport's walkways, the vibrant color of hibiscus and porcelain roses standing bright against the man-made backdrop.

In the exterior of the arrival area, minivan drivers waited patiently for their charges, many holding neatly printed signs announcing the names of the passengers they awaited or the hotels they represented. They were each dark complexioned, skin tones ranging from deep chocolate-brown to a deeper blue-black. All were dressed conservatively, cotton slacks in navy, black or khaki, complemented by button-down dress shirts in pastels and whites.

The wide smile of Jericho's former college roommate and best friend, Peter Colleu, greeted him warmly, the man waving his hand excitedly in Jericho's direction. The man's deep voice and familiar accent called out his name as he rushed over to wrap his friend in a brotherly embrace.

"My friend," Peter chimed. "Welcome to my home."

Jericho grinned back, patting his friend's protruding stomach. "You look good, Peter. I see that wife of yours is feeding you well!"

Peter laughed. "You should find a woman to do the same for you, my friend."

The two continued laughing as Peter led the way to his vehicle and ushered Jericho into the passenger seat.

"So, how was your flight?"

Jericho sighed. "Long. I'm glad for it to be over."

"Well, you are here safely. Are you now ready to work? I have much work for you to do."

Jericho nodded. "Just say when."

Peter nodded his head. His expression became serious as he began to speak. "We are grateful to have you here with us. Our children need a good doctor."

"How many are with you now?"

"We have twenty-seven orphans plus too many to count in the villages. They have been abandoned because their parents had no way to feed them or disease has wiped out their families."

"How are you getting funding to take care of them?"

Peter glanced quickly toward his friend, then returned

his gaze back to the road. "Donations have helped. Your parents have been very generous. Their last check helped with the construction of the school."

Jericho smiled, nodding his head ever so slightly. "My mother believes in what you are doing. You know that all you have to do is ask and it is yours."

His friend grinned. "Did she send me that package?"

Laughter filled the interior of the car as Jericho chortled wholeheartedly. "She sent boxes of Butterfinger candy bars and Ding Dongs. More than enough to rot their teeth out."

"Whose teeth? That candy is for me!"

The two men continued chatting excitedly, catching up on the time that had elapsed since Peter had last been in the United States. As Peter maneuvered his vehicle along Gaba Road, the rising city stood out against a backdrop of plush, white clouds floating against a vibrant blue sky.

Conversation waned as Jericho's attention shifted to the views outside the window. An ebony-toned woman stood roadside, an infant clinging to her back. The mother's garments were well-worn, a purple, floral print skirt and green polo shirt hanging against her thin body. A large bowl of newly-picked bananas rested against the top of her head.

Peddlers traveled the length of roadway, some by foot, others riding on mopeds or pedaling bicycles. Peter caught him staring, then gestured with his head. "They are *bodas,*" he said, pointing to the young men on minibikes. "*Bodas* will deliver anything, anywhere."

Jericho smiled, turning his attention back toward a group of craftsmen gathered around a display of iron works, an assembly of newly fashioned iron gates lined in a neat row. As Peter continued their drive through the suburban streets, Jericho was struck by the abject poverty of the residential areas. Running water in the dilapidated homes was nonexistent. Children ran barefoot, threadbare clothing barely fit for dirty rags. A little girl, no more than five years old, stood alone, her thumb pulled into her mouth, a dusty-yellow cotton shift skimming the lines of her malnourished frame. Jericho heaved a deep sigh.

Noting the change in his friend's disposition, the man's initial excitement defusing quickly, Peter offered commentary. He pulled the vehicle off to the side of the road and shut down the engine.

"My homeland is still recovering from our days of political oppression and the subsequent war. Tribal animosity, corrupt politics and military tyranny had crippled us. Some parts of the country are still too volatile to think about traveling. But we are slowly becoming stabilized. Look at the city of Kampala. It thrives! It is the new Uganda! It is what this whole country shall one day become."

Jericho nodded his head slowly. "But the children look so dejected."

"Our children are hungry and homeless and there is no money to care for them. Thousands have been abducted by the Lord's Resistance Army to be child soldiers or sex slaves. Many more have been orphaned by the AIDS pandemic. Our sons and daughters have had a hard road to travel."

"Why isn't more being done to help them?"

Peter paused, a flicker of a tear rising to his eyes. "We are doing all we can," he answered, his words falling into a whisper.

"What can I do?" Jericho asked, turning to look his friend in the eye.

Peter smiled. "You are doing it, Dr. Becton. You are here, my friend."

Chapter 9

The two friends sat in quiet reflection as the waiter carved slices of slow-roasted meats onto their plates. The tradition of best friends' night had begun in high school, the monthly ethnic dining sessions initiated by Leila's obsession with foreign cultures and supported by Talisa's simple desire to hang out with her best friend.

That first year, on teenage allowances, or lack thereof, each monthly meeting had revolved around Oriental food, Yum Yum's Chinese Takeout the main staple of each event. A library screening of an Oriental art film featuring Chinese actor Yao Kim had ended with egg rolls and wonton soup. Sidewalk seats at the Chinese New Year's Day parade, complete with fireworks and the traditional dragon float, had been capped off with a shared order of beef lo mein and fried noodles. The following years, with the help of part-time jobs after school and a flux of creative energy, the activities and meals had become much more interesting.

This night was Brazilian night. With tickets to an Afro-Latino music festival, the two women had imbibed the cultural experience of Brazilian and Peruvian musicians, dancers and singers. The evening wasn't complete until they'd taken their seats at Fogo de Chao, a local Brazilian restaurant, to experience the culinary artistry of *churrasco*—large cuts of meat slow roasted over an open pit.

As the last slice of filet mignon was placed on her plate, Talisa palmed the dining chip that had been issued to them when they'd been seated. Twirling the coin between her fingers, she flipped the chip from green to red. The waiter stopped just as quickly and backed away from the table.

"Here, try the *liguica*," Leila said, reaching to place one of her spicy pork sausages onto Talisa's plate.

"The food is incredible," Talisa exclaimed, swallowing a mouth full of potatoes before she spoke.

Leila nodded, unable to speak, her own mouth a forkful away from overflowing. She reached for the chip, flipped it back to green and gestured to the waiter who rushed to their sides to refill the water glasses. As the last drop of fluid fell into her friend's crystal container, she flipped the chip back to red and the pleasant-looking man disappeared to the other side of the room.

"So, are you excited about your trip?" Leila asked, grinning in Talisa's direction.

"Yes. I'm also scared," Talisa answered, leaning back against her seat.

"I'd go with you if I could. You know how much I'd love to see Africa."

"You'd love to see Africa from a five-star hotel with an

experienced guide. Not with ten college students and a sleeping bag on a schoolroom floor."

Leila laughed. "So, next year you and I will go and we'll use my travel agent instead of yours."

Talisa laughed with her, her head bobbing up and down against her shoulders. She reached a palm into the air, her fingers waving excitedly. "Oh, oh, oh!" she exclaimed. "Did I tell you what my mother did?"

Eyebrows raised, Leila shook her head from side to side. "No. What's happened this time?"

"The hottie doctor called me. Not once, not twice, but three or four times. And she forgot to give me the messages."

"Your doctor from the auction? *That* doctor?"

Talisa nodded, pulling a forkful of salad to her lips.

Leila giggled. "I told you your mother was losing her mind. You don't get half the messages I leave for you. That's why I only call your cell now."

"I was so upset with her."

"Did you call him back at least?"

"I tried. Dr. Becton has left the country for the next twelve months," Talisa said, mimicking the only response she'd been able to get out of his nurse.

"Where did he go?"

Talisa shrugged, dejection painting a look of frustration across her face. "I don't have a clue. No one will say."

Her friend shook her head. "Oh, well. You win some and you lose some."

"Damn, Leila," Talisa muttered, tossing her hands into the air. "First, I didn't think he was interested. Then he calls and my mother ruins it for me. I've lost him twice now and we haven't even managed a conversation long enough to make a date."

Leila reached for the chip, flipping it to green for service. "Lord, have mercy! You cussed. This definitely sounds like a bottle of wine problem, if you ask me."

Their server smiled as Leila requested two glasses of wine. The two paused momentarily as they watched him head toward the bar and return quickly, a newly-opened bottle in hand. Leila resumed the conversation after the waiter poured them each a glass of cabernet. "So, how do you think your parents will do with you gone?"

Talisa shrugged. "My father will be fine. I've got some concerns about my mother though. Something's not right with her and I don't know what it is."

"Talisa, there's been something not right with your mother since before you were born. Your mother's borderline crazy. You just don't want to admit it. Maybe it's time she saw a doctor."

"Okay, maybe she's got some issues."

"*Some* issues? Girlfriend, I know she's your mother but you need to take those blinders off. I love your mother dearly, but she has a lot more than *some* issues."

Talisa sighed, her gaze meeting Leila's. She reached for her wineglass and took a sip. "They're still fighting like cats and dogs. I'm afraid of what might happen when I'm gone."

Leila reached out a hand, dropping her palm against the back of Talisa's clenched fist. "Your mother has an explosive temper. You and your father have both ignored it and now it's getting worse. It may very well be a chemical imbalance. Take her to see a doctor," the woman said more emphatically.

"I tried, remember? She had a fit and the next thing I knew, we were rolling on the floor while she tried to pull my hair out. For a month afterward no one got any sleep.

She was like a lunatic ranting through the house at all hours of the night. I don't want to go through that again."

"Talisa, your mother is grown. So are you, and for once you need to think about you. You can't make your mother get help and you don't have to take her abuse. You know my opinion. You and your father enable her behavior by trying to hide it. You might be keeping the neighbors from finding out, but she still isn't getting better. It's like I recommended before—when she gets like that you need to call the police. Then call me and we need to have her committed so that she can be evaluated."

Talisa chuckled, a nervous laugh to mask her sudden desire to cry. "I think I'll just go to Africa instead."

Her friend nodded. "But she's still going to be crazy when you get back."

Mary London was pacing the floor, her stress evident on her face. Every few minutes she would pause and tap her foot against the linoleum flooring, her arms folded harshly across her chest. Talisa tossed the woman a quick smile, attempting to alleviate the tension that surged anxiously throughout the home.

"Mom, you're going to wear out the floor. I promise you everything is going to be fine."

"I don't think you should go on this trip, Talisa. It's not safe."

"Nothing is going to happen to me. I have to go. It's my job."

"You don't know what could happen in them jungles. I don't like this. I don't like this at all."

Talisa reached to wrap her mother in a warm embrace. "You worry too much, Mommy."

"I should call that Reverend and tell him you can't go. That man doesn't know what's good for you, Talisa. You need to listen to me."

Her daughter smiled, shaking her head from side to side. Just then her father entered the room, reaching for the oversized backpack sitting on the floor by the entrance. "You ready to go, pumpkin?"

Talisa nodded. "Yes, sir."

Mary tossed her hands up, anxiety causing her to shake. "Herman? This ain't good. Talisa should stay home. She don't have no business going over to no Africa!" she exclaimed excitedly.

Her husband rolled his eyes. "Talisa has to go do her job, Mary. Stop giving her a hard time. She doesn't need that from you right now."

The tone of his reprimand stalled the woman's next comment, her mouth opening and then closing as she sputtered air.

Talisa took advantage of the moment, leaning to kiss her mother's cheek. "I'll call you when I get there to let you know I'm safe," she said, rushing behind her father as he exited the house. "I love you, Mom!" she called, closing the door behind her.

Still frozen where she stood, Mary bristled with anger. Talisa was hardheaded, she thought, always had been. Shaking her head in frustration the woman rushed to the door, pulling it open just as her husband and child pulled out of the driveway. She watched as they headed out of sight, knowing that this trip would be the worst thing that could happen to Talisa and she would probably be the one to fix the mess when the girl eventually came back home.

* * *

As the airplane came to a smooth stop at the end of the runway, the noise level inside the cabin rose to a high pitch. The ten students were cheering excitedly and although many of the passengers were eyeing them all with a curious stare, Talisa found their excitement infectious. She was grinning broadly as they collected their luggage and were processed through customs.

A small minivan was waiting in the arrival area, their host chaplain, Reverend James Oloya, greeting them cheerfully. "Welcome," Reverend Oloya chimed, reaching to shake everyone's hand.

"Thank you for having us, sir," Talisa said as the man embraced her warmly.

"No, my dear. It is we who are so grateful. We are very pleased to have you here with us."

"When do we get started?" Clarissa, the senior intent on practicing pediatric medicine, asked excitedly.

Their host smiled. "Tonight you'll be guests at the American Embassy while we prepare you for your duties. In the morning we will take you on a tour of the country and then in the afternoon, over to the village where you'll be spending the next two months."

As they climbed into the vehicle, Talisa locked eyes with another driver who was waiting patiently for his passengers. The mahogany-toned man smiled broadly, white teeth gleaming in her direction. He nodded his head ever so slightly as he appraised her, his gaze sweeping from the top of her head down to her feet. The overt gesture swept a wave of nervous tension through Talisa's body and she felt herself blushing profusely as she pulled her tote bag to her chest.

* * *

Despite a full night's sleep, Talisa was exhausted. The day had been long and there didn't appear to be an ending anywhere in sight. The morning had started with a two-hour history session about the country, then the minister and his staff had warned them against traveling north toward Sudan, where rebels were committing heinous crimes against civilians. Duly noted, Talisa had reiterated to her group the importance of none of them ever traveling unaccompanied and without letting her, or Reverend Oloya, know where they intended to venture. The rest of the day had been a whirlwind of activity, so much so that Talisa could barely remember one point from another.

Nakasero, the residential area where the embassy sat, wasn't much different from any other upscale community in the United States. There was an energy that resounded through the streets of Kampala, a direct reflection of the culture's growth and thriving independence. They'd been driven to Gaba, where the waters of Lake Victoria had seemed to welcome their arrival. Colorful boats sat invitingly against the dark waters. The shoreline was a wealth of nonstop activity. Black men were auctioning the morning's catch to fishmongers near the lake's shore, baskets overflowing with tilapias and Nile perch. Not far from the activity of buying and selling, the women were smoking meals of fish and fresh vegetables under heavy brick structures.

They'd traveled the road from Kampala to Jinja, stopping to admire the lush green landscape of the tea plantations that lay like thick blankets atop the rich, dark earth. In Jinja, they'd noted the dilapidated homes that had once housed Uganda's wealthy, now only empty, stagnant structures that looked out over the Nile.

Talisa had actually cried at the edge of the river Nile where bare-breasted women cleansed themselves and their laundry, children splashing in play in the cool waters. One of the students had asked for prayer and so they'd all stood in a circle, hand in hand, heads bowed as Clarissa led them in litany.

Talisa was grateful for the assortment of cameras that had captured the sights; memories she could reflect back on at a later time, in a different place. Her only memories at that moment were the stares and gazes of the women and children who would never know the privileged lifestyles she and her students took for granted. The van was quiet. Everyone was lost in deep reflection as Talisa stared out over the landscape. She was struck by how alone she suddenly felt.

"We're here," Reverend Oloya called out to them, pointing toward the village that was awaiting their arrival. Talisa leaped up to see a circular enclave of thatched roof huts, bordered by fields of sugar cane and manioc, a fruit much like the tropical cassava root. As they slid out of the automobile, a crowd was gathered in the center of the village and they were greeted with the excruciating screams of a small child in pain. Children were racing about as if lost and the women were wailing at the top of their lungs.

Reverend Oloya pushed his way to the center of the commotion, Talisa close behind him. The young girl was writhing on the ground, clutching her protruding abdomen as intense hurt contorted her face. The child's mother was beside herself, pleading in Bantu for someone to help them.

"There is a doctor at the orphanage down the road," Reverend Oloya shouted to Talisa.

Instinctively, Talisa tossed her tote to one of the young adults in her party and reached for the child, lifting the little girl into her arms. Her legs seemed to have a mind of their own as they propelled her straight toward the vehicle, Reverend Oloya and the crying mother close on her heels.

It was a short drive and as they entered the gates of the Home of Compassion Orphanage, Talisa's heart was racing. She brushed at the tears on the toddler's face, cooing softly into the small person's ear.

"Hold on, baby. Help is coming, sweetheart," Talisa murmured under her breath.

As Reverend Oloya pulled open the car door, another man rushed from nowhere to guide them to the clinic. The child's mother was still moaning and crying, words spewing out in her native tongue. Talisa understood the woman's grief, but had no understanding of what she was trying to tell them.

"This is Peter Colleu," Reverend Oloya said, the quick introduction meant only to ease the anxiety racing between them. "Peter, this is Talisa London, visiting with us from America. She is leading the mission team that will be lending you their services."

The man nodded politely. "Thank you. I'm sorry that your arrival is marred with sudden trauma."

Talisa could only nod her head, the weight of the ailing child bearing heavy on her shoulders and her spirit.

"This way. Our doctor is inside."

The strong smell of antiseptic greeted them in the entrance. Inside the white concrete building, a very tall, very elegant black woman guided them into an examination room. Talisa barely noticed the doctor who stood with his back to them as he pulled instruments and syringes from a locked cabinet. His tone was firm and commanding as he barked out orders and asked questions.

"What happened?" he queried from behind her, turning just as Talisa leaned down to cradle the child against the examination table.

The man named Peter answered as he and Reverend Oloya stood in the doorway, his arm wrapped consolingly around the mother's shoulder. Glancing up, it was the first time that Talisa noticed how young she was, her exquisite, deep chocolate complexion creased with worry.

"The mother says the child hasn't been well for a few days. She won't eat and last night she started screaming in pain. The mother walked all night to bring her to our village."

The doctor pushed Talisa aside as he began his exam, spinning her to stand against the wall behind him. So intent on his work, the man didn't even bother to focus a gaze on her, almost oblivious to her presence. Talisa eased out of the way as she watched him work on the child, the other woman following his orders effortlessly. His palm pressed gently against the child's stomach. The baby screamed and the doctor reached for a syringe, filling it with medication that he quickly injected into the little girl's arm. Talisa could sense him counting to himself as he stalled, waiting for the pain medication to take effect. Talisa found herself counting silently herself.

The second time the doctor pressed hard against the child's stomach, there were no screams, barely a whimper from the child. And just as quickly the little girl ceased crying, her gaze flickering back and forth in interest across the man's face. From where she stood, Talisa could see the child smile ever so slightly and she sensed the man must have smiled first as he stared down at her. They all stood in anxious anticipation for his diagnosis.

"What's her name?" the doctor asked, looking up for the first time, his eyes locking on the adults standing in the doorway.

Peter repeated the question in Bantu.

The mother answered, her fingers twisting nervously in front of her. "Juji."

The doctor nodded. "Juji has an abdominal hernia. There is a small hole in her stomach muscle and her intestines became trapped. I've pushed it back in but I'm going to have to operate to repair it, otherwise it will only happen again."

"She's going to be okay, isn't she?" Talisa asked, speaking out loud for the first time.

Turning an about face in her direction, Jericho Becton saw her for the first time. Recognition wafted like a current of electricity between them and both stared in disbelief.

"Yes," Jericho finally answered, his excitement seeping like a tidal wave of water from his glazed eyes. "Yes, Miss London. She'll be just fine."

Talisa grinned. A rush of color warmed the brown tones of her complexion, the tint of red flushing her cheeks. "Thank you, Dr. Becton. That's very good news."

Chapter 10

Talisa sat patiently in the clinic's waiting room. She had no idea of the time, but was certain that at least two hours had passed since the surgery had begun. Juji's mother had crawled onto a corner of the wooden bench against the other wall and had fallen into a deep sleep, forty-eight hours of sheer exhaustion overcoming her. Talisa had searched out a blanket from the clinic's sparse supply cabinet and had wrapped it snugly around the woman's lean frame.

Her own eyelids were heavy, beginning to get the best of her. Images of the handsome doctor had occupied her mind since he'd greeted her, the two of them offering a quick explanation to the others about the nature of their acquaintance. When he'd asked her to wait with Juji's mother, she'd nodded willingly, not bothering to pause for a second thought. She was finally succumbing to the burden of exhaustion that pressed heavy against her shoulders. She closed her eyes and leaned her head back against the wall, the pattern of her breathing shifting gears toward slumber.

Jericho came to a stop in the doorway, watching as Talisa fought to keep her eyes open, losing the battle as she sank lower in her seat. She was breathtaking in the simple white blouse and khaki trousers that fit her nicely. He was in awe, unable to comprehend how the exquisite creature could actually be there. Talisa London was so close that he could smell the light essence of vanilla in her perfume, the aroma of fragrance scenting the air around her. He heaved a deep sigh, a heavy shiver coursing through his bloodstream. Pulling the green surgical cap from the top of his head, he moved to take the seat beside her, brushing his palms against the matching green surgical scrubs he wore.

Jericho pressed a warm palm lightly against Talisa's knee, gently stroking the flesh beneath her cotton slacks. The woman jumped with a start, her gaze flickering with disorientation until focus finally settled on Jericho's smiling face. Talisa smiled back, her hand moving over her mouth as she tried to suppress a yawn with her palm.

"Excuse me," she whispered, her voice low so as not to wake the sleeping woman.

"I didn't mean to scare you," Jericho whispered back.

"How's Juji?"

"Sleeping. That one's a fighter. We probably won't be able to keep her still when she wakes up."

A pregnant silence suddenly filled the space between them as they both continued smiling nervously.

"What are you doing here?" Jericho finally asked. "And why didn't you return my telephone calls?"

"I'm so sorry. My mother forgot to give me your first

messages and by the time she remembered, your office said you were gone. What are *you* doing here?"

"Volunteering. I came to help my friend Peter and his wife get this clinic operating. Now back to you. What are you doing in Uganda?"

"I'm here with a college work team. We're here on an eight-week, church-related, missions program."

Jericho nodded with approval as he processed the knowledge that not only was Talisa there in the flesh, but that she would be there for an extended period of time. He glanced down at this watch, the hands on the timepiece approaching the midnight hour.

"I can't believe I've kept you here this long. Have you eaten? Are you hungry?" Questions raced a mile a minute from Jericho's mouth.

Talisa smiled, the warmth of the gesture suddenly stalling the man's words. "Thank you, but I'm too exhausted to be hungry. It's been a long day."

"You can stay here if you'd like. We've got a few empty beds in the back."

"Well…" Talisa hesitated. Certain that most in the village compound were probably sound asleep, and having no idea where it was they'd arranged for her to stay, she surmised staying at the clinic was probably the better option. "If it won't be a problem, I should probably stay here," she concluded.

"No problem at all. The beds aren't overly comfortable, but it's quiet. Juji is our only patient tonight and she should sleep straight through the night."

"I'm sure I'll sleep like a rock myself."

Jericho came to his feet, extending a hand to help Talisa to hers. As she rose, Talisa became acutely aware of just how close his body was to hers. So close she could study the chiseled lines of his profile with ease, noting the faint brush of new growth that painted the beginnings of a new beard across his face. His smooth, caramel complexion had tanned deeply beneath the intense African sun. But what was most apparent was that he looked much more at ease than Talisa remembered from their last encounter. He'd been out of place at the auction, but there, within the clinic walls, he was in his element: secure, confident and in total control.

The exchange of energy permeated with an eroticism that had them both breathing too heavily for comfort. It was an unspoken wanting that pulled them closer, Jericho taking an unconscious step toward her and Talisa meeting him with one of her own. Jericho reached his arms around her and pulled her close, his face brushing against the softness of her curls. Talisa reached out to hug him back, pressing her body comfortably against his.

"Welcome to Uganda, Talisa London. I'm very glad you're here."

Talisa awoke from a sound sleep just as quickly as she had fallen into it. Her gaze focused instantly on the little girl sitting upright in the bed across from her and the child's mother who lay beside her daughter, humming softly. Juji smiled and lifted her hand in a slight wave. Talisa pulled her body upwards and waved back. Juji's mother sat up and grinned in her direction, greeting her warmly.

Looking around, Talisa took in her surroundings beneath the morning light. The room was sparse, two rows of twin beds lined neatly against the walls with a small nightstand between each one. There were no curtains at the windows and sunlight flooded the interior. Someone had placed a new toothbrush still wrapped in cellophane, a sample tube of toothpaste, a washcloth and a bar of soap on the small nightstand at Talisa's side. As Talisa swept the items up into her arms, the woman from the night before entered the room.

"Good morning, Ms. London."

"Good morning. I'm sorry, but I don't know your name."

"Angela. Angela Colleu."

"You must be Peter's wife?"

The woman smiled, a brilliant display of straight, white teeth. "Yes."

"It's very nice to meet you, Angela. And please, call me Talisa."

Angela nodded as she reached to check Juji's temperature. There was a brief exchange of conversation between them and Talisa listened with amusement at the quick, lyrical linguistics of the language.

"Juji says you are very beautiful. She has many questions about you," Angela said, coming to sit on the bed beside Talisa.

Talisa smiled in the little girl's direction. "Thank you," she said, nodding at the grinning child.

"The rest of your group has just arrived from the village. Peter has breakfast ready for everyone. There is a bathroom and shower down the hall where you can freshen up. One of the students placed your luggage inside for you."

"Thank you. I definitely need to get into some clean clothes."

Angela smiled. "Jericho wanted to come wake you, but I would not let him. Now he is pouting. He is such a man."

Talisa laughed. "I'm glad he didn't see me like this. I'm sure I don't look that good this morning."

"That one will think you look beautiful no matter what. He is very excited about you being here. You and he are old friends, no?"

"We actually just met recently and only for a few minutes."

Angela clapped her hands together. "That would explain it then. You have both been touched."

Talisa looked at the woman questioningly, her gaze meeting Angela's dark eyes in query. "Touched by what?"

Angela rose to her feet, gesturing for Talisa to follow. The woman smiled smugly as she answered. "Touched by the light of love, of course."

Jericho paced the concrete floor of the clinic's small office. He was weary, his energy level nearing an all-time low and his body was feeling it from his shoulders down to his lower back. His sleep had been less than restful, his mind overwhelmed with anxiety. Anxiety plaguing his dreams. What had he been thinking? He'd been so consumed by his excitement that he had blundered about like an adolescent. As innocent as it was intended, it was sheer boldness that had prompted him to pull Talisa into his arms.

She had fit against him as though they'd been made for one another and all had felt right with his world. Even when they'd both pulled back, embarrassment tingeing the moment, things between them had seemed copacetic. But Jericho knew things weren't always what they appeared and what had seemed very right between them could easily turn very wrong. Shannon had taught him that harsh lesson.

Jericho shook a quiver of coldness through his body, the sensation sweeping down the length of his spine. Clasping a hand over his fist, he cracked the knuckles of each appendage. A deep inhale of air blew mournfully past his lips. He suddenly remembered the feel of Talisa's cheek pressed against his, the gaze that had caused him to melt with wanting, and the laughter that had warmed him from the pith of his center. He smiled, hope settling easily into his bloodstream. Talisa London was nothing like Shannon.

Peter's presence in the doorway pulled at Jericho's attention.

"Good morning, Peter," Jericho said, acknowledging his friend's arrival.

Peter smiled. "How are you this morning?"

Jericho nodded his head, then shrugged his shoulders. A wide grin spread across his face as the other man appraised him all-knowingly.

"The volunteers from Wesley are here. They are having breakfast with the children this morning. Their arrival is special to us so the women have made *mkate mayai.*"

Jericho's grin widened as he thought about the breakfast meal. Originally an Arab dish, *mkate mayai,* or bread eggs, was a rare treat for them all. Made from wheat dough spread into a thin pancake and filled with minced meat and raw egg, the concoction was then folded into a neat little package and fried over hot stones until done. Suddenly realizing just how famished he was, Jericho dropped a hand to his abdomen, hunger growling loudly for attention.

Peter laughed. "It would seem your appetite will be just fine. How about your heart?"

Jericho cut an eye toward his friend as the two men headed out the office door into the courtyard. "My heart is just fine," he said sheepishly.

"Miss London is very special to you, I see."

"I barely know the woman."

"But you will. Angela says you two are sharing the same heart. She is ready to see the two of you married already."

"Tell your wife to stay out of this."

"You know my wife will do as she pleases, and it would seem to please her to see you and Miss London together. She says you two have been touched."

Jericho rolled his eyes. Angela Colleu was the perfect complement to his friend. The duo had met in England, both doing graduate work at Oxford University. After an intense political debate about the theologies shared by Prime Minister Tony Blair and President Bill Clinton, the two had been inseparable, marrying one year later. It had been love at first sight.

Wherein Peter had immersed himself in Western culture, Angela had instead clung to the ancient ways of the Ugandan tribe she'd been raised in. It made for a perfect match when they'd chosen to return to their homeland to dedicate themselves to helping their fellow countrymen improve their lives. Side by side the two made a handsome couple, both tall in stature with lean builds, blue-black complexions, and the same intoxicating smile that made you feel as if you'd known them forever. Jericho had great admiration and respect for Angela and he loved her like a sister.

As the two men stepped inside the doors of the orphanage's dining room, Jericho couldn't help but notice the quiet exchange that passed between husband and wife, followed by the intense look Angela was giving him. He smiled nervously, then shifted his eyes around the room searching for Talisa.

"She is not here," Angela said with a smile as the two men took a seat at the table.

Peter laughed.

Reverend Oloya reached out his hand in greeting. "Good morning, Dr. Becton. Are you looking for Miss London?"

Jericho could feel himself blushing. "Good morning, Reverend. I was told the volunteers had arrived already."

The man nodded his gray head. "They're in the chapel. Miss London wanted to meet with them before they started this morning."

Jericho nodded. "Have they been fed?" he asked.

"Yes," Angela answered, still staring intently in Jericho's direction. "You are the only one who hasn't eaten yet. Your breakfast has gone cold waiting for you."

Jericho's disappointment swept across his face and Angela tossed Peter another silent message. Peter laughed again, pushing himself up and away from the table.

"Reverend Oloya, will you join me for a walk?" Peter said, his gaze focused on the senior member of their group. "I'd like your opinion about some of our future plans."

Jericho watched as the two men headed out the door. He suddenly lost his appetite, pushing his barely eaten plate away from him. He could feel Angela still staring at him, but he refused to meet her gaze. Pulling the plate back ever so slightly, he forced himself to take a bite of his breakfast, feigning interest in peeling a banana that lay across his plate.

"What?" Jericho said finally, spinning in his seat to face the woman. "What do you want to say, Angela?"

The woman smiled. "Nothing. Why are you behaving so strangely?"

Jericho sneered and then the two laughed loudly.

"I like her, Jericho," Angela said after catching her breath. "I think you and Talisa will be good for one another."

Jericho shook his head, waving it from side to side. "We barely know each other."

"It is like you've known her a lifetime."

"Maybe in a past life."

"Perhaps, but you greeted her with your heart when you saw her. The Nigerians have a saying that when a handshake goes beyond the elbow, it becomes something else."

Jericho rolled his eyes. "You don't know what you're talking about."

"I know you, and I can see the energy the two of you share. She has stepped into your light and you into hers. You are both brighter together than you are apart. I don't need to know anything else." Angela stood up. The warmth of her appraisal seemed to rain down over him and any weight of doubt felt as if it was being lifted from Jericho's shoulders.

Angela placed a large hand against his arm. "When you're ready, Talisa and her students need to know what you need them to do. I told her the two of you would decide together who needed to go where. She'll be waiting for you in your office." Angela turned to leave, stopping to take one last glance over her shoulder. "Now, finish your breakfast. We do not have food to waste around here."

Eyes wide, Jericho watched as his friend headed back in the direction of the clinic. Her words washed through him, seeping deep into his pores. He found himself wanting to believe in her confidence of him and Talisa as a couple, to believe it as true as Angela's intuition believed it to be true. Inhaling the last of his food, Jericho rushed toward a new beginning, hurrying to meet Talisa.

Chapter 11

She was standing in the corner of his office, staring out the window at the children who played happily in the courtyard. Jericho stopped short in the entranceway to watch her. His gaze skimmed the length of her body, his senses awash in the length of chestnut hair pulled into a tight ponytail that hung down to her shoulders, the pale pink cotton polo shirt which complemented the brown of her complexion, waving past the khaki slacks that neatly fit the round curves of her buttocks, stopping at the slip-on sneakers that adorned her feet.

His mind whirled. The magnetic woman thrilled him. As Angela had just said, it was as if he'd known her for a lifetime and Jericho was suddenly awestruck by the possibilities a future might hold for them. He took a deep breath, straining to stall the sudden rush of excitement that had encompassed his body. He felt his heart leap when she turned, her gaze meeting his.

Talisa smiled warmly, sunlight gleaming along the lines of her profile. Outside, the rising sun was already hot in the clear morning sky, floating against the crystal backdrop like molten gold. Just minutes before, she'd been thinking how idyllic the day had begun. As her eyes locked with Jericho's, confirmation of that thought reflected back at her.

His stare was intense, swallowing her whole. Hesitation, then resolve, danced in his eyes, willing her to fall head-first into the emotion spilling from his spirit. She could feel a faint line of perspiration beading between her breasts and the air in the room had suddenly become heavy. Dropping her gaze to the floor, Talisa had to catch her breath, nervous excitement infusing butterflies in her stomach.

"Good morning," Jericho said, his lips pulling into a deep smile that flooded his face with joy.

Talisa smiled back. "Good morning, Jericho." She took a deep breath. "How are you this morning?"

The man nodded as he came to stand at her side. He took a quick glance out the window, then back toward Talisa. "Excited. It feels like it's going to be a good day. How about you?"

Talisa beamed. "I was just thinking the very same thing."

"Did you sleep well?"

She nodded. "I did. I slept very well. Thank you."

Jericho gestured for her to take a seat in the empty chair behind the desk. He sat down in the wooden chair opposite her.

"So, I'm told that most of your group are medical students?"

"Correct. Two of the young men are research scientists doing graduate work at the university, but the others are all second, third and fourth year students."

"How about you?" Jericho asked, personally curious more than anything else.

"Actually, I am the only nonmedical member of the group. But I do a lot of volunteering at the women's clinic in Atlanta and the hospital so I have some experience around medical personnel and procedures. Typically, I deal mostly with teens and young mothers, teaching parenting courses, safe sex, that kind of thing."

Jericho nodded. "Your responsibilities here won't be as glamorous. A good deal of what we need to do is grunge work. I'm trying to get as many children immunized as we can but we're limited in staff and our drug supply is exceptionally low. I'm hoping we'll be better stocked by next week and with the help of your group we can spread out to some of the villages. I think your skills will come in handy and we'll need your help with AIDS awareness. It's a definite problem here and education is sparse.

"Peter and Angela also need extra hands repairing some of the structures here at the orphanage. Some of these buildings were just slapped together with paper and glue and they're starting to fall apart. Every warm body that can help get something done is appreciated."

Talisa smiled, her head bobbing up and down. "We are eager to pitch in wherever you need us. Most of the students have limited building experience. We work with Habitat for Humanity every year. And, if there isn't someone who can show us how to do something we're more than willing to give it our best effort."

Jericho smiled back. His gaze shifted around the room, his sudden awareness of a rise in his body temperature causing him some discomfort. When his eyes fell back on

Talisa, her gaze had fallen to the floor, her hands twisting nervously in her lap.

He cleared his throat. "I…um…just want to apologize again for last night. I didn't intend to make you feel uncomfortable when I hugged you."

Talisa blushed. "You didn't. Don't give it a second thought. We hugged each other. It really was nothing," she said, trying to make light of the incident. As she reflected back on the moment she kicked herself for the little white lie that had slipped past her lips. His arms around her had been much more than nothing. She had wanted him to hold her, had walked willingly into his embrace, her head dropping easily against his chest as they lost themselves in the moment. The warmth of Jericho's body pressed tightly against hers had definitely been something. Something exceptional. Something special. Something she'd been yearning for without even realizing it. As she met his stare again, her lips parted ever so slightly, her breath coming in a quick gasp, she sensed that he had thought so as well. Then she worried that her own imagination was getting the better of her, control being lost to the heat raging in the body parts that made her female.

Jericho came to his feet, the emotion filtering through his body unnerving. The look she gave him mirrored his own, desire painted in the warm coloration of her face, wanting spilling from her eyes like water from a faucet. He so wanted to give in to the waves of emotion flooding between them. Shaking the sensation from his head, he heaved a deep sigh, imagining her giving him a resounding slap to his face were she to read the erotic thoughts that had just crossed his mind.

"Well," Jericho said, struggling to contain the anxiety

in his voice. "Why don't we go get started. I'm sure we won't have any problems working together."

Talisa nodded, brushing her damp palms against her cotton shorts. "I'm sure we won't," she concluded as she followed him out of the room.

The morning had sped by and before Talisa knew it the sun was starting to set over the horizon. She and the students had quickly settled in, finding more things that needed to be done than any of them could have imagined. The lengthy to-do list ran the spectrum from assisting with medical care in the clinic, doing minor repairs to the cottages, helping with English lessons for the children, to planting a garden in the rich soil that bordered the edge of the orphanage property.

Talisa stretched the length of her body. The day had been long and she was weary from the never-ending activity that had consumed her since she'd left the doctor's office that morning. As she unpacked the last box of books onto the shelves in the storage room, she couldn't help but think about the man. Thoughts of him had consumed most of her day, fiction and fantasy flickering through her mind like snapshots in a slide show. So deep in thought, she barely noticed the woman who stood in the entrance watching her.

Angela's warm voice startled her out of her daydream. "Jericho will be like a spoiled child if you miss dinner with us tonight."

Jumping to attention, Talisa clasped a hand over her heart. "Angela, you scared me," she said, chuckling lightly.

The two women stood smiling at each other as Angela nodded. "My apology. I came to tell you it is time for supper. We are having a welcome meal tonight to thank you and the others for volunteering. Jericho has been like the big cats pacing the floor for you to arrive."

Talisa blushed. "He's been very helpful."

Angela laughed. "He is a good man, our doctor. And he has eyes only for you."

Talisa could feel the color flushing her cheeks. Her eyes skipped around the room fighting not to stop on Angela's intense gaze. Angela was amused by her nervousness and said so.

"You are as silly as he is. You and Jericho are meant to be. It is written in the stars for you. I can see it. Come, we shouldn't keep them waiting."

Following behind the woman, Talisa couldn't find any words to respond to Angela's pronouncement. There was a part of her that wanted to wave off the prediction as nothing but wishful thinking on Angela's part. But there was a much larger part of her that wanted to believe that the woman might have known what she was talking about.

As they crossed the courtyard the tap-tap of the Acholi drum sounded through the evening air. A large fire burned in a pit and the small community was gathered around it. The savory aroma of marinated meat filled the air as chicken sat soaking in a broth of olive oil, wine, spices and pineapple juice. Talisa smiled as she noted the Wesley students holding hands with the children, the youngest tots negotiating for space on someone's lap. Everyone was laughing and smiling as the music played, toddlers danced, children sang and the warmth of a traditional tune resounded in the air.

Talisa stopped in her tracks, overcome by a wave of emotion that she had no explanation for. It was a happiness that was so intense, so encompassing that it seemed to choke the breath from her. Her expression was painted with the brilliance of it and as she stood staring from one face to another, Jericho felt himself being consumed by the sheer beauty of it.

He had watched her as she followed behind Angela, his friend's long strides quickly leaving Talisa behind. And then she'd stopped, her gaze racing from one corner of the gathering to the other, her eyes wide with wonder. Reverence had washed over her expression, dancing in the lines of a slow smile that had quickly overflowed with joy across her exquisite face.

As he stood watching, her eyes suddenly locked with his, holding him captive in his seat. They stood staring and it was as if time stopped, the hands of the clock adjusting itself to register a moment of absolute perfection. Peter's voice suddenly pulled him from the moment, fighting for his attention.

"There is our guest. Talisa, come sit here," Peter called, gesturing for the woman to take the seat across from Jericho.

As she made her way to the low table and took a seat, Jericho clasped his hands in his lap, wiping at the perspiration that had dampened his palms. He nodded in greeting, his voice lost deep in the nervous tension in his midsection. Talisa smiled sweetly, fighting not to stare at him, then turned to observe the children who were performing up on the stage.

Six of them stood side by side, the oldest no more than twelve years old. To the accompaniment of drums, a xylophone and a fiddle, they danced and sang, performing a traditional dance. Talisa listened intently as Peter explained the historical and social origins of each number. With his elbows on the table, his chin resting in his palms, Jericho leaned toward her, every so often asking a question of his friend.

Talisa watched in awe as two of the teenagers performed a soft dance number, the easy movements engaging their lithe frames. The beauty of the tempo was subtle at first, rising to an impassioned intensity that was eerily captivating. She suddenly sensed Peter and Angela watching her closely and she turned to see why it was they stared. Jericho, who had been equally immersed, was suddenly pulled from the moment.

Angela smiled as she began to tell them a story about the dance being playing out on stage. "There is old folklore about the history of our people. In the beginning of time when the earth was bare and darkness filled the sky, the great Creator came forward to bless the land. He washed rivers of blue water from one end to the other and made the land fertile for the plant life and animals to grow. Uganda was as the Garden of Eden in the Christian Bible. The first black man was placed on one edge of the country and the first woman on the other. They existed alone searching for what was missing, knowing that there was something special that awaited them at the end of their journey."

Angela paused to stare at the couple up on the stage, limbs entwined in the fluid motion of the dance. Her eyes widened as she continued. "One day a hint of light flickered in the dark sky and both were drawn to the beauty of it. They walked for days, eager to reach its center, watching as it grew larger, beginning to fill the whole of the sky. The day came when the light was shining brightly from one corner of the world to the other, no darkness found anywhere and beneath that light the man and the woman found each other. It was the light of love that drew them to each other and washed down over them. It was beneath this light that their children and grandchildren were conceived. That light was their strength and it magnified the beauty of what was meant to be between them." Angela stopped, settling back against her seat, her stare focused back on the stage as the dance came to an end.

Peter nodded his head slowly, looking from Talisa to Jericho. "The old people say that only a special few are touched by this light because it is the will of the Creator that brings them to it. It just is and nothing and no one can keep them from finding each other beneath it."

Across the table the couple locked eyes, falling into the moment. Talisa felt as if she had fallen waist deep into the blue gaze that seemed to own her, calling her possessively. Neither could find the words to respond to their hosts, marveling at the significance of their story.

As the show wound down, Peter clapped his hands excitedly. "You two will enjoy this last one also," he said, grinning from Jericho to Talisa and back again.

"This is the *orunyege,* a courtship dance performed among the Banyoro-Batooro people of western Uganda. In the past, young men and women would be brought together in front of the community to choose their future mates. This ceremony was very important, especially for the boys because if they were poor dancers they risked being rejected from the girls."

The drums were intoxicating, the deep rhythmic beat reigning control. The dance was demanding, an exuberant showcase of talent and style. When the performers were finished, applause resounded through the air, cheers and shouts filling empty space in the stratosphere.

Turning back to face Jericho, Talisa tried to ignore the

nervous flutter that danced in her stomach. Peter grinned knowingly as he patted his friend on the back, leaning back in his own chair.

"I am told, Talisa, that Jericho is a very good dancer. Perhaps one day you can convince him to dance for you."

"He's cute, isn't he?" Clarissa asked, her voice low as she whispered to Talisa.

"Who's cute?"

The young woman gestured with her head, her gaze moving from Talisa's face to Jericho and back again.

Jericho stood in the exam room, changing the bandages on an old man's legs. Ulcers had blistered the man's flesh and he was visibly agitated by the annoyance of his predicament. Angela stood at Jericho's side, translating the senior citizen's complaints and the doctor's instructions.

A wave of warmth tickled Talisa's stomach. Fighting not to stare, she turned her attention back to the inventory of medical supplies. "He's nice-looking. I guess," she said, feigning disinterest.

Clarissa laughed at her. "You think he's cute, too!"

"You are trying to throw off my count."

"We're actually finished," Clarissa responded. "Everyone is ready to go," she said, pointing to the plastic containers filled with medical supplies. She leaned to secure the lids on each.

"Good. Why don't you let Reverend Oloya and Peter know."

"Are you joining us?"

Talisa shook her head no. "Peter is taking you, John, Barry, Tara and Adam with him. Everyone else is going with Reverend Oloya. I'm staying here to help in the clinic.

I'm also going to be teaching an English class at the school. I don't have the medical training the rest of you have so I think I'd just be in the way out in the fields. I'll get more accomplished here."

Clarissa nodded. "I wouldn't be so sure about that. Once these kids realize we're here to inoculate them, we might need an extra hand to hold them down."

Talisa smiled. "I'll pass. I want them to still like me when we leave here."

Clarissa pulled a large plastic bag from a zippered pouch in her backpack. She shook it in Talisa's direction.

"What's that?"

"Bubble gum and lollipops. Once the guys stick 'em, I plan to cheer 'em right up."

Talisa laughed. "Get going and remind everyone to please be careful."

Jericho grinned as Talisa joined them, a wide smile across her own face. Angela looked from one to the other, nodding her head. She said something to the old man in their native tongue that made him stare first at Talisa, then Jericho, before offering commentary that only Angela understood. The two laughed, the patriarch seeming to nod his approval.

"They are laughing at us," Jericho said, cutting his eye toward Talisa.

"How could you tell?" she asked facetiously.

Angela smiled. "We are laughing for you, not at you. We are just rejoicing in the wisdom of what will be."

Jericho pulled the rubber gloves from his hands, discarding them into the trash. "Talisa and I are just going to ignore you. Now, what's next on our agenda, Mrs. Colleu?"

"You are scheduled to visit the AIDS hospice this morning. Talisa will be joining you. She needs the exposure."

Talisa nodded slowly, taking a deep inhale of air. "I'm ready when you are, Dr. Becton, but I would like to check on Juji before we leave."

Jericho nodded. "Juji is at the school. I told you we wouldn't be able to keep that one still."

"Is that safe?"

The man smiled. "She'll be fine. We're keeping a close eye on her."

Angela pointed a finger toward the door, dismissing them. "You two need to get going. Drive safe, Jericho. We'll see you later for dinner."

There was no denying the beauty of Uganda. It ran deeper than the lush, fertile shores of Lake Victoria, the dusty desert of the northeast lands, or the mountains of the western borders. The magnitude of Uganda's beauty coursed deeper than the bloodlines of its people, gleaming its intensity out of its children's eyes.

As they made the drive back toward Kampala, Jericho and Talisa sat in quiet contemplation. Conversation was sparse as both sat absorbing the picturesque views, inhaling the aromas of the landscape, and reveling in the comfort of just being at each other's side.

Jericho broke the silence. "I don't think we should consider this our first date. I was hoping for something a little more romantic myself."

The comment was unexpected, coming with a quiet conviction that made Talisa smile. Jericho watched her out of the corner of his eyes, his gaze shifting back and forth between her and the road.

He continued. "I really can be very romantic," he said, his low voice dropping even lower.

Talisa could feel the inflection of his words filtering through her bloodstream, causing her to quiver in her seat. "Is that so?" she responded, trying not to choke on the sudden rise of desire that swept over her.

Jericho nodded. "I like to give it my best shot. And, I haven't had too many complaints over the years."

"But you've had complaints?" Talisa asked, a slight smirk gracing her face.

Jericho shrugged, tossing her a wry smile. "Only two. First time was in third grade. Vivian Kelly had some issues with the bullfrog I gave her for her birthday. Then again last month. I didn't pay enough attention to my auction date. My mind was on the woman who didn't win. The woman I really wanted to be with. My date wasn't happy. Go figure."

Talisa laughed out loud. "Maybe we shouldn't count those. Seems like you were at a disadvantage."

"See, I knew you'd understand."

Talisa took advantage of the moment to ask a question that had crossed her mind countless times since the evening of the auction. "Was that woman a friend of yours?"

Jericho pursed his lips, reflecting on his answer before responding. "We were friends once. We grew up together, then started dating in college. We were engaged to be married, but broke it off. Things didn't work out."

Not at all what she'd expected or had hoped to hear, the statement came like a harsh right cross to her abdomen. Talisa struggled not to let Jericho see her obvious discomfort, turning to focus her attention out the window. The gesture failed.

"I'm sorry," Jericho said, turning to stare directly at her.

The vehicle they were riding in slowed, dropping well below the speed limit.

Talisa shook her head. "No, don't be. I asked the question. You only answered it. I don't know why it bothered me."

A pregnant pause filled the space between them.

"No, I take that back," Talisa said suddenly. "I do know why that bothered me. It hasn't been that long since you ended an engagement. You were going to marry this woman and it seems that she's still very interested in that idea. I don't want to be a rebound relationship while you're trying to figure out what you want."

Jericho sighed, blowing warm breath past his lips.

"Shannon and I are finished. I don't have any feelings for her. You can trust that. Whatever develops between you and I will be something we both want for the right reasons. I'm not trying to get over Shannon. I've been over Shannon for a long time."

"But clearly she has feelings for you. Twenty thousand dollars' worth of feelings, to be exact."

Jericho pulled off the road, bringing the car to a complete stop before shifting the gear into Park. He twisted his body to face her, pulling her hands between his. "Talisa, I know we don't know each other very well, but I think you and I made a great connection back in the States. Whatever it is you want to call it, we both felt it. Now, tell me if I'm wrong, but I think you and I are still feeling it."

Talisa's head bobbed up and down slowly as she nodded her agreement. Jericho paused as his gaze fell to the views outside the car window before returning to Talisa's face. His eyes flickered about trying to capture each detail to memory, the exact shade of her brown complexion, the arch of her eyebrows, down to the curve of her nose and how her ears lay against the side of her head. His gaze rested on the fullness of her mouth and the tiniest of tongues that peeked through every so often to moisten her lips.

His heart was racing at rapid speed, his conscience urging him to share everything. The initial flirtation between them was clearly something more and Jericho was suddenly hungry for it, wanting to claim it as his and his alone as he wrapped himself in the magnitude of it. From what he saw as she stared back at him, Jericho was certain Talisa was feeling the same way.

"This isn't easy for me," he said, his voice coming low. "But I need for you to know everything." As he spoke, the story of him and Shannon, and the history they shared, clouded the air between them. When he finished, he studied Talisa's expression, wary of her reaction. He so wanted her to believe and understand him, that desperation fell like rain from his eyes.

Talisa pulled her hand from beneath his, pressing her palm to the side of Jericho's face. She wiped away the tears from his cheek and said nothing, falling back against the car's seat as silence wafted between them. Unnerved by her silence, Jericho shifted the car back into Drive and pulled back onto the main road to resume their trip. Talisa stared out the passenger window, still not saying a word. The silence suddenly felt like a knife through Jericho's heart, his own anxiety twisting the handle.

"Please, Talisa, say something," he finally implored. "Anything, please."

"You're right. I don't think we should consider this a first date."

Jericho tossed her a cautious smile. "Does that mean you'll give me a chance?"

"It means I don't like bullfrogs and I do want to find out just how romantic you can be."

"I promise I'll never give you anything slimy, green and bug-eyed for your birthday."

"Thank you." Talisa hesitated a quick minute before continuing. "Jericho, I'm sorry you had to go through that. I can't begin to imagine why a woman would do that to a man but I know that there are women who have, no matter how wrong they knew it was. And you're right, we don't know each other well. I don't know anything about you, but I know enough to believe that you could never violate any woman that way. And I know that there is something happening between us. Something special, and I want to know what that is."

With one hand on the steering wheel, Jericho reached the other across the center console to hold Talisa's, entwining his fingers between hers. Talisa could feel her heart skip a quick beat at the sensation of his touch.

When Jericho pulled into the parking area of the Hospice center, both he and Talisa had settled into a comfortable space with one another. The quiet between them exuded an intoxicating warmth. Gone were the tense waves of nervous energy, the unsettled feelings between new couples fighting to put their best faces forward. Theirs was a shared aura of newly placed confidence, an innate understanding that whatever was developing between them was as close to perfect as they could get.

As she stepped out of the vehicle, taking in her surroundings, Talisa sensed a sudden change in the atmosphere. She could feel an air of tension spread through Jericho's body and subsequently hers.

"What's wrong, Jericho?"

"Have you ever been through an AIDS home before?"

Talisa shook her head. "No."

Jericho reached for the black medical bag in the back seat, leaning back against the car after closing the door. "Just like in the United States, some care facilities are better than others. This is one of the best in Uganda, but you'll see that they are just as underfunded, and under-staffed, as the rest of them.

"You need to understand that this won't be easy, Talisa. The patients here are dying and that's a hard thing for some people to deal with, especially when you know so much more could be done if we could just get them the drugs and medication they need. The best the doctors are able to do here is keep their patients comfortable. They draw their strength from us, so you will need to be as strong as you can. Sometimes that's not so easy to do. Being in the medical profession I've seen a lot, but I have to be honest with you, this place has been one of the hardest experiences of my life."

Talisa nodded. "I may need some help from a higher source." She reached for Jericho's hand. "Will you pray with me?"

Jericho nodded, then closed his eyes as he bowed his head, his chin coming to rest against his chest. The lilt of Talisa's voice was a gentle breeze against his heart as she whispered a prayer skyward, asking God for guidance and strength to do whatever would be required of them.

As Jericho guided her through the doors of the hospital, he marveled at how easily the litany had come to her, noting that he could barely remember the last time he had offered up a prayer so readily.

* * *

The sun was just minutes from setting when Jericho parked the car back in front of the clinic's door. The duo had been silent for most of the return drive. His only acknowledgment of her tears had been to wipe them gently with his fingers. Jericho had understood her need to cry, remembering his own tears just weeks before.

Talisa had impressed him with her composure. She'd held many a fragile hand, had wiped foreheads, assisted the nurses with baths and feedings, even clearing away a bedpan or two without being asked. Seven hours of nonstop work and there hadn't been one word of complaint from her. He'd expected her tears when they'd been unable to resuscitate a young mother, no older than Talisa herself, who'd finally succumbed to the hateful disease. But Talisa had held them, relying on that God-given strength to help the woman's two young children comprehend that their mother was gone. Without skipping a beat, she'd moved on to the nursery to hold and rock the infants infected with the virus, humming each a soft lullaby as they fell asleep in her arms. On the drive back, when she'd finally let go of her emotions, he'd understood better than anyone the need for her low sobs. Jericho moved to the passenger door, pulling it open to help Talisa to her feet. She had dried her eyes, the last of her angst wiped away with a tissue.

"Are you okay?" Jericho asked as they stood side by side.

Talisa nodded. "I will be. I'm glad you're here with me, Jericho."

Talisa lifted her gaze to stare into the man's eyes. Jericho wrapped his arms around her body and pulled her closer. He leaned over and gently kissed her on the lips. His touch was easy, a faint brushing of his flesh against hers. As

Talisa's hands pressed against his back, Jericho lightly teased her lips apart with his tongue. When Talisa opened her mouth, he pressed his tightly over it, his tongue probing deeply into the warm cavity.

From the doorway of the clinic, Angela and Peter stood arm in arm watching. Squeezing her husband's hand, Angela pointed skyward. Following the line of her hand, Peter stood staring at the star-filled sky that shimmered overhead, the full moon a beacon of light cascading down over the embracing couple. Angela turned to go back inside and Peter followed closely behind her.

Chapter 12

Herman London could hear his wife's screams as he stepped out of his Ford pickup truck. As he made the short walk to his front door he prepared himself for the onslaught of ire waiting for him on the other side of the entrance. These episodes were too familiar, his wife's frequent outbursts beginning to take their toll. He was battle weary, way too tired after a long day of work to deal with the woman's instability.

As he pushed his key into the lock, he could feel every nerve ending in his body tense. Mary stood screaming at the foot of the stairs as he closed the door behind him.

"Talisa Michele London! I know you hear me. Girl, you better get your behind down here now. You hear me calling you! Talisa! Talisa!"

"Woman, what is your problem? You know Talisa's not home."

The woman snapped her head in her husband's direction. "I know you didn't let her go out. I told her she couldn't go out on school nights."

Herman shook his head. "Mary, Talisa is in Africa for her job. Don't you remember? Talisa done finished school."

Confusion washed over Mary's face. "Africa?"

"Yes. You remember? She went with them medical students from the church center. How long you been standing here screaming like you done lost your mind?"

The woman bristled. "I'm not crazy, Herman London. I just forgot is all."

The man pushed his way past her, allowing a wide palm to fall against his wife's broad hip as he stopped to kiss the side of her face. "Okay, Mama. Do you remember now?"

Mary nodded, giggling as she followed him into the kitchen. "Lord, I'd forget my head if it weren't attached to my body!" she exclaimed as she reached for the pots on top of the stove.

The telephone ringing pulled at her attention, interrupting her thoughts and their conversation.

"Hello?"

"Hi, Mrs. London. This is Leila. How are you?"

"Hello, Leila! I'm doing just fine. How are you doing, baby?"

"I'm well, thank you."

"Talisa's not home at the moment, baby. I can tell her you called though."

Leila chuckled softly. "I know, Mrs. London. I told her we'd check up on you while she was gone. My mother wants to know if you'd like to go out with us Friday night. She has tickets to the Ebony Fashion Show and I thought we could all go to dinner."

The excitement rang in Mary's voice. "Ohhh! That sounds like a good time. You tell Nellie I said thank you. I'd love to go."

"Good. I'll call you on Friday and let you know what time to meet us and where."

"Thank you, baby. Goodbye."

As Mary moved to place the evening's meal onto the table, Herman watched her closely. Talisa had shared her concerns about her mother before departing on her trip, begging him to contact their family physician for advice.

There had always been problems between him and Mary, but their baby girl had been the glue that had kept them together. Talisa, and plain, old-fashioned till-death-do-they-part love had been the lifeline that kept them hanging on. Admittedly, his wife had always been high-strung, her nerves wound just a touch too tight for comfort, but he loved her. He had loved her for over forty years. And Herman still loved her, crazy and all, whether he said so or not.

Because he and Talisa had been the only witnesses to Mary's erratic behavior, he'd learned to ignore it once he escaped out the front door each morning. Talisa had learned the art of ignoring her mother's bizarre behavior from him, and now it was Talisa, miles away in another land, who was insisting they give their albatross a name and let it out for the whole world to see.

Their mother-daughter excursions had been another Leila brainchild, initiated their first year in college to celebrate Mother's Day, and followed with some reluctance by Talisa and Mya. Over the years it had been expanded to include birthdays, various holidays, and any celebratory event one or the other could plan a meal or evening out around.

The friendship between Talisa, Leila and Mya had also ignited a sisterly camaraderie between their mothers, and so there was nothing unusual when the three elderly women greeted each other with hugs and kisses as they met at the entrance of the Toulouse Bistro.

"Mary, how are you?" Nellie Brimmer gushed as she wrapped her arms around the other woman's shoulders.

"I'm doing just fine, Nellie. Hello, Miss Hazel!"

Mya's mother, Hazel Taft, joined in the embrace. Mya and Leila stood off to the side. Both women rolled their eyes at the three matriarchs giggling their excitement in loud whispers.

"Our table is ready," Leila said, gesturing in the direction of the hostess.

"Thank goodness," Mya said with a deep sigh, leading them toward a large table in the rear dining room.

An eclectic mix of local artwork decorated the restaurant's neutral walls. One in particular, an impressionist landscape caught Leila's eye and she pointed it out to her mother, asking the woman's opinion.

"Does this child buy everything she sees and wants?" Hazel asked with a laugh, fanning her hand in Leila's direction.

Nellie laughed with her. "Child keeps telling me she can't take her money with her when she dies so she might as well spend it while she's alive."

"My Talisa saves every dime," Mary chimed in. "She'll be more than ready for a rainy day."

Mya shrugged her shoulders upward and scoffed. "I'd save too if I still lived at home."

"No one told you to move out," Hazel responded. "You were the one in such a hurry to be grown."

"No, Mother. I didn't leave because I was in a hurry to be grown. I *was* grown. It was time for me to leave," Mya said curtly.

The three mothers each raised an eyebrow in Mya's direction. Mya's mother shook her head, waving it from side to side.

Leila's mother sucked her teeth.

A tall, young woman with vibrant red hair made her way to the table and introduced herself, handing them each a menu as a busboy hurried to fill their empty water glasses with fluid. As the woman turned away to give them some time to consider their order, Mary London broke the tense silence by changing the subject.

"That sure is a nice-looking man eating all by himself over there."

Everyone at the table turned to see where she pointed, each nodding in agreement.

"He's probably on the DL," Mya stated, sizing up the sienna-toned man with a mountain of black, silk curls sitting atop his head. "He looks pretty like that."

"DL? What's that?" Mary asked.

Leila giggled. "The down low. It means he dates women, in fact, he may even be married, but he sleeps around with men in secret."

"That's just plain nasty," Mary said as she skewed her face in disgust. "What about the poor women they're with?"

"It's a definite problem, Mrs. London. Makes it hard for us girls to find a good man," Mya answered.

The three older women shook their heads.

"Well, I'm glad my Talisa isn't thinking about some man who might do her wrong like that," Mary stated emphatically. "My girl is focused on her career doing God's work. I think she might even go into the ministry and preach. Talisa's not thinking about no man. They ain't nothing but trouble anyway."

Leila and Mya both chuckled, cutting an eye toward one another.

"I don't know about all that," Mya laughed.

Mary turned, squinting her displeasure in Mya's direction. "What's that supposed to mean?"

"I thought you told me there's a man Talisa is interested in?" Nellie asked, her gaze falling on her own daughter.

"What man?" Mary queried, a rise of tension washing over her body.

"The doctor she met at that charity auction," Leila answered casually, pulling a menu into her hands and feigning interest at the listings.

"Talisa is not interested in that man," Mary stated.

"Leila, you told me when Talisa called you that she said things were really good with her and that man," Nellie said, a look of confusion crossing her face. "What did she call you from Africa and tell you that for if it wasn't true?"

"Talisa called you from Africa?" Mary asked, her voice rising an octave.

A wave of anxiety crossed Leila's face and she looked toward Mya for assistance.

"I'm sure she tried to call you, too, Mrs. London," Mya said. "Leila said she tried to call us all, but the phone lines were funny and she had a hard time connecting."

"That's right," Leila added. "I'm sure you'll hear from her soon."

Mary looked from one girl to the other, her expression less than pleased. "Is that man in Africa with Talisa, Leila?"

Leila bit down against her bottom lip. Her gaze met Mya's and both knew they'd stepped right into it with both feet with no way out, and poor Talisa would suffer for the infraction. Before Leila could answer, Mary London jumped out of her seat and stormed straight out of the restaurant.

"Have mercy!" Hazel exclaimed, shock registered on her round face. "Talisa didn't tell her mama about this man?"

Mya shrugged.

"Leila, baby, you should have told me Mary didn't know what Talisa was up to," Nellie said, her tone chastising.

"Mama, Talisa's not up to anything. I told you, she and Dr. Becton had no idea the other one was going to be in Africa. I also told you that Mrs. London hasn't been acting right, but you didn't want to believe me."

"I think she was just upset about Talisa calling you and not her," Hazel interjected.

"I don't think so, Ma," Mya responded. "Mrs. London has always been controlling and she has some real issues with Talisa dating. Remember when Talisa was going out with that guy in college and things didn't work out for them? Mrs. London told her it was all her fault. Ever since then, no matter who Talisa is interested in, Mrs. London keeps telling her it will end up bad, that Talisa's a fool, and how she's going to have to pick up the pieces and fix things because Talisa's not capable."

"Mary is not that bad, Miss Mya," Nellie said.

Leila shook her head. "No, Mama. She's worse. You two have just never seen her the way Mya and I have. Mrs. London can be pretty cruel toward Talisa when she wants to be. Personally, I think she needs professional help."

Nellie tossed Hazel a look. "Well, you two stay out of

it. Hazel and I will run by the house and make sure Mary's okay before we go home."

"Mama, Talisa really likes this man and from what she says I think he likes her, too. It would be a shame if Mrs. London messed this up for her."

"Mary only wants what's best for Talisa, Leila. That's all any of us want for you girls."

Mya nodded. "But in this case, Mrs. Brimmer, I don't think Mrs. London has a clue what's best for Talisa."

Herman was hanging up the telephone receiver when Mary slammed through the front door, cursing a long string of expletives. Their daughter's name was peppered between each negative comment and Herman couldn't begin to imagine what wrong thing Mary could possibly believe Talisa had done.

"What's wrong, Mama?" he asked as she pushed past him, her face bloated with rage.

His question was met with continued ranting, not one word of it making an ounce of sense. His tone raised, he asked again. "Mary, what is wrong with you?"

"Nothing. Leave me alone."

The man heaved a deep sigh, sucking in oxygen as if it were an injection of patience. "Talisa called. She said to tell you she's sorry she missed you. She's doing fine. Working hard, but she's having a good time."

"I just bet she is," Mary spat. "Did she tell you she's there with some man? How could she disrespect us like that? What will the women at church think if they find out?"

Herman paused, reflecting back on the brief conversation he'd just shared with his daughter. Her excitement had rung through the telephone lines as she'd told him about the doctor who was also volunteering his time over there. The girl had been overly anxious to share the news with her mother. There had been a hint of disappointment in her voice when he'd had to tell her that Mary wasn't home, promising to pass her good news on to his wife the minute she came through the door.

He took another deep breath before he spoke. "Talisa's a good girl, Mary."

"You're always sticking up for her."

"And you always want to think the worst of her."

"I do not!" the woman screamed, her shouts vibrating around the room. "I just want her to do what's right."

Herman stood frozen as Mary seemed to fall apart before his eyes, her strength and spirit breaking into pieces around them. Tears gushed from the woman's eyes as she sobbed uncontrollably. He reached out to wrap his thick arms around her, pulling the fullness of her against his chest. His own eyes misted ever so slightly.

"It's okay, Mama. You just miss our baby girl, that's all. Everything is going to be A-OK."

Chapter 13

Had she given it half a thought, Talisa could have easily succumbed to exhaustion, but her mind was instead focused on Jericho. Their day had been long, and at moments difficult, and while the others had given in to the calls of slumber that claimed them, she and Jericho were still wide-eyed and awake, lost in the spirals of conversation that had become their nightly ritual.

The duo sat on the concrete floor in Jericho's office, their legs stuffed into an oversized sleeping bag, their backs resting against two pillows Jericho had snatched off two beds in the clinic.

"My father is white," Jericho was saying as Talisa shifted her body against his, her head resting comfortably on his shoulder. "He came from a very privileged, wealthy, Bostonian family."

"What about your mother?"

"Mom was born in a very small South Carolina town called Garnet. She was the youngest of twelve children. Her parents owned a small farm."

"How did they meet?"

"College. Mom earned a scholarship to Yale and they became friends her first year there. One day Mom didn't have money for lunch and Dad bought her a sandwich. Dad says it was love at first sight. Mom says it was empathy that turned into friendship, and then love. They came from very opposite ends of the spectrum and somehow trying to meet each other in the middle, brought them as close together as any two people could imagine being."

"Your mother's a beautiful woman," Talisa said, remembering the woman from the auction. "She carries herself with such grace and dignity that it's no wonder your father would have been attracted to her."

"They're good for each other, but enough about me and my family. Tell me about your folks," Jericho said, changing the subject.

Talisa sighed. "My mom and dad are like oil and water. No matter how much you shake them up they still go their separate ways when things settle down. My dad drives a bus for the city of Atlanta and Mommy use to teach. She retired years ago but Daddy still works. He says it's the only thing that will help him stay sane because my mother would drive him crazy otherwise."

Jericho laughed and the warmth of its sound made Talisa smile.

"Your parents sound like quite a pair."

Talisa nodded. "My dad is the sweetest man in the world. He'd give you his last penny if he had it to give. Unfortunately, my mother would do whatever she could to keep anyone else from having it."

There was a hint of bitterness in Talisa's tone and Jericho noted the look of dejection that washed over her face.

"Sounds like you and your mom don't get along?"

"We do, most of the time, but my mother's not always an easy woman to get along with. She loves me though. It's just that sometimes I think she has no control over her behavior. It's strange and I don't know that I can explain it."

"How old is your mother?"

"Sixty-nine."

"She had you late in life."

Talisa nodded again. "And she reminds me regularly."

"Age can have an impact on our emotional behavior. A change in her diet or maybe even medication can help. You should discuss it with your doctor if you think it's a problem."

"That's what my best friend Leila said."

"Smart friend."

Night sounds filtered through the warm evening air as the two fell into an easy moment of silence. Jericho wrapped his arms tightly around her torso, pulling her back against his chest. He liked the feel of her in his arms, the warmth of her skin beneath his palms. They fit comfortably together like two matching spoons in a spoon drawer.

Jericho caressed her arms, his hands running a slow race from her wrists to her shoulders and back. The sensation of his touch sent the shimmer of a chill down the length of the young woman's spine, awakening butterflies in the pit of her stomach. Talisa clasped his hands beneath her own, stalling his exploration.

"Are you all right?" Jericho whispered into her ear, allowing his full lips to brush like a whisper against the line of her flesh. He ran his tongue across the delicate lobe of her ear.

Talisa nodded as Jericho planted a line of moist kisses on her neck. "But I won't be if you keep that up," she managed to whisper, the words blowing with the exhale of air that escaped past her lips.

"Keep what up?" Jericho murmured against her skin, his mouth creeping across the palette of her brown flesh.

Talisa giggled as she twisted around to face him. "We need to get some rest, Jericho. We've got a long day tomorrow."

Jericho hummed incoherently into the soft pocket just beneath her chin, his tongue flitting like a feather across her skin. A stray hand dropped like mist against the outer curve of her breast and Talisa inhaled swiftly, the air catching in her throat. Just before they brushed against the protrusion of nipple that had risen hard against her cotton shirt, Talisa caught his fingers between her own.

"Jericho, if you keep this up we're not going to be able to stop."

He smiled, the seductive bend of his mouth piercing straight into her heart. "Would that be a bad thing?" he asked, catching her face between the palms of his hands.

Talisa could feel herself falling into the intensity of his stare, the warmth of it drawing her into its intoxicating cavity. Jericho dropped his mouth against hers, his lips drawing the breath from her body as he kissed her with an intensity that had her body playing havoc with her mind. It was mutiny at best as every sensitive region begged to be touched. Talisa could feel her self-control weakening as a volcano threatened to erupt between her thighs.

With the last of her willpower, Talisa pulled away, breaking the connection between their mouths. Her lips were starting to swell from the attention and Talisa pushed the tip of her tongue out to moisten them. Jericho was still staring intently as he pressed his thumb lightly against her mouth, her cheek cradled in the palm of his hand. Their eyes locked for just a brief second, but it seemed to last forever. Leaning his forehead against hers, Jericho closed his blue eyes. He heaved a deep sigh, feeling as if every drop of his blood were pulsating in his groin, the engorged organ crying for relief.

Neither wanted to break the connection, Talisa still leaning against his chest, his arms locked around her body. She closed her own eyes, wallowing in the warmth emanating from his body and within minutes both were fast asleep, each still clinging hungrily to the other.

Jericho woke first, opening his eyes to find a crowd staring down at them. Talisa was still cradled tightly in his arms, her head resting against his chest. The two of them were propped awkwardly in the office corner.

Peter stood just behind his wife, a broad grin spread across his face. Angela's arms were crossed tightly over her chest, her head waving from side to side. Amusement was painted across her expression. Reverend Oloya's gaze shifted from one side of the room to the other, fighting not to focus on anything in particular. Clarissa rounded out the group, the young woman clearly amused by the turn of events.

Angela cleared her throat loudly, which caused Talisa to jump out of her state of sleep. Jericho eased her quick moment of anxiety by brushing his hand against her back.

"I think we overslept," Jericho said softly, meeting her anxious gaze.

As Talisa looked from one face to another, acute embarrassment washed over her. Blushing profusely, Talisa could feel the wealth of color that flooded her face. "Well, this is a little awkward," Talisa said, kicking her legs from the sleeping bag. She ran her palms across her thighs, brushing lint from her denim jeans.

Jericho shook his head. "No. It would have been awkward if we were naked. But we still have our clothes on so this is just comical."

Talisa's hands flew to her face. "Just shoot me now!" she exclaimed in jest.

Jericho gave her a quick hug, joining in the laughter that rang through the room. Angela glanced over her shoulder toward Clarissa, fighting her own desire to laugh out loud. Her comments were directed at her husband.

"Peter, why don't you take Jericho to our quarters so he can shower and change," she said, her tone just shy of commanding.

Jericho rolled his eyes as his friend laughed at him. He gave Talisa's shoulder a squeeze before making a quick exit with the other man.

Noting Talisa's discomfort, Angela dropped down onto the wooden chair in front of the desk, propping her chin against the back of her hands and her elbows against the tabletop. "You and Jericho have no privacy here. We must do something about that."

The profusion of blush continued to wash over Talisa's face. "Can we please just forget about this?" Talisa said, rolling the sleeping bag into a tight package.

"I think it's great," Clarissa gushed. "You two are so cute together. This is so exciting!"

"You and Jericho are meant to be together. It is written in the stars," Angela stated matter-of-factly.

Talisa opened her mouth to respond, then closed it, the words lost somewhere between Angela's pronouncement and Clarissa's agreeing nod. She smiled instead.

"I need to wash up and change," she finally said.

Angela nodded. "Clarissa and I will figure out a plan while you dress. Our doctor loves you, and you love him, and we must take full advantage of it while we can."

For the second time Talisa sputtered like a fish out of water gasping for air. Her gaze locked with Angela's, joy smiling in the woman's dark eyes, then as if on cue both turned to stare out the window, watching as Jericho and Peter strolled easily across the yard.

Peter was still chuckling to himself when Jericho stepped out of the bathroom, showered, shaved and dressed. His friend stopped short as he entered the room and the two men locked eyes. Jericho could only shake his head and Peter laughed out loud.

"Leave me alone, Peter." Jericho grinned.

Peter shook his index finger at the man. "This woman is very special to you. We can all see it. You two aren't hiding your attraction to each other very well if that is what you wanted."

Jericho dropped down against the well-worn sofa, taking a seat beside the man. "Would you leave me alone if I said there isn't any attraction between us?"

Peter smiled. "If you said that then you would be lying. You are too honest a man to tell such a lie."

"And what if I said I didn't want to talk about her?"

"I would respect that."

Jericho nodded, clasping his hands together in his lap. "But I don't think my Angela will let you off as easily,"

Peter finished, giving his friend a sly grin. "I'm sure Angela will have much to say about the two of you."

Jericho couldn't help but laugh, knowing just how right Peter was about his wife. "So, how do I get that woman of yours to leave me and Talisa alone?"

"Marry Talisa today and have beautiful babies. That will make Angela very happy. She says it is your destiny."

Jericho tossed his head back against the sofa, his body sinking into the thin cushions. "My destiny, huh?"

Peter shrugged, the broad grin still filling his very round face.

"Well, Talisa and I are just getting to know each other so I think a wedding is going to be a while."

"Getting to know her is a good thing." The conversation was interrupted as Angela entered the room. "That is a very good thing," the woman stated, looking from one to the other.

Jericho sat back up, his spine straight. "Angela, I know—"

Angela cut him off in midsentence. "Peter, I need you to pack the tent and two sleeping bags. Clarissa is already preparing the medical supplies for your trip. Jericho, you need to go ready yourself. The boats leave Entebbe at four o'clock and you and Talisa need to be on time. There's a lot for you guys to get done this weekend."

Both men stared at her questioningly. Jericho stammered. "On time...? Does Talisa...? What's going...?" He rose to his feet, his hands resting against his lean hips. "Where are we going?" Jericho finally managed to ask, his eyebrows raised in query.

Angela smiled, a broad grin spreading over her ebony face. "The Sese Islands, of course!"

Chapter 14

There was static and then the telephone line clicked rapidly in her ear, dialing the international exchanges and then her home telephone number. Nervous excitement filled Talisa's midsection as the phone finally rang on the other end. After four rings, her mother answered, her deep voice echoing over the other end.

"Hello?"

"Hi, Mom. It's me!"

"Talisa! Where are you, baby?"

"I'm still in Africa. How are you? I called last week, but Dad said you'd gone to dinner with the girls."

Mary didn't answer.

"Mom? You still there?"

"Talisa, are you in Africa with that man?"

"What man?"

"That doctor who's been calling here for you?"

Talisa giggled softly. "His name is Jericho, Mom, and he's incredible. Can you believe it? All those times we missed each other and we finally meet here in Uganda of all places!"

"I'm sure that was convenient," Mary said, her tone curt. "How stupid do you think I am, Talisa? Did you think I wouldn't find out about this?"

Shock and confusion filtered from one end of Talisa's body to the other, her mother's deprecating tone flooding her with dread. "I don't know—"

Mary screamed into the receiver. "Don't lie to me, Talisa!"

"Mom, I don't know what you're talking about."

"If you act like a whore, Talisa, God will see. You will reap what you sow, girl!" Mary spat, punctuating each word with venom.

Talisa could feel her body tensing, her fingers tightening around the telephone receiver. "Mom, are you feeling all right?"

"You're the one messing up. Not me. There is nothing wrong with me."

Talisa took a deep breath. "Mom, is Dad home?" she asked, her tone as even and as controlled as she could manage.

"You need to come home, Talisa. You need to come home now. I'm going to call that Reverend Warren and let him know about this. Yes, I am."

"Mom, everything is going to be fine. I promise. I'll be home very soon and things will be just fine. Okay, Mom?"

"You're coming home?"

"Yes, ma'am."

"You need to forget that man, Talisa. He's no good for you. He's evil, Talisa. I can feel it. The man is evil and I can't let no evil get into my house."

"I know, Mom. Everything is going to be okay. I promise. Can I say hello to Dad?" Talisa questioned, asking about her father for the second time.

"Hold on," Mary answered, her demeanor suddenly calm.

By the time Herman London picked up the telephone, Talisa's soft tears had risen to a low sob.

"Talisa, baby? What's wrong?" the man asked, concern ringing in his words.

Talisa's voice was soft as she sobbed into the telephone. "It's Mom. What's wrong with her, Dad? What is wrong with my mother?"

The car radio was playing softly as Peter guided the vehicle past the perimeter of the orphanage onto the main roadway. The man drove toward the lakeside market of Entebbe. As Angela detailed their itinerary, Jericho jotted quick notes into a pocket-sized notepad. The three were chatting easily as Talisa stared out the window, her concentration broken by thoughts of her mother and the earlier conversation between them.

Although Peter and Angela seemed oblivious, Jericho could sense that something wasn't quite right. He dropped a hand against her knee, squeezing the flesh gently, and when she turned to face him, he gave her a warm smile, comfort gleaming past his blue gaze. Talisa smiled back, entwining her fingers beneath his as she turned back to stare out the window, not wanting him to see her cry.

"Tonight and tomorrow you will stay in Bukasa. After that you can go to Buggala," Angela stated, giving them both a quick glance over her shoulder as the names of the smaller islands rolled effortlessly off her tongue.

As Peter parked the car, Talisa wiped her face with the

back of her hand. Angela stepped from the vehicle and headed toward the fishermen who stood at the shoreline preparing their canoes for the ride home. Nothing remained of the day's catch and the men gathered were anxious to set out for their homesteads.

Talisa and Jericho followed behind them, standing just off to the side, as their friends negotiated a method of travel for them. Bantering back and forth in their native tongue, an agreement was quickly reached with a tall, charcoal man whose bright white smile was breathtaking. The man gestured in their direction, greeting them warmly as he guided the duo to his motorized canoe, accepting the cash Peter handed to him.

"Enjoy your time away," Angela called out to them as the boat eased away from the shore, skipping along the bright blue water. As she and Peter stood waving their goodbyes, Jericho leaned to whisper in Talisa's ear. "I don't know what's wrong, sweetheart, but I promise you, I'll do whatever I can to help."

As the warmth of his breath blew like an easy breeze against her skin, Talisa wanted to believe him more than anything else she had ever wanted before.

Their guide chatted eagerly, his English as broken as Jericho's Bantu, but the two seemed able to communicate comfortably as they made their way across the waters to Bukasa, one of eighty-four lush, green, untouched isles in the Sese Islands in the Ugandan quarter of Lake Victoria. As they reached their destination, coming ashore at the jetty where the ferry came and went twice weekly, the man pointed them in the direction of shelter and bid them goodbye.

Jericho reached for their baggage, turning to pass a canvas sack to Talisa. As his eyes met hers, he stopped in his tracks. She was beautiful, and the fact that she carried herself as if she could not see it, made her even more attractive. He stood staring for only a quick minute until the sad look that crossed her face lifted him from his trance. Dropping his gaze to the ground, Jericho tossed his backpack over his shoulder as Talisa adjusted hers comfortably against her back. Holding out his hand, Jericho waited until she took it, entwining her fingers beneath his. Lifting her hand to his lips, he kissed her palm, then turned toward the dirt road, pulling her along beside him.

"Where are we going now?" Talisa asked, speaking for what seemed to be the first time since they'd departed on their trip.

"Agnes's Guest House. It's supposed to be at the top of the hill here," Jericho answered, pointing ahead of them. Quiet filled the space between them until Jericho spoke again. "So, do you want to tell me what's wrong?" he asked, cutting his eyes in her direction.

Talisa heaved a deep sigh, but said nothing.

"Do you not want to be here, Talisa?" Jericho asked. His tone was soft, comfort rolling off his tongue. "We can go back if you're uncomfortable with all of this. I know Angela meant well but it was quick and we really didn't talk about it first. I'd understand if you didn't want to be here."

Talisa forced a smile, shaking her head from side to side. "That's not it at all, Jericho. I want to be here with you. I just…" Talisa hesitated.

"You just what, Talisa?" Jericho asked, the two of them stopping in their tracks.

His gaze was questioning, determined to make whatever was wrong, right again. Talisa could feel herself falling headfirst into the promises of his stare. As Talisa repeated the conversations she'd had with her mother, and then her father, Jericho listened intently. As Talisa finished, he pulled her into his arms and gently kissed away the tears that had dripped against her cheeks.

"Do you think you should go home?" Jericho asked.

Talisa shook her head. "My father told me to stay. He said there's nothing I can do and since I only have a few more weeks that I should just stay."

"What can I do?"

"I'm just scared for her, Jericho. One minute she's ranting like a wild woman and the next minute she's the sweetest person in the world. I don't know what's wrong with her."

"Well, your father may have some answers by the time you return. It's good that he was able to convince her to go see a doctor."

"I guess."

The two resumed their walk, easing slowly up the dirt road.

"I'm sorry," Talisa said. "I didn't mean to let my mood spoil this for us."

"You have nothing to be sorry for," Jericho replied, squeezing her hand. "We'll call your father as soon as we get back to see what the doctor said. I'm sure everything will be fine."

As they reached the top of the hill, Agnes's Guest House, the only place to stay on the small island, came into view. Once a prosperous display of wealth, the house sat surrounded by a stunning garden that looked north out across the vast lake. What was once a grand estate had long since disappeared, a ransacked shell of a building with no electricity or running water remaining. Presidents Idi Amin and Obote's troops had destroyed the luxurious homestead back in the seventies when they'd taken everything of value, including the generator. The home was now dark and damp, yet filled to capacity with guests. Jericho and Talisa were greeted warmly at the entrance by Agnes, the owner, and directed to an empty corner of the courtyard. As Jericho pitched the small tent in the gardens, sunbirds flitted among the bushes and white-faced vervet monkeys chattered in the trees. The sun was setting to the west, the last shimmer of light filtering off the water's surface. Talisa pulled two sandwiches and a bag of fruit from her backpack, offering half to Jericho.

"I'm beginning to wonder what Angela had in store for us," Jericho said as he took a bite out of a deep red apple.

Talisa smiled. "It's actually quite beautiful," she noted, taking in the last views of the flora that blossomed around them.

As they finished their meal, Jericho adjusted their possessions and the sleeping bags inside the tent. Searching inside his knapsack, he pulled a wide-tooth comb and paddle brush from an interior pocket. "Can you braid?" he asked, looking over his shoulder toward Talisa.

"Excuse me?"

"Hair. Can you braid hair?"

The woman chuckled softly, nodding her head. "Yes, I can."

"Would you mind cornrowing my hair, please? I need to get it out of the way," Jericho asked softly, running his fingers through the thick length of black strands.

Talisa nodded, extending her hand to reach for the comb and brush. A large boulder sitting in the garden space made for a makeshift stool, and Talisa gestured for Jericho to come sit on the ground between her open legs.

As Jericho made himself comfortable, draping his arms over her legs, both were acutely aware of the emotions sweeping between them. With his shoulders pressing against the insides of her thighs, Talisa was overcome by the waves of heat generated from his body to hers. As Talisa gently brushed his hair down the length of his back, she tried to ignore his fingers which were skating easily along the back of her calves, gently caressing and kneading her flesh through her cotton slacks. As she slowly parted his hair into segments to be braided, she pretended not to notice the growing intensity in his strokes, each pass sliding higher to the back of her knees. By the time she was finished with the third braid, she refused to acknowledge the warm palms that had pushed under her pant leg to bear down on her bare flesh.

With his chin leaning forward against his chest and his eyes closed tight, Jericho was enchanted by the gentleness of her touch, the light scratching of the comb soothing against his scalp. Even the slight pulls as she plaited the neat braids tight to his skull were lost to the sensation of his hands against her skin, and her hands against him. He fought the sudden urge to turn his face and lightly bite the inside of her thigh. With the last cornrow, Talisa twisted the length of ends down the center of his back, capturing the strands into one large braid held together by a rubber band. As her fingertips gently grazed the back of his neck, neither of them said anything, lost in the heat of each other's touch.

Talisa broke the moment, giving his torso a quick squeeze between her knees. "That should last you a while," she said softly, passing him back his comb and brush.

Jericho nodded, thanking her for her help. "I appreciate

this," he said, still not moving away from the warmth between her thighs.

"So, why do you keep your hair so long?" she asked, willing conversation to stall the rise of wanting that was quivering for attention in the center of her womanhood.

"No special reason." Jericho shrugged, pausing for a brief moment as he reflected on her question. "No, take that back. I haven't cut it because Shannon hated it long. I think not cutting my hair was my way of dealing with that hurt in my life."

Talisa nodded slowly. She gently stroked the sides of his face with her fingers, running her fingertips against the edge of his hairline. Jericho leaned his head back against her, looking up into her face. "If you want me to cut it, I will," he said, his gaze dancing against hers.

Talisa smiled down at him, leaning to kiss his lips gently. "Cut it because you want to, Jericho. I want you to do what feels right for you," she answered, pressing her mouth to his one more time.

Jericho lingered in the kiss, allowing the emotion of it to sweep through his body. Energy pulsed from his heart out into his limbs, willing life into his manhood. As a full erection suddenly pressed hard against his leg, he couldn't help but imagine the length of himself nurtured between her thighs. A rustle of noise from campers on the other side of the rock wall reminded him of where they were and he reluctantly pulled himself up and away from her.

"We should get some sleep," he said softly. "We've got a long day tomorrow. Agnes said they've already sent word that I'm here. I'm sure patients will be lined up bright and early."

Easing herself inside the compartment beside him, Talisa suddenly felt nervous. The proximity of their bodies, and the full moon shimmering overhead, was inciting a rush of warmth through her bloodstream. As Talisa settled into her sleeping bag, still wearing the clothes she'd arrived in, Jericho wrapped an arm around her torso, pulling himself and his own sleeping bag against her. Talisa eased into the warmth he offered, closing her eyes as he whispered good-night, his lips brushing ever so lightly against hers.

When the first ray of sunlight landed across her face, Talisa was pulled from the much needed sleep that had consumed her. Jericho had risen some time before and his sleeping bag lay empty against the ground. Pulling herself up and out, Talisa stretched her body upward, her arms elongated over her head, her spine stretching skyward.

"Good morning," Jericho greeted as he came from the main house back out to the gardens. "Did you sleep well?"

"I did," Talisa said, smiling sweetly. "How about yourself?"

The man nodded. "It was great until someone's snoring woke me up."

Mortified, Talisa's eyes widened. "Did I really snore?"

The man laughed. "Like a freight train," he said teasingly.

The woman shook her head from side to side, laughing with him. "So, what's on our agenda for the day?"

Jericho leaned down to pick up his bag. "Unfortunately, it's going to be a short hike through the woods first. There's no running water here but there's a small waterfall at the end of the trail over there where we can shower and bathe. Agnes says the water's clean and the area is fairly private."

Following Jericho's lead, Talisa repacked her possessions, helped him dismantle the tent, and then followed as he led the way through the forest. The thirty-minute trek was fairly easy as they maneuvered through the dense trees, the sounds of natural wildlife filling the air around them. Birds chirped, monkeys chattered, and a cool breeze blew the sounds through the morning air.

There was little sunlight peeking past the tall trees that hovered above them. The air was just shy of being cold and as the two of them stepped in sight of the waterfall, Talisa was in awe. The small flow of water was tucked neatly away on the other end of the island, moisture gushing naturally around them.

"It's a little chilly," Jericho shouted above the sound of the water's spray as they both leaned over the edge of the wet pool to brush their teeth.

"It'll warm up once we get in it," Talisa said, rinsing the toothpaste suds from her mouth.

Jericho grinned. "Oh, really?"

Talisa blushed. "I didn't mean it like that!"

Jericho wrapped his arms around her. "How did you mean it?" he asked, pulling her close.

Wrapping her own arms around his neck, Talisa clasped her fingers together behind his head. "I don't remember," she said, just as he pressed his mouth to hers, his lips pulling anxiously at hers.

Breaking the kiss, Jericho pulled his gray T-shirt over his head, dropping it to the ground. "You ready to get wet?" he asked.

Talisa grinned, shaking her head at him. "You go first," she said, toying with the buttons on her cotton blouse.

Jericho's gaze was locked on her face as he stepped out of his cotton slacks, his boxer briefs hugging the round of his hips. His mouth fell open ever so slightly as Talisa eased her shirt off her shoulders, dropping it and her denim jeans to the ground. The matching bikini bottoms and lace bra lay like a second skin against her body, the bright yellow of the fabric complementing her complexion. Her youthful breasts stood high and firm beneath the sheer garment, defiant in the open air. His eyes traveled eagerly across her flesh, the sight of her inciting a rage of emotion across his groin. Jericho turned quickly to shield the sudden rise in his shorts from her view.

Stepping cautiously behind him, Talisa eased into the water, moving to stand beneath the spray of liquid that showered from overhead. The fountain was chilling, but invigorating, and when Jericho pressed his hand to her back, massaging a bar of soap against her skin, she could focus on nothing but the heat from his fingers radiating through her.

His touch was electric, its fire burning with fierce intensity. Jericho drew a slow trail across her shoulders, down the length of her arms, to the lace edge of her brassiere. He continued past her belly button, and finally rested his hands teasingly against the shelf of her buttocks, his fingers itching to sneak beneath the elastic of her panties to press against the round of her behind.

Talisa pressed herself tightly against him, her pelvis caressing his in a slow grind as her own hands danced like butterflies over his chest and around to his broad back. Jericho's mouth danced a tango against hers as he kissed her greedily, his tongue sneaking past the line of her lips. The kiss was hard and deep and when Talisa finally pulled away she could barely breathe from the sheer beauty of it. Jericho pulled her hand to his lips and kissed the tips of her fingers, his wanting dropping like rain from the intense stare between.

Talisa laughed softly, dropping her forehead against his chest. "Jericho, this water is freezing."

Jericho laughed with her. "I hadn't noticed until you stopped kissing me," he said, rinsing the last of the suds from her skin before easing her out of the spray of fluid.

Reaching for his T-shirt, Jericho brushed the moisture from her body, buffing warmth and color back into her skin. He stopped as his fingers rubbed against the scar line that ran a short length across her abdomen. Curiosity, then awareness, crossed his face as his eyes moved from the dark blemish to Talisa's face, and back again. Flush from his discovery, his excitement filling his spirit, Jericho wanted to jump up and down with joy.

He laughed loudly, tossing his head back in glee. "I can't believe I didn't remember it before this. You told me I had beautiful eyes. Then you said that you thought you could love me."

Talisa laughed with him, rolling her eyes. Color rushed to her cheeks.

"So," Jericho asked, a smug expression on his face, "did you mean it? Do you really think you can love me?"

Talisa grinned widely. "I guess we'll just have to wait and see, won't we, Dr. Becton?"

His expressive lips curled in an indulgent smile as Jericho grinned back. He watched Talisa kneel down to pick through her bag for a change of clothes. Fighting the sudden urge to lay her across the grass-covered land and cover every inch of his maleness with the softness of her femininity, Jericho struggled to maintain some self-control. He turned his back to her, offering her a semblance of privacy as he moved to hide the rise of his erection.

"Don't you peek," he chimed jokingly, easing the moment for them both.

Talisa responded with a low giggle, her own excitement

coloring her cheeks a vibrant red. The two of them stepped quickly out of their soaked undergarments and into a dry change of clothing before turning back around to face each other.

Hand in hand, they strolled back toward the guest house, easy conversation passing the time. When they were in sight of the home's entrance, Agnes stood gesturing excitedly in their direction, calling out for the doctor.

The little boy who lay on the floor inside could not have been more than seven years old. Rail-thin, the child was as tiny and as fragile as a piece of fine china, his dark skin as dark as pure onyx. The flesh against his pencil-thin legs was blistered raw and the sight of it made Talisa gasp in shock. Agnes was pressing a damp cloth to the little boy's head as she offered him a sip of warm fluid to drink.

"What happened?" Jericho asked, leaning down to inspect the wounds as Talisa pulled supplies from his medical bag.

Agnes clucked softly under her breath before answering, her English quite adept, the words punctuated by her thick accent. "His mama live up country and has no money to care for him. Sent him to her family here on Bukasa but they too poor also. Had no bed for him to sleep in so he sleep outside by the fire last night. Baby roll into the hot embers and burn himself awake. The mama's relatives send him here to me for medicine."

As Jericho cleaned the charred flesh and coated it with an antiseptic burn cream, Talisa held the little boy's hand. Tears of pain misted in the child's eyes but he did not cry. Talisa wanted to cry for him but she didn't, holding back her own hurt. As Jericho taped the last bandage, they could feel the gratitude wash over the little boy's spirit.

The child was the first of many patients the two aided that morning, the elderly and the infirm coming one behind the other to see the blue-eyed, black American doctor who would help them for free. Later in the afternoon, when Talisa went to check on the little boy, the child was gone, roaming back to his relatives for the promise of shelter.

It was late when the two of them finally crawled back inside their sleeping bags for another night of rest. Jericho's stomach rumbled with hunger and it was only then that Talisa realized neither of them had stopped long enough for a full meal.

"Jericho?" Talisa whispered his name into the cooling air.

The man wrapped his arm around her, brushing his fingers against her cheek. "Yes?"

"I'm glad I'm here with you. I can't think of any other place I would want to be."

Jericho smiled, pressing his face into her neck, then leaned to kiss her shoulder, dropping off to sleep with his body pressed close to hers.

The ferry departed early the next morning. Talisa and Jericho sat side by side, his arms wrapped protectively around her shoulders as they hopped from one island to another, headed in the direction of Buggala. The sun was shining brightly, and in combination with the rising temperature and the clear sky, Talisa knew another beautiful day was promised to them. She settled her body closer to Jericho's, reaching to hold his hand. Both stared out to the waves of water that splashed against the sides of the ferry, falling into low swells behind them.

As Talisa inhaled the rich essence of the culture, she

realized that not only was she enamored with the country, but also its people. The friendly inhabitants of the cluster of islands had welcomed them warmly, opening their arms in hospitality. Only the inner beauty of its people overshadowed the exterior beauty of the land. As she sat beside Jericho she could sense that he was as taken with their surroundings as she was. His eyes were closed, his head tilted slightly back, enjoying the movement of the air and the fine mist of water that rained around them.

From the ferry dock, the duo hiked down to the white sand beach and Hornbill, the guest residence that would be home to them for the next few days. Within minutes Jericho had secured a private *banda* right on the beach, the round, open-sided, grass-roof structure affording them a semblance of privacy. As Talisa dropped her possessions against the double bed situated in the center of the room, Jericho eased his way toward the entrance, staring out into the open air and the water. The sun shimmered down over his face, warm light caressing his skin. Talisa eased up behind him, wrapping her arms around his waist as she leaned her cheek against his back.

"I think we should get started," Jericho said, brushing his palm against the back of her hands.

"Do you think we'll have as many patients to see today?" Talisa asked.

Jericho chuckled softly. "No, not at all. We're not here to work today. We're here to just relax and enjoy each other," he said, turning around to pull her into his arms.

Surprise carved a look of confusion across Talisa's face. "You're kidding, aren't you?"

Jericho shook his head. "No. I'm very serious. We've worked hard this week, and we deserve a chance to rest up for the upcoming week. Plus you and I need this time between us. Think about it, Talisa. We met under some unusual circumstances. Then we reconnected under unusual circumstances. This is so incredible that it's almost unreal. We need this time to just talk about nothing as we get to know one another. Besides," Jericho said as he kissed her quickly, "the more time we spend together, the more time I spend thinking about making love to you, and that was never going to happen at the orphanage."

Talisa smiled coyly. "And that might happen here?"

"A man can hope, can't he?"

Jericho kissed her again, a multitude of quick pecks that teased her cheeks, her forehead, her eyelids, and finally her lips. His mouth was searching, his lips dancing a slow two-step against hers. His touch was so soft, so gentle, that Talisa could feel herself slide into the beauty of it. When Jericho pulled away, taking a step back from her, Talisa still stood with her eyes closed, and her head tilted back ever so slightly. Her breathing was slightly elevated, her breasts ballooning up and down in rising exhilaration.

"Let's go canoeing," Jericho whispered, the sudden comment spinning Talisa out of her moment of reverie.

Opening her eyes, Talisa stared into Jericho's, swimming headfirst into the emotion embodied in his gaze. His longing was undeniable, desire painting his excitement across his face. Sweat had beaded across his brow and both his hands were cupped nonchalantly in front of his crotch, attempting to hide the telltale sign of pure lust. A seductive smile blossomed across Talisa's face as she stepped in toward him, her hands falling against the waistband of his slacks. Nodding her head, Talisa's gaze was still locked with his. Her wanting was just as clear as she pressed her lips to his, allowing the words to ease past her lips in a rushed whisper. "Whatever you want, Dr. Becton."

Chapter 15

Angela was folding gray flannel blankets into a neat pile when her husband slid into the room, easing up behind her. He hugged her tightly, his embrace reflecting the anxiety sweeping through his spirit.

"What is wrong?" Angela asked softly, her instincts sensing that all was not well. Turning around in his arms to return the hug, she studied the tense lines of the man's face. "What has happened, Peter?"

"The fighting in Sudan and the northern border has intensified. The rebels are killing everyone in their wake. The refugee camps are overflowing. Families are trying to make their way down from Kitgum and Gulu. We need to prepare to help as many of them as we can. The children will need us. They will need our help."

Angela shook her head, tears misting in her eyes.

"When will this war end, Peter? How much more can Uganda endure?"

Peter tightened his grip around her torso. "Uganda is growing stronger each day. One day soon we will know our wealth again. Our people will be healthy. What we have accomplished thus far is just one of many miracles that has blessed our people. Our children will learn and they will grow to help us rebuild our country. If we put our faith and hope in our children, they will not disappoint us. We have to believe that." Peter wiped at a tear that had fallen against Angela's cheek.

Angela sighed, the gesture reflecting the deep despair she was suddenly feeling. Peter kissed her forehead, allowing his full lips to rest against the softness of her skin. "We will need Jericho," the man said as he turned to walk back out the door. "Many of the children will need a doctor."

Angela nodded her agreement. "I will send word for him to return immediately."

The day could not have been more spectacular, Talisa thought as she lay across the bed waiting for Jericho to return from the bathhouse. She pulled her arms over her shoulders, crossing them behind her head.

They had gone canoeing, laughing easily as they shared stories of childhood antics and teenage dreams. As they sat alone, surrounded by the waters of Lake Victoria, the morning had passed too quickly. Time had rushed past, leaving them behind as the sun shifted its position in the clear blue sky. There was magnificent birdlife on the beach with white-headed fish eagles fishing some thirty feet from the shoreline. Kingfishers, storks, herons, and hornbills flew above the trees around them.

They had strolled the length of beach hand in hand, caressing each other idly. Jericho had run his appreciative palms along her curves, acquainting himself with the lines of her body. Saying little, they'd taken in the abundance of their surroundings and each other.

An early dinner had been incredible, freshly caught fish grilled right on the sand, their plates overflowing with a cornucopia of pineapples, mangos and papayas. After a full meal, they had gone hiking through the tall trees, then had rested by the shore, watching the antics of Punky, Hornbill's resident mascot, a small monkey notorious for stealing food and trinkets left unattended. Punky's comedic battles with the large German shepherds and a few of the other guests had kept them laughing until their sides ached. And now, after watching the most incredible sunset Talisa had ever seen, she was waiting for Jericho to join her, to spend the night alone beneath the star-filled sky with no one near enough to disturb them.

Not realizing Jericho had reentered the room, Talisa still lay with her eyes closed, her relaxed body sprawled against the cotton sheets, memories of their day together dancing behind her eyes. Her full breasts pushed like ripe melons against the cotton fabric of her thin tank top, and the very round curves of her buttocks peeked past the short line of the boy-cut boxers she wore.

Jericho inhaled her beauty, enamored with the bliss that shadowed her face. Talisa was breathtaking and Jericho was suddenly overcome by the heat that rushed from one end of his body to the other. He shivered with longing, scarcely able to restrain himself. Her name caught in his throat as he whispered it into the warm air, the lilt of it resonating throughout the room.

Rising up onto her elbows, Talisa's gaze met his, the swell of her breathing answering his call. As Jericho crawled over her, his towel-clad physique hovering easily above the length of her body, Talisa felt as if the moment was unreal, a sweet dream born from a lifetime of fantasy. Jericho's lips skating across her lips, his tongue anxiously seeking out hers, lifted her into the moment, the reality of it burning like fire through her womanhood.

Talisa pressed her palms to Jericho's bare chest as he eased her back against the mattress, reclining his weight against her. She kissed him hungrily, eager to satiate her sudden appetite. Her sexual experiences had been limited, one brief relationship in college with a man who had promised her the world, and had left her feeling empty when all was said and done. Jericho had promised his heart in exchange for her own, and the overwhelming reality of that suddenly filled her soul beyond reason.

She wrapped her arms around him, her hands racing the length of his broad back. His flesh was still damp, the rising heat of his body simmering the moisture beneath her palms. Jericho was whispering her name against her skin, blowing promises with every kiss that touched her. Every touch was a sweet caress, feathery lashes against her flesh that made her nerve endings tingle with anticipation.

Jericho leaned up on his forearms, shifting the bulk of his weight to his arms as he leaned down staring into the depths of her gaze. His heart beat heavily against her own. Her breathing was as strained as his, oxygen fueling their sensual desire. He pulled his hands through her hair, releasing the barrette that held the length of brown silk in a ponytail at the nape of her neck. His face fell into the fresh scent of coconut oil that coated each strand, his lips searching the length of her neck, licking at the lobe of her ear, then falling back to her mouth.

Pulling at her top, Jericho removed it from her torso as she lifted her arms high above her head. Nothing could have prepared Talisa for the sensation of his hands as they reached to cup her breasts, his palms dancing against the hardened nipples. The sudden feeling of his touch fired energy from the top of her head straight down to her curled toes. When he dipped his head down to take her into his mouth, suckling lightly, it left her breathless. Talisa had barely recovered from the exhilaration when she realized that they were dancing naked against the bedsheets, Jericho in full control as he guided her in an erotic slow drag across the mattress. When he reached for a condom off the small nightstand that sat against the edge of the bed, Talisa was completely lost in the ecstasy, her mind a haven of sensual desire. When she reached to take it from his hand, Jericho pressed his mouth back to her breast, giving in to the sensation of her hands against him as she sheathed him slowly. As Jericho tasted every inch of her body with his own, both savored the enormity of the moment, suddenly aware that they had reached a point of no return. Knowing there would be no turning back for either of them.

Chapter 16

Punky was chattering excitedly, his brown fur standing stiff against his neck as his high-pitched shrill filled the early-morning air. Talisa woke with a start as Jericho jumped from the bed, lunging headfirst at the small creature scampering toward the entrance.

Her gaze fell on Jericho's naked backside. As he turned around to face her, she inhaled swiftly, gasping at the beauty of the man who had captured her heart. Jericho blushed as she appraised him so wantonly.

"Sorry," Jericho said, crawling back onto the bed as he moved to kiss her lips. "I tried to keep him out so he wouldn't wake you."

Talisa pulled back, drawing her fingers to her lips. "I have morning breath," she said softly, blushing ever so slightly.

Jericho shrugged, pulling her into his arms. "So do I," he said, dropping his mouth down to hers and kissing her hard. Talisa kissed him back, her tongue dancing across his lips.

"Thank you for trying to let me sleep," she said after lifting her mouth from his.

Jericho nodded, smiling down at her. She leaned to press a kiss against his chest, drawing a line of wet pecks down the length of his torso. Jericho wrapped himself around her, cradling her nakedness tightly against his own. His body was ultra-sensitive to her touch, the nearness of her heightening all of his senses. He felt as if he were drunk with wanting.

They lay curled against each other, taking in the rise of sounds filtering in from the outside, both lost in their own thoughts. Talisa had no sense of time, the moment almost too surreal to be believed. She opened her eyes to study the easy curvature of his profile, her finger tracing a line across his brow, down the slight slope of his nose, across the soft tissue of his lips. She inhaled, drawing the scent of him deep into her nostrils, wanting the essence to linger through her spirit. Taking a second deep breath of air, Talisa broke the silence, propping her head against her elbow as she leaned up to speak.

"I'm feeling very guilty," she said softly, her gaze meeting his.

"Why?"

"Because this isn't what I came to Africa for." Talisa bit down against her bottom lip. "The foundation sent me here to assist their students, and here I am, playing honeymoon with an incredible man. I should be out there somewhere, helping to change bandages or something. This wasn't supposed to be a vacation and I'm not being very responsible."

"Aren't you and your students allowed some personal time to yourselves?"

"Yes, but—" Her gaze dropped to the floor.

"Do you regret making love to me?"

"Not at all, Jericho," Talisa said, looking back up as she reached to caress the side of his face. "Being with you has been the most incredible experience in my entire life. I have loved every minute you and I have shared."

"Then you have nothing to be guilty about. You have more than honored your commitment to your students and your job. You've done an amazing job, Talisa. I am so proud of you. And, you deserve this time to yourself. There couldn't possibly be anything wrong with our being together, sweetheart. We've been touched by the light, remember?" The warmth of Jericho's gaze billowed through her body.

Talisa reached to kiss him one more time. "Thank you, Jericho," she whispered softly, allowing her lips to linger lightly against his. "That means a lot to me."

Jericho grinned, pulling her down over his torso, his excitement pumping through every muscle in his body. "You're welcome!" he said, the echo of his voice bouncing around the room and out toward the body of water that kissed the shoreline outside.

The day's sun was perched midsky when the pair finally made their way out of the *banda*. It was a glorious day, the brilliance of sunshine against the cloudless blue sky shining as brightly as the light that cascaded from Jericho's eyes. They were strolling the shore locked arm in arm when a young man hurried excitedly in their direction, calling out to them with a lyrical accent that rang like music through the air. His words were a mix of English and his native tongue, the words "doctor, doctor" ringing clearly in the wind.

As the man reached their side, both sensed his urgency as he introduced himself quickly, insisting that they both hurry to follow him. The man's gaze lingered for just a brief minute on Talisa's face before turning toward Jericho's intense stare, and then he turned, gesturing for them to follow.

"What's wrong, Jericho?"

"We need to get back to the orphanage. Something has happened and they need a doctor."

Without uttering another word, both Jericho and Talisa raced down the beach to gather their belongings, following the lead the man called Bongo had taken.

The boat ride back to Entebbe took no time at all and Peter stood waiting for them at the pier. His smile was warming, but worry had creased the lines across his forehead, and both Jericho and Talisa could sense that all was not well. Bongo shook Jericho's hand before waving goodbye as he turned his boat back toward the islands.

The man leaned to hug Talisa warmly. "Welcome back, Talisa. Did you enjoy your stay on Sese?"

Talisa smiled. "I did, Peter. But what's wrong. What's happened? Are my kids okay?"

Peter nodded his head. "The students are all well," he said as he dropped their bags into the back of the car and lifted himself into the driver's seat.

"There's nothing wrong with Angela is there?" Jericho asked, his own concern rising in his voice.

"No, my friend. My wife is well also." Peter took a

deep breath then explained what had happened, his words darkening the good mood the lovers had arrived with. "We hated to have to send for you," Peter concluded, nodding his head at one and then the other.

"We understand completely," Talisa said from the back seat, dropping her palm against the man's shoulder. "I would have been upset if you didn't call for Jericho."

"So, have the refugees started arriving yet?" Jericho asked.

Peter shook his head. "No. We are going to have to go to them. There is a hospital in Gulu that needs us. The children are marching in every day for help. They go there to sleep at night to hide from the rebels and then they walk back home in the mornings. Food is scarce and many of them are very sick."

Jericho nodded as concern washed over Talisa's expression. "Is it safe in Gulu with the rebels so close?" she asked.

Peter heaved a deep sigh. "I will not ask you or any of the Wesley students to help us, Talisa. There is more than enough for you to do here."

"But I want to help, Peter."

"He's right, Talisa. It's probably better that you stay here."

"I'm going, Jericho."

"No, you're not."

"Yes, I am and you don't have anything to say about it," Talisa said firmly, sliding back against the seat, her arms crossed over her chest. Defiance clouded her expression.

Peter chuckled softly. "I see you have met your match, Dr. Becton. This one sounds much like my wife."

Jericho looked over his shoulder, his gaze meeting Talisa's. The look on her face was stern, resolve dancing in her eyes. For a quick moment they locked eyes, an unspoken understanding passing between them. There was nothing he could say or do to change her mind. Talisa was as committed as he was to do whatever was required to help those in need. If he chose to fight her decision it would be a battle he would surely lose. When she smiled, a slight bend to her lips, he could only smile back, silence his only response as Peter sat laughing at his side.

Chapter 17

"There really is nothing wrong with me," Mary exclaimed for the umpteenth time, her words seeming to fall on deaf ears.

The doctor in attendance only nodded his graying head slowly, continuing the exam that he had already started.

"Your blood pressure is exceptionally high, Mary. That's a cause for concern. How is your diet?"

"I eat just fine. There is nothing wrong with me."

"Your husband seems to think you may be under a great deal of stress. Has something happened lately to upset you?"

Thoughts of her daughter crossed her mind, but Mary shook them from her head, her jaw setting in a tight line that pinched her face awkwardly. "No," she said, her tone rising defensively. "Like I said before, everything is just fine."

The doctor spun around in his seat, scribbling notes into the file of medical records imprinted with Mary London's name.

Mary had just about had enough as she scooted her body to the edge of the examining table. Her gaze met the man's as he turned back to stare at her.

"I'd like to run some further tests, Mary."

"What kind of tests?"

"Just some blood work, nothing too uncomfortable. I'd also like you to go see an associate of mine. Her name is Dr. Wentworth. She's a psychiatrist."

"A head doctor! I don't need to see no head doctor!" Mary said, beginning to shout.

Her physician held up his hand to calm her, his palm dropping heavily against her forearm. "I just want you to talk to her one time. We need to get some additional information to know how to help you and Dr. Wentworth has the qualifications to do that."

"I'm not crazy!" Mary professed, ire rising in her gaze.

The man shook his head. Patience glimmered in his pale green eyes, his tone even and controlled. "No one is saying that, Mary. Not at all. I just think it's important that we run all the tests we can to make sure there is nothing wrong with you. I think that's the smart thing for us to do. Don't you agree?"

Mary studied his expression, her own pensive stare reflecting her thoughts as she weighed all her options. "Fine," she said matter-of-factly. "If it will get my husband to leave me alone, then I'll do it. But once you see that there is nothing wrong with me, you need to tell him to just leave me alone."

The doctor smiled, patting her arm gently. "I promise I'll do just that, Mary. As soon as we have some answers."

Mary paced her kitchen floor, wearing a thin path against the aged linoleum. There was something she needed to do but for the life of her she couldn't begin to remember what it was. Herman's foolishness with the doctor had her out of sorts and the confusion of it all had seeped into the cavity of her mind like water into a sponge.

From where he sat on the living room sofa, Herman could sense the sudden shift in his wife's mood and he felt the muscles tense throughout his body. "What's wrong, Mama? You seem upset."

Mary twisted her fingers anxiously, still pacing from one side of the room to the other. She said nothing, not even bothering to acknowledge his question with a quick glance.

The man repeated himself. "Mary? What's the matter?"

Mary stopped short, suddenly looking up to meet her husband's stare. Her gaze was questioning, confusion wafting over her face.

"Are you all right?" he asked again, sliding forward in his seat.

"I'm fine. I forgot…"

"What, Mary? What did you forget?"

Mary smiled, chuckling softly as she shook her head from side to side. "Heavens me," she said with a light laugh. "I swear, Daddy, I'd lose my head if it wasn't attached."

Herman smiled a faint smile, his lips bending upward unconsciously. Mary suddenly reached for her purse and the car keys.

"I have to run an errand, Herman. I don't know what I was thinking. You and that doctor done messed with my head today. I'm about to forget what I'm supposed to be doing."

The man rose to his feet. "Do you want me to come with you, Mary? I can drive you wherever you want to go."

Mary flipped her hand in his direction. "I'm not feeble, Herman London. Ain't nothing wrong with me. I should be back in a while. We're having fish for dinner. Thought I'd make you some hush puppies and coleslaw to go along with some fried catfish."

"That sounds good, Mama," he said softly, watching as she rushed out of the front door, waving casually toward the window as he stood staring out at her. Herman heaved a deep sigh, air filling his lungs, and nervous energy suddenly flooded through his body.

She had expected the rear entrance into the Wesley Foundation to be locked, but the door was open, a clear invitation that everyone was welcome, no matter what the hour. Stepping inside the air-conditioned building, her arrival was greeted with a gust of cool air that felt as if it was pushing the afternoon heat back to where she'd just come from. As she made her way down the length of narrow corridor, she was anticipating someone or something to jump out and stop her but with each step it was as if there was no one else present in the building.

She stopped at the entrance to the sanctuary, easing her head in first to look around. Sunlight streamed through the stained-glass windows, filtering streams of light across the vibrant red carpet and massive oak pews. A single podium rested on the altar, an open Bible covering the wooden tabletop. From the balcony above her, someone was practicing on the large pipe organ, the mesmerizing sound filling the open air around her.

Dropping into a rear pew, Mary closed her eyes and inhaled the beauty of the moment, relishing the sense of peace that overcame her. Her moment of reverie was interrupted by the call of her name resounding through the room.

"Mary London! How are you?"

Mary looked up to find Reverend Warren smiling down at her. "Reverend, how are you?" she responded, extending her hand to shake his.

"Please, call me Edward. You know we only stand on so much formality around here." He dropped down into the pew beside her. "So, what brings you over to see us today?"

"My Talisa, Reverend. She needs your prayers. My Talisa is in serious trouble."

The man's stare was perplexed as he twisted his body around to face her, cocking his head slightly to the side. "I don't understand, Mary. The mission trip is going exceptionally well. I've gotten glowing reports from the team and they tell me Talisa is doing a wonderful job. Has something happened I don't know about?"

Mary nodded her head slowly. "She has you all fooled, Reverend. But it's not her fault. Satan is working to ruin my baby girl."

"Tell me what's going on, Mary," he said, suddenly sensing that he needed to tread carefully. The woman before him was shaking, her face contorted with anger, a sudden rage that seemed to swell from her eyes into the room. The minister studied the woman carefully, cautiously assessing the situation before him as she told him what was weighing heavily on her spirit.

"He's the devil, Reverend. I cannot allow that evil into my house. I have tried to make Talisa understand that he is no good for her. He's working his devilment on her there in Africa and we need to pray for her. You need to bring Talisa home."

Reverend Warren reached to take Mary's hand into his own. "Why don't we pray together, Mary," he said softly. "Talisa can never have too much prayer in her life."

"Then you understand why Talisa needs to come home right away?"

The man smiled sweetly. "Talisa will be home very soon and I'm sure that you'll feel much better then. We're going to pray for her safe travels and for everyone and everything in her life. Will that make you feel better?"

Mary returned his smile. "We'll beat this evil, Reverend. Your prayers will help me save my child."

An hour later, Mary sat in the student lounge laughing with Johanna and Stevie as if all were well in her world. Reverend Warren stood in the doorway of his office watching them as they shared family tales and Mary caught up on the students' many antics. This was the Mary London that he and his staff had come to know so well, the Mary London who was adored by her only daughter. The woman he had sat with in the sanctuary had been a stranger to him, her bizarre obsession about her daughter a definite cause for some concern. Turning an about-face, he eased the door closed behind him, taking a seat in the leather chair behind his desk. Reaching for the telephone, he dialed Talisa London's home and waited for the young woman's father to pick up the line.

Leila and Mya sat at Mrs. Brimmer's kitchen table giggling over a plate of freshly baked oatmeal cookies and cups of hot chocolate topped with fresh whipped cream. The younger women were laughing as Leila's mother gave them advice on their respective love lives.

"Your problem, Mya," Mrs. Brimmer was saying as she slid a pan of cookies into the oven, "is that you're chasing after the wrong kinds of men. You think a man is supposed to be the answer to all your problems. And Leila doesn't want a man to be the answer to any of her problems. Wants to solve everything all on her own. Both of you need to readjust your standards and maybe you can catch yourselves a husband."

Leila rolled her eyes. "Weren't you the one who raised me with those standards?"

"I raised you to be smart, girlie. And you can be smart without scaring a man off. I caught your daddy by being smart. Caught 'im good, too!" The woman chuckled loudly before she continued. "But these boys are afraid to even approach you the way you carry on sometimes. I'm not ever gone have no grandbabies at the rate you're working."

"Well, if it's grandbabies you want, I don't need a husband to do that. I can get right on that grandbaby thing for you." Leila winked at her friend who was grinning widely at both of the women.

"Oh, no you won't! We won't be having any of that around here. I sure enough didn't raise you to be thinking no foolishness like that."

"Well, you need to make up you mind, Mama. Either you want me to find a man or you want grandbabies."

"I want both and I want them the old-fashioned way, in the proper order. Don't be cute, girlie." Mrs. Brimmer waved a finger in her daughter's direction. "And, Miss Mya, what's this I hear about all these boys you keep dating. When you gone find you a decent man to settle down with?"

Mya sighed, her eyebrows lifting toward the ceiling. She shrugged. "Who knows, Mrs. Brimmer. Maybe you can introduce me to a nice guy."

Leila's mother took a seat in the empty chair across from the two younger women. "You need to come to church more. We have some nice young men who've joined the church."

Mya winced. "Those are usually the worst ones," she exclaimed as she and Leila both burst out into laughter.

"Honey, hush," Leila giggled, reaching for another cookie to stuff into her mouth.

Mrs. Brimmer waved her head from side to side, her gaze resting on one woman and then the other. "What am I going to do with you two?" she said, joining in the laughter. Rising from her seat she leaned to peer into the oven, keeping a close eye on the pan of sweets inside the hot cavity.

"So, what's going on with Talisa? Have you talked to her since she called last?" Mrs. Brimmer asked, peering up to look at her daughter.

Leila nodded. "I have. She called me the other day. She's having a great time. This doctor seems to have swept her right off her feet."

"Why can't I ever find a doctor?" Mya asked wistfully.

"You can't catch quality, Miss Mya, when you're not acting in a quality fashion," Mrs. Brimmer professed, meeting Mya's dark eyes with a stern stare.

Mya blushed ever so slightly, dropping her gaze to the tabletop in front of her.

"Have you spoken with Mrs. London?" Leila asked, trying to redirect the conversation. "Is she doing any better?"

Mrs. Brimmer's expression changed, the age lines in her brown complexion hardening with intensity. Her attention seemed diverted as she fell into her own thoughts. The two younger women stared curiously, waiting for a response.

The older woman sighed before she moved to respond, first removing the last tray of cookies from the oven and onto a wire cooling rack. She tossed a dishrag against the countertop before returning to the seat she had left empty just minutes before.

"Mary's going through a difficult time. I don't think she understands what's happening with Talisa. Talisa needs to talk with her mother more so Mary doesn't feel so left out. That might help."

"Mrs. London just needs to let Talisa go. She is grown," Mya professed.

Mrs. Brimmer tossed Mya a scolding glare but didn't bother to respond to the young woman's comment.

"I don't know if that will help, Mom," Leila said. "Talisa and her mother are close, but Mrs. London doesn't like it when Talisa tries to make choices for herself. I think Talisa could talk until she was blue in the face and her mother would still have a problem with Talisa getting involved with a man. Any man."

"Maybe this man isn't right for Talisa. Her mother may know something we all don't."

Leila shrugged, tossing Mya a quick glance before she replied. "I don't think Mrs. London knows anything more than what we all know, Mom. She knows that Talisa is interested in this man and the man is interested in Talisa. The very idea that Talisa may leave home and find happiness elsewhere is the problem Mrs. London is having."

"It's like I said," Mya repeated. "Talisa is grown and her mother just needs to let her go."

Mrs. Brimmer shook her head. "Yes, she is, Mya. Talisa is an adult, but since she's living under her parents' roof, she owes her mother a certain degree of respect."

"Does that mean she should give up her own life until she moves out?" Leila asked.

Her mother waved her head again. "She just needs to be honest about her actions. I think that is all her mother expects."

"Talisa is the most honest person I know, Mrs. Brimmer. I don't think being honest with her mother is her problem. If you ask me, Mrs. London is just crazy."

Mrs. Brimmer swatted her palm in Mya's direction. "Well, girlie, I didn't ask you and you need to hush that nonsense. Mary may have some issues, but that doesn't give you any cause to disrespect her like that."

"Well, whatever the problem is, I think it's only going to get worse before it will even begin to get better," Leila said.

The matriarch met her daughter's serious stare, mulling over the young woman's comment, knowing in her heart that both Leila and Mya were probably right.

Herman sat perched on the edge of a kitchen chair, his elbows pressed into his thighs and his head resting in the palms of his hands. His day had been long and from the minute he'd entered his home, he'd sensed that the worst of it was yet to come.

Mary had not moved once from her seat on the padded chair that rested in the corner of the kitchen beneath the wall-hung telephone. For over an hour, the telephone receiver had rested between her ear and her shoulder, the appliance in use every minute except for the few seconds it took for her to disconnect one call and dial another.

Each of the woman's conversations had been the same, long-winded dissertation, bemoaning Talisa's alleged crimes against her and God. Herman had lost count of the number of times Mary had claimed that Talisa was being deceived by Satan and now considered her mother to be the enemy. As he sat listening it had become easy to tell which conversations were going Mary's way and which were not. It was easy to discern who was giving an ounce of validation to her craziness and who wasn't.

As Mary slammed the receiver back onto the hook, it was clear that she was not happy with her friend Nellie. Knowing Nellie Brimmer's straightforwardness, Herman could only imagine what she'd said to Mary to have made her so angry. As Mary reached to dial another number, he'd witnessed more of her nonsense than he cared to. He couldn't allow it to go any further. Rising to his feet, he crossed the room to his wife's side and pulled the receiver from her hand, dropping it back onto the hook.

"What in the—?"

"You've gone too far with this foolishness, Mary. No more."

Anger pierced the room, rising like a new day's sunrise. "Don't you dare tell me—"

The man raised his voice. "I am telling you. This is going to stop and it's going to stop now. Talisa hasn't done anything wrong. You have no business carrying on the way you are."

The woman's hands fell to her hips, her lips pursed out to give her husband lip. It was the look he gave her that stalled the bitter words, trapping them against her tongue. His glare was hard and angry, and nothing like she had become accustomed to over the years. His left hand was clenched in a tight fist at his side and he shook his right index finger in her face, almost daring her to say or do something he didn't approve of. Mary took a step back, falling into the chair beneath her. The duo continued to stare each other down until Mary finally dropped her gaze to the floor. Only then did Herman relax the muscles in his body, easing his way slowly out of the room. He stopped in the doorway, turning to stare over his shoulder.

"We need to fix this, Mary. You need help. I love you with all my heart, Mama, but you need help and we're going to figure out where we need to go to get it. Now, I need to change my clothes. Then we're going to go get some dinner. Tomorrow, we're going back to the doctor for some answers. Until then I don't want to hear another word about Talisa. Do you understand me?"

Without waiting for a response, Herman London made his exit, tears filling his eyes as he climbed the flight of steps to his bedroom.

Chapter 18

The clinic was exceptionally quiet, one of few evenings where none of their patients had required overnight attendance. The room was dark, just a shimmer of moonlight gleaming into the side windows. Outside, night noises filled the damp air, thunder rolling across the black sky as the last remnants of a rain shower fell from overhead.

Talisa lay curled against the mattress of a twin bed. Jericho sat at the foot of the bunk, slowly rubbing the tension from her aching feet. Talisa marveled at the relief his large hands were affording her size sevens as he slowly caressed the flesh from her toes, across her arches, over her heels, and up to her ankles. Talisa could hear herself moaning ever so slightly and when she opened her eyes to see if Jericho had noticed, the man's mouth had raised up into a smile, the seductive gesture sending a wave of wanting surging through her body. Talisa wiggled her toes and laughed softly, pulling her foot from Jericho's grasp.

"That tickles," she whispered, needing to distance herself from the rise of heat as a half truth fell from her mouth.

Jericho winked, dropping his body against the bed to curl himself around her. "If we could lock the door I'd massage the rest of you," he whispered back, his warm breath blowing gently against her ear.

The very thought combined with the sweet kiss of his breath, caused Talisa to shudder with excitement, her teeth biting against her bottom lip as she pressed her knees tightly together. Jericho pressed his face into her neck, his mouth dancing against her flesh. She smelled sweet, like fresh berries in the springtime, he thought. His hands glided like a feather down the length of her body, coming to rest against her abdomen.

Talisa rolled, carefully turning her body around to face him. She lifted her mouth to his and kissed him softly at first, her tongue tasting his top lip and then his bottom. She could feel his heartbeat quickening against her breasts, keeping time with her own. The swelling of his male tissue pressed eagerly against her feminine quadrant. The kiss became more intense as her tongue probed deeper and deeper, brushing ever so gently against the roof of his mouth. The motion was teasing and Jericho could barely contain his own excitement.

His breathing began to come in gasps and then he remembered where they were. Reluctantly, he pulled his mouth from hers. Talisa smiled sweetly and he couldn't help but press one more kiss against her nose, her eyelids and her lips.

"We should get some sleep," he said softly, shifting his

pelvis away from the touch of her body. "We've got a long day tomorrow."

Talisa heaved a deep sigh, nodding her head in agreement. She leaned her head into his chest and closed her eyes. Sleep came quickly, dancing in on the beat of Jericho's heart.

Talisa was not at all prepared for the devastation in Gulu. The drive to the government rehabilitation center had started very early in the morning and though Peter had gone to great pains to ready her and Jericho for the experience, she was taken by complete surprise.

Southern Uganda, Kampala and the Sese Islands had spoiled her. Kampala's new shopping mall and large self-service food store and supermarket had been no different from home. The city had been relatively safe and not once had she or Jericho ever felt threatened or been made to feel uneasy. Their friendly faces had been met with friendly faces. The friendship they'd offered had been offered in return. Life had been very comfortable.

As Peter drove through the steel gates that bordered the center and parked his Mitsubishi Pajero, a four-wheel drive jeep, Talisa realized that she had been too comfortable. For the past month it had been as if she'd forgotten that she was in central Africa, residing just miles from a low-intensity war zone. The view outside the car window was a harsh reminder. Jericho sensed the wave of panic that suddenly consumed her, reaching to wrap his arm around her shoulder as they stepped from the vehicle.

Their arrival was met with curious stares, children and some adults eyeing them cautiously. This particular day was food distribution day and villagers stood in a lengthy line awaiting a handout. Peter explained that though the area was one of Africa's most fertile regions, farmers were unable to work their lands, fearing retribution from the rebels. Countless survivors had come to depend on food aid from the World Food Program, the only organization that the rebels allowed to work in the area and only because they stole most of the supplies after the food was delivered to its distribution point.

As Peter left them to inform the center of their arrival, Jericho and Talisa went to offer their assistance. A young, blond man with a deep British accent greeted them warmly, stepping out of an armored car to hand them both a bullet-proof vest. Talisa's eyes widened with discomfort as the man helped her strap the protective garment around her chest.

"Is it always like this?" Talisa asked, gesturing with her head toward the food convoys and their military escorts. Almost fifty soldiers in trucks, multiple armored cars and an automatic cannon mounted on a platform truck sat in a clean line, one behind the other.

The young man nodded. "We need as much protection as we can get. Some days are better than others."

Joining in, Talisa and Jericho immediately went to work, helping to move cartons from the back of the truck to the front. The crowd was growing anxious, impatience filtering through malnourished bodies and it was as if the level of nervous energy swelled thickly in the humid air. Talisa smiled warmly as she passed powdered milk and bags of rice to outstretched hands, mothers and fathers nodding their heads in gratitude.

Minutes later, Peter gestured for their attention, calling them toward the makeshift hospital. As the duo sauntered in his direction, Talisa noticed a group of children gathered at a communal water pump. They had looked no different from children anywhere else until she noted that many of the young girls were pregnant, bellies in varying stages of new growth, and that most of the boys were nursing wounds, battle-hardened expressions tainting the youthfulness of their faces.

"They're just babies," Talisa heard herself say, the words falling out of her mouth before she could catch them.

Peter squeezed her shoulder. "They are only children in age. They have endured far too much to ever be children again," he said, the sadness of the truth haunting his words. "If they find their way here they are lucky. The rebels stole many of them from their beds, killed their families, and then made them fight. Taught them how to kill. Many of the girls will live the rest of their lives with the reminders of their kidnappers, raising the children of men who took away their innocence." Peter waved his hands in the air. "This is the tragedy of my homeland."

"How long do they stay here?" Jericho asked.

Peter shrugged. "A few months, maybe. Here they have someplace to sleep, food and medical care. But sooner or later they leave again. Sometimes they can go home to family and sometimes their families reject them for what they've been made to do. Most have no family to go back to. They will tell you their stories," Peter said, his gaze meeting Talisa's. "But some of their stories will not be easy for you to hear." Peter's voice quivered as his composure was threatened by his own tears.

Jericho patted his friend on the back as the trio stepped inside the small concrete building. The makeshift hospital was filled to capacity, injured bodies filling every conceivable cot. Jericho instantly stepped into doctor mode, reaching for his black bag and the medical supplies they had lugged with them from Kampala. For the next six hours they moved from one injury to another, helping to treat patient after patient, many of them barely past the age of eleven.

During their third hour, a young boy named Moses began following Jericho from one point to another. Talisa smiled as the youngster chatted nonstop, words flowing a mile a minute from his mouth. His questions were endless, one long list of how comes, and what fors. The medical personnel who staffed the facility had grown weary of shooing the boy off and eventually had left it up to Jericho to decide what to do with him.

"I will be a doctor some day," Moses said, his thin chest pushing out proudly. "I will study medicine and make people well."

"That's very good," Jericho replied, stopping to take a seat in an old wooden chair as Moses stepped between his legs, taking a seat on Jericho's lap.

"Where is your family?" Jericho asked.

Moses shrugged his narrow shoulders. "My father is dead. I don't know where my mother is. I have a sister. Her name is Susie. Me and Susie live here. We don't want them to get us again. They did bad things."

Jericho nodded slowly, lifting his eyes to give Talisa a quick gaze. His hand reached for the boy's leg, lifting it straight out in front of him. "Did they do that?" he asked, pointing to a large bandage wrapped around the child's calf.

Moses waved his head up and down. "Me and Susie run from the bad man when he not looking. He shoot his gun and hit me in the leg. I didn't cry," the child exclaimed, puffing his chest our farther. "My sister got beat in her head. She don't remember things good no more."

Jericho inhaled, filling his lungs with air. "Well, I think we need to change that bandage. Is it okay for me to look at it, Doc?"

Moses grinned. "I'm strong. It won't hurt me."

"I didn't think so." Jericho smiled as he reached for the sterile gauze and antiseptic that Talisa was passing to him.

Talisa spent the rest of the afternoon helping where she could. Whenever she had a quick moment she would stop to carry on a conversation with some of the young women, their new friend Moses translating when necessary. His sister Susie had barely talked at all, smiling shyly as Talisa asked questions that the girl sometimes answered and sometimes didn't. She had understood Talisa's prayers though, bowing her head and holding tight to Talisa's hand as the woman had asked the good Lord to shower his blessings down upon them.

As the sun prepared to settle down for the evening, dropping low into the horizon, there was a sudden rush of noise through the front gates. Stepping back outside, Peter, Talisa and Jericho stood watching as a stream of children marched into the compound. Hundreds of them seemed to appear out of nowhere, some having walked miles from their villages to seek shelter for the night. Both Talisa and Jericho watched in awe as they made their way to the safe haven of the small community. Seeking out a space on the floor of the hospital and the outside grounds to sleep, they made beds from the sacks and thin blankets they had carried in with them.

"They are our night commuters," Peter said, his voice low. "There is safety here. They will sleep tonight and go home in the morning."

"Do they do this every night?" Jericho asked, his own voice barely a loud whisper.

Peter stood silent for a brief moment before responding. He nodded, his words coated with anguish. "More nights than they should have to," he said, turning back around to go inside.

For the entire week, Moses trailed Jericho's every step. The child had even bonded with Talisa, coming to hold her hand or wrap his arms around her waist as she hugged him back. In the evenings, Talisa read to him and his sister from her Bible and an assortment of well-worn children's books that were scattered around the center. Nine-year-old Susie was harder to reach. The little girl was quiet and withdrawn, prone to panic attacks, and both children suffered from fitful sleep and nightmares. It was the rare moment when Moses was able to make his baby sister smile, a glimmer of joy shining from her large black eyes. Too often Susie would only stare out into space, her mind blank to keep from remembering her pain-filled experiences.

It was on their eighth day there that Susie sought Talisa out, shadowing the woman's moves as Talisa made her rounds through the center. As Talisa helped to prepare lunch, Susie stood at her elbow overly anxious to lend a helping hand. Talisa smiled down at the young child, reaching to wrap her arms around the little girl's shoulders. Talisa was surprised when the tiniest of voices spoke to her.

"Can I...home...with you?" Susie asked, her broken English a soft whisper. She stared down to the ground, her bare feet sifting the dirt between her toes. "I promise be good girl," Susie implored, glancing up for a brief second to meet Talisa's gaze.

Talisa had to fight back her own tears as she laid the spoon she was using against the table. Dropping to her knees she pulled the little girl to her and hugged her tightly.

The frail creature was barely skin and bones in Talisa's arms, her petite frame feeling as if it would break beneath the slightest pressure. Talisa kissed the child's cheek and said nothing, unable to find the right words to explain to the child her inability to fulfill the little girl's request.

Hours later, Talisa and Jericho lay side by side. Talisa could barely sleep, too tired from the emotional stress to allow her body to relax in comfort. Jericho was feeling it also, the strength of his palm gently massaging her shoulder. Neither said anything, no words necessary to explain the flood of emotions washing over them. Talisa had broken down when she had relayed her conversation with Susie, and as Jericho had shared her feelings of despair and hopelessness, he had cried with her, the duo holding tight to each other for support.

As Talisa floated in and out of slumber she found herself questioning the choices she had made for herself, wondering if she would ever find the answers to calm the unrest washing over her. She rationalized that she was only one person and could only do but so much, and it ripped her spirit to be unable to do more. As she rolled over to her side she realized that Jericho was no longer lying beside her, having risen from his resting spot during one of her moments of rest. She lifted herself up, her eyes searching the dark room to see where he might have gone.

The darkness was suddenly breached by a flash of light bursting through the door of the hospital. Within a short span of time, the quiet outside was disturbed by the sounds of gunfire and children screaming. Talisa jumped from her sleeping bag, rushing outside to see what was going on. Peter stood in the center of the compound, shouting in one of the Nilotic languages. As Talisa struggled to focus her eyes on where Peter stood staring, Jericho rushed out from somewhere behind her, sprinting across the compound toward the front gates which stood wide open. Talisa's eyes adjusted to the darkness, following the stream of the flashlight, as she recognized Moses's slight frame racing into the night. As Jericho and the child disappeared into the dark, someone else slammed the gates closed behind them. Over the commotion of another burst of gunplay and the children's screams and cries, no one heard Talisa calling out for Jericho to come back to her.

Chapter 19

Joss Stone was playing in the CD player, *The Soul Sessions* CD spinning continuously. Elijah Becton lounged on a teak recliner that sat beneath the window of the screened sunporch. The temperature was rising outside, heat and humidity battling for control. He reached for a cotton towel that lay across his lap, swiping at the rise of moisture that dampened his forehead and gray hair. Irene stood in the doorway, eyeing her husband with amusement. Her head bobbed in time with the music.

"Why don't you come inside, Elijah? The air-conditioning is on and it's much cooler."

"I like the heat," the man replied, giving her a broad grin. "Why don't you come out here and get hot with me?" he said with a perverse laugh.

Irene laughed with him, shaking her index finger in his direction. "Don't be fresh." She glanced down to the watch on her wrist. "We're having lunch with the Houstons. I thought we'd dine at the club. What do you think?"

The man shrugged. "There are a dozen other things I'd prefer to do with my Saturday afternoon. Personally, I'd rather skip lunch and go right to the desserts," the man said, his voice dropping low and deep. "Why are you standing over there?"

"Because you're being fresh and we don't have time for that. We'll never make it on time if you don't go upstairs to dress."

The man squinted his eyes, feigning a look of annoyance. "You're not fair," he said, pouting.

Irene laughed again. "You remind me of our baby boy with that look on your face. Now go get ready, Elijah. We can play later."

"We can play now *and* we can play later. What do you say? I'm game if you are!"

Before Irene could respond, the telephone rang, the chime resounding through the air. Elijah moved his mouth as if to cuss and Irene's eye widened in reprimand, pointing at the telephone that sat on the glass tabletop beside him. "Answer the phone, Elijah."

The man sighed loudly, clearly unamused as he reached for the receiver. "Hello?"

Irene, who had turned to exit the room, spun back around as she caught the beginning of her husband's conversation. She moved closer, stepping into the space toward him.

"Peter, hello! I didn't recognize your voice. How are things in Uganda?"

There was a quick pause. "What do you mean—? How could this—? Do we know—?" Elijah's ruddy face had lost all its color as he sat upright in his seat. He met his wife's gaze, visibly agitated. His expression was painted with fear, and as Irene stood staring at him, the rank emotion seeped like morning mist into her spirit.

Elijah ended the conversation. "I understand. We'll be there on the first flight we can get out. I'll call you back as soon as I know our plans."

As he dropped the receiver back onto its hook, tears leaked from his eyes. He struggled to hold his wife's gaze, his words catching in the back of his throat.

"Where's my son?" Irene asked, panic ringing in her voice. "What has happened to Jericho?"

Elijah brushed at the moisture against his cheek with the back of his hand. "Jericho's missing. They think he's been abducted by the rebels." Elijah rose to his feet, reaching to pull the woman into his arms.

"Go pack," he said finally, releasing the tight hold he'd had on her. "I'll call the airport and arrange for a flight. Make sure you grab our passports. Peter will get us visa clearance through the U.S. Consulate. We can run by the hospital for yellow fever vaccines. I'll give us the injections if I have to."

Irene nodded, racing from the room. Elijah stood with his eyes closed, holding onto the wisp of breath he'd just inhaled, fighting to maintain a semblance of calm. "Lord, help us," he whispered into the air as he reached for the phone and began to dial.

Talisa was beside herself, pacing the floor from one end of the room to the other. She struggled not to cry, wanting to scream out in rage.

"I don't understand this, Peter," she said. "Where can he be? Why isn't someone out looking for him?"

"They are looking for him, Talisa. You need to stay calm."

"Stay calm? How can I stay calm? It's been two days now." Her voice had risen in anguish. She clutched at her chest, pulling the button-front shirt tight against her throat. "How could this have happened, Peter?" she said finally, her gaze meeting his. "How?"

Peter sucked in air, breathing heavily as he struggled for the umpteenth time to understand the few details they had any knowledge of, repeating them over as if it were the first time. "The child went racing after his sister. For some reason she'd wandered past the gates and he heard her screaming. Apparently the rebels had grabbed her. We didn't know they were that close to the compound. Jericho saw Moses running and just took off after him. There was no way we could have stopped him, Talisa. They were all gone before we realized what was going on."

"This can't be happening," Talisa muttered, dropping her head into her hands and pulling at her hair. "Why is this happening, Lord?" she cried, her gaze lifted skyward.

Peter wrapped her in a comforting hug. "We have to be strong, Talisa. For Jericho, we have to be strong."

She nodded her head. "Have you called his parents?"

"I did."

"What about my students? Things are still safe at the orphanage?"

"Everyone is well and they send their prayers. Clarissa said for you not to worry about them. They are keeping busy with the children."

Talisa blew a sigh of relief, grateful for one less thing she would have to worry about. Her eyes misted with water, unable to still the fall of saline that pressed heavy against her lashes. As her tears finally fell in swells, Talisa didn't know how to make anyone understand how unbearable her hurt was. She was beset with visions of Jericho in pain, injured, in distress, alone, and her not being there to help him. The past two nights she had been unable to sleep for want of him, desperate for his warmth and protection. For the past few hours she'd tried to focus on his patients, to help where an extra hand was needed, but every time she stopped, he was there in her mind's eye, haunting her. It was unbearable. Their being together, their delight in each other was still so new and so intense that not being together was like a physical pain she could not explain.

Talisa stood frozen at the center's gate, staring out toward the distance. Her mouth was dry, her eyes clouded from crying. Fear coursed through her veins, rushing in toxic waves over her spirit. She was afraid Jericho would never be found. She panicked that he might not ever return. And she feared how he might come back to her. It was those all-consuming seeds of doubt that were trying to steal her spirit.

Chapter 20

Jericho had walked for hours. His bare feet were blistered raw but he knew there would be no rest anytime soon. They had traveled mostly at night, hiding and sleeping in the brush during daylight. The dirt path they followed was a long stretch of land occupied by a wealth of thorny bushes and thick trees.

As his captors pushed him along, Jericho understood that Moses was the only reason he was still alive. The child's fast talking was the sole reason he had not been left for dead days ago. The insurgents were in need of a doctor and Moses had made them understand that Jericho could serve them well, but only if he was unharmed. The leader of the group, a young man who barely looked twenty had eyed the two of them with much apprehension but had eventually relented. Moses had not asked once about his sister and Jericho sensed that for him to do so would only make things far more difficult for the little girl wherever it was she was being held.

As Jericho struggled to stay standing on his weary legs, Moses reached for his hand. Despite the hardened lines that painted the young boy's face, the small hand beneath Jericho's was shaking ever so slightly. Neither of them spoke, fearful that they might be heard by one of the young men following close beside them. Not far ahead of them, rows of tents and cone-shaped huts painted the hillside. As they approached an abandoned village that was being used as a rebel camp, Jericho was grateful. His body was exhausted and even a few minutes of rest would serve him well.

Someone slammed him in the shoulder with the butt of a rifle and he fell hard to the ground, unable to catch his balance. The soldiers all laughed, amused by his predicament. A heavy boot slammed into his ribs and excruciating pain rippled through his body, the blow slamming every ounce of air from his lungs. As he struggled to pull himself upright, gasping for oxygen, Moses was pleading to their captors to leave him be. The boy stood protectively, placing his own small body between Jericho and his attackers. The gesture earned the child a harsh slap across his face, but Moses stood firm, refusing to be bullied as he professed their need for a doctor.

The leader, a teenager whose name was Onen, was duly impressed with the boy's bravery, thinking that if properly trained he would be of great use to them. Moses had the demeanor of a warrior and once they were in control of his mind he would serve them well. Onen uttered orders that the rest quickly followed, the group turning to amuse themselves elsewhere.

Onen watched as Jericho came to his feet, fighting his

own hurt to lift himself up on his legs. As Jericho stood upright, his hands bound tightly in front of him, the young man stood in front of him, both of them staring at each other intently. Onen sneered, then lifted his filthy T-shirt for Jericho to examine his torso. He pounded a fist against his chest, pointing to a red rash that was crawling from his belly button up to his shoulder and down his back. Jericho instantly recognized the parasitic infection, common in those who lived in areas with no clean water and inadequate hygiene facilities.

"Tell him I need fresh water, clean rags or bandages, and an antiseptic," Jericho said to Moses who quickly translated for him.

The man suddenly became agitated, yelling loudly before lifting a clenched fist to strike Moses down. Jericho moved quickly, stepping between the man and the boy. He spoke quickly, his words rushing past his chapped lips. "Tell him I can use leaves from that banana tree over there, but I have to have clean water. We can boil whatever he has and I'll figure out the rest."

Onen stood with his hand still raised to strike, dropping it slowly to his side as Moses translated for a second time. His gaze darted from the doctor to the boy and back again, then he nodded his head, turning an about-face toward one of the empty huts. Jericho breathed a sigh of relief.

"Do you know where we are, Moses?"

The boy nodded. "Close to Sudan."

"Do you know a way for us to get help?"

Moses shook his head. "We will try to run the first chance we get. Susie will let them know where we are headed."

"Susie? You know where Susie is?"

"That boy over there beat her," Moses said, pointing to

a thin child who was probably only eleven or twelve years old himself. "When he stop I tell her to pretend to be dead. She do and they leave her body there. I tell her to walk back for help. Susie will tell them to come," Moses whispered. Jericho sensed the child was trying to convince himself as much as he wanted to assure Jericho that things would soon be well for them.

An hour later, Onen returned with supplies and two metal plates of food. After Jericho cleaned his rash, coating the bruised area with the sap from the banana leaves, he and Moses were allowed to eat. The meal was sparse, boiled sorghum and weeds, and slices of overripe mango. The first meal since their capture, Jericho and Moses both ate until their plates were empty, their bellies barely feeling full when they were done.

The evening air had grown cooler, the threat of rain billowing dampness overhead. Jericho settled himself against the hard earth, curling himself around Moses to afford the child some warmth. His eyes were heavy, exhaustion trying to consume him. Every so often one of the young girls in the group would scream out, something or someone doing them harm. Only the tight ropes that bound his feet and hands kept Jericho from leaping to their rescue.

As darkness settled around him he thought of Talisa, hoping that Peter had taken her back to safety in Kampala and the orphanage. He would have given anything, he thought, to be with her one more time, to hold her in his arms and feel the tender caress of her skin against his. As he lay listening to the hushed whispers of his captors, he couldn't help but wonder if he was ever going to have the chance to kiss the sweetness of her mouth again. Jericho could feel his tears falling down his cheeks. Moses was

snoring lightly beside him and so Jericho lay still, not bothering to try to wipe his eyes lest he wake the child from
his few minutes of rest.

He could only imagine what was going through Talisa's
mind. He knew that if their positions were reversed he
would be crazy over the loss of her. If it took a lifetime,
nothing and no one could have kept him from finding her.
He imagined Talisa was thinking the very same thing.
Jericho sighed. He knew enough about Talisa to know she
was holding on to hope from a higher source. "Let go, and
let God," she had said to him once, that sweet smile
washing over his spirit as she lifted herself in prayer.
Talisa's faith was unfailing. He closed his eyes, filling his
lungs with oxygen as he took a deep breath. Staring back
out into the darkness, Jericho began to pray.

Talisa noticed the lone figure limping toward the
compound before anyone else. The thin frame was so small
against the dusty horizon that she almost thought it an
illusion. As it drew closer, Talisa could feel her heart skip
a beat, anxiety suddenly washing over her.

"Peter! Peter!" she yelled loudly as she gestured for some
of the men to open the gates for her. "Hurry, Peter!" she
called as she raced to catch Susie's bruised body into her arms.

The child was barely recognizable. Her face was
swollen, having been battered black and blue. Talisa
pressed her fingertips to Susie's forehead, fighting back the
flood of tears that suddenly spewed from her eyes.

"Shhh, you're safe, baby girl," Talisa whispered into the
child's ear. "I'm right here, Susie."

Susie squeezed an eye open to stare up at Talisa. The
edge of a smile blessed her face. Her mouth moved open

and then closed as she struggled to speak. Talisa leaned to hear as the child whispered into her ear.

"Just rest," Talisa responded, lifting the child into her arms and heading back into the compound. "You just rest now."

Running to meet her, Peter and one of the nurses reached to lift the girl from Talisa's arms.

"She's burning up with fever," Talisa stated, still holding tightly to the child's hand as they rushed her into the infirmary.

Talisa stepped back out of the way as the medical staff leaned in to work on the girl's injuries. She turned to stare toward Peter who was watching just as intensely.

"We have to go find them, Peter," she said matter-of-factly. "Jericho and Moses are both okay, but we have to go find them before it's too late."

As Peter stood staring at her, his resolve melding with hers, he nodded his understanding. With much to arrange, Peter headed out the door, Talisa following closely behind him.

Later that evening Talisa pulled her chair up against the cot, settling herself comfortably beside the sleeping child. Susie rested uneasily, tossing about as nightmares coursed through her dreams. If it had been possible, Talisa would have taken every ounce of the child's hurt onto herself and it pained her to see the small body so tormented. She ran a soft hand against the child's arm.

She and Peter would be headed toward Sudan in the morning, hopeful that Jericho and the boy would be found before they crossed the borders into hostile territory. She understood that the trek would not be an easy one, but finding her man was all she could think about.

Despite the distance between them, Talisa could feel

Jericho as if he were standing beside her. He was thinking of her, worried about her being safe from harm. He missed her as much as she missed him and it was if the emotions they carried for one another were being carried on the gentlest of breezes blowing through the African air.

Rising from her seat, Talisa eased her way outside, taking great care not to disturb anyone from their sleep. Standing on the porch of the building, she took a deep breath, inhaling the essence of Jericho from the midnight air. High in the dark sky overhead, the sliver of a new moon glimmered in the distance. A spattering of stars twinkled against the black backdrop, shimmering reverently for attention. Talisa could feel her spirit smiling as Jericho called her name, telling her he was alive and fighting just as intensely to get back to her. Lifting her gaze skyward, Talisa could feel the pull against her heart and answered it, her arms hugging her body tightly. "I'm coming, Jericho," she said, her voice barely a whisper out into the dark. "We'll be together very soon."

Jericho leaned up in the darkness. The village had finally gone quiet for another night, the troops preparing to leave for Sudan in the early morning. The faint moonlight and glitter of stars above shone down upon him, easing the anxiety that had plagued him for much of the day. Talisa was in his heart, and he could feel his spirit holding on to hope that they would soon be together again. He could taste her, his tongue flickering out over the coarse skin that covered his dry lips. The scent of her filled his nostrils, her honeyed essence billowing through his bloodstream. Jericho smiled, whispering softly into the night air. "I love you, too, Talisa. I love you, too."

Chapter 21

They were stocking the jeep with supplies when the convoy of military vehicles pulled into the compound. Both Peter and Talisa diverted their attention as officers from the local militia and the Ugandan army pulled into the empty spaces beside them. Angela drove the fourth jeep, stepping quickly out of the car as Jericho's parents followed closely on her heels.

As Talisa's gaze locked with Jericho's mother, she smiled, nodding her head softly. The older woman smiled back, her nervous anxiety flooding her dark complexion.

Angela reached to hug her husband first, then leaned to wrap her arms around Talisa. "Any news yet?" she asked.

Peter nodded. "We're headed to the border. We think we can catch him before they cross."

Angela nodded, her gaze shifting from one to the other. "Well, I've gotten you some assistance," she said, gesturing in the direction of the military presence. "The consulate is calling in a number of favors on our behalf."

Peter smiled as he was quickly introduced to the officials. Turning his attention to Jericho's parents, Peter extended his hand toward Dr. Becton. "I am sorry that we must meet again under these circumstances, sir," he said, pulling the man into a warm embrace as they greeted each other.

Jericho's father nodded his head. "So am I, Peter," he said, as Jericho's friend reached to hug and greet his wife.

"Do you think he's okay?" Irene asked, the worry tainting her words, Peter's arms still wrapped around her shoulders.

Peter turned his gaze toward Talisa. All eyes followed his as everyone's attention suddenly fell on the young woman who stood standing off to the side.

"We're going to bring him home, Mrs. Becton," Talisa said softly.

The woman studied her momentarily. "You must be Talisa," she said finally, reaching for Talisa's hands. "We've heard so much about you."

Talisa nodded. "Yes, ma'am."

"Well, I'm going with you," Dr. Becton said, looking from one to the other.

Peter shook his head. "I do not think that is a good idea, sir. I think it would be safer for you to stay here."

"Well, I don't care—" the man started.

Talisa lifted her hand to interrupt him. "Jericho wouldn't want that, Dr. Becton. They can use your help here. The hospital is filling up and there aren't enough medical personnel to help all the patients. Jericho would want you to help out here until he can get back. I promise you, sir, we will find him and bring him home."

"How can you promise me that?" Dr. Becton said tersely. "What do you know?"

Talisa pressed her palm against her heart. "I know that I love your son and he loves me. And I know he's going to be just fine. He's strong and he'll guide us to wherever he is. But we don't have time to argue about it. He would want you to stay here, to be with his mother. He would want both of you to help with the children. That's what Jericho would want you to do."

Dr. Becton moved to argue, tossing an angry look in Talisa's direction. His wife stalled the motion, moving to press her fingers to her husband's lips. The man eyed her curiously as she stepped back toward Talisa, clasping the younger woman's hands between her own.

Talisa noted the damp tears that pressed at the woman's eyes. She reached to give the woman a hug. "I can feel him, Mrs. Becton. I can feel him in my heart and I know he's going to be fine," she whispered.

Irene nodded. "I believe you," she whispered back. She wiped at her eyes, the moisture brushing against the back of her hand. Reaching for the necklace around her neck, she undid the clasp, pulling the chain and pendant into her hand. She studied it for a quick minute then pressed it into the palm of Talisa's hand.

Talisa looked down to study the large gold cross embedded with a line of four diamonds and the heavy chain that supported it. She wrapped her fingers tightly around it as she glanced back up to stare at Jericho's mother.

"When you find my baby boy, give him that, please. Tell him his father and I will be right here waiting for him. Tell him, please, that we love him."

Nodding, Talisa linked the chain around her own neck.

"I promise, Mrs. Becton," she answered as the woman leaned to kiss her cheek.

Irene pressed a palm to Talisa's face. "They have work to do, Elijah," she said, directing her comment to her husband. "Peter and Talisa do not need us in their way. We can do more for Jericho right here. Talisa's right. That's what Jericho would want."

The man sputtered as his wife turned to clasp his arm in her own. "Angela, why don't we three go see where we can be of service. These two need to get out of here," she stated, leading the way toward the hospital, pulling her husband along behind her.

Angela smiled, reaching to hug and kiss her own husband one more time. She turned to Talisa and grinned. "Just follow the light," she said, nodding her head slowly. "It will take you in the right direction."

Talisa grinned back. "I know."

Minutes later, Angela and the Bectons stood watching as the rescue caravan exited through the gates. In the seat beside Peter, Talisa turned to wave back as Jericho's mother lifted her hand in the air. Watching the woman who clung closely to her husband for support, Talisa couldn't help but wish for her own mother.

Onen was giving orders, his troops falling into line as they prepared to move camp. Jericho knew they were quickly running out of time. Beside him, Moses had grown anxious, shifting nervously from side to side. His gaze shifted focus quickly, trying to take in everything and everyone around him.

"What's happening, Moses?" Jericho whispered.

"We have to run soon," the boy responded. "We can't

let them take us across the border. But if they catch us, they will kill us."

Jericho nodded his head. "We won't let that happen," he said firmly. The rope around his wrists was cutting into his flesh, cutting off his circulation. He wiggled his fingers, trying to motivate the blood flow through his arms. "I need my hands free, Moses."

The boy nodded, then called out to the leader. Onen gave them a hostile gaze and they could almost see the vile thoughts racing through his mind as he contemplated what he wanted to do. He stomped toward them, a rifle raised high, ready to fire, as he shouted obscenely.

Moses leaned against Jericho's leg, his body tensing. "The doctor wants to check your bandage," he said, not a quiver in his young voice.

Onen stared first at Moses, then Jericho, then back to Moses. The gun dropped down to his side. He spoke quickly, casting a glance over his shoulder to watch that his troops were acting on his orders.

Moses spoke again. "The doctor says he needs to check the infection. He doesn't want you to get sick. You can't lead if you are sick." Moses pointed to where the young man stared. "They will not listen to you if they know you are getting weak," the boy added.

Onen grunted, then gave the okay for Moses to release the bindings. He stepped forward, gesturing for Jericho to examine his rash. Cleaning the flesh and applying the balm had significantly soothed the raging infection. Jericho could see marked improvement in the teenager's condition, but he did not say so. Instead, he shook his head, a look of serious concern crossing his face.

"Tell him this is getting worse," Jericho said to Moses.

"We need to treat it for another day or two before he leaves. If it gets any worse it will poison his blood and kill him. Tell him if he continues to travel in this heat, it will make the rash spread faster."

Moses nodded and translated. Onen grunted, looking down at his chest, his hands reaching to touch his flesh. His skin burned ever so slightly but not nearly as much as it had before the doctor had treated him. The two men locked eyes, studying each other intensely. Pointing his gun for a second time, Onen gestured for the duo to take a seat back on the ground. He turned, heading back to the gathering of boys who stood readying themselves for travel.

"Do you think he believed me?" Jericho whispered.

Moses said nothing, listening closely as Onen shouted. The rebel turned to toss them one last glance before storming into the hut he'd spent the night in. Moses nodded. "They're splitting up," he said, whispering back. "He's sending most of them on ahead. The rest of us are going to follow in a day or two."

Jericho smiled ever so slightly. "That's good," he said softly. "That's all the time we need."

By midafternoon the summer sun was shining brightly overhead. The heat was intense, flooding over them. Onen and three of his soldiers were lazing around doing nothing. None of them were paying any particular attention to Jericho and Moses, having almost forgotten that they were still there. Onen had allowed Jericho to change his dressings just before lunch, then had left them as he sought out shelter away from the scorching heat. Deluded by their compliance, Onen hadn't bothered to retie Jericho's hands.

"They will be sleep soon," Moses said, gesturing with his head toward the four young men who were settling down for an afternoon nap, their bellies full from the food they'd not bothered to share.

Jericho nodded, lying back against the dark earth as if he, too, were tired. His mouth was dry, the back of his throat and his tongue hardened tight from the dust that clung to the lining of his tissues. He yearned for just a single drop of water but knew none was coming. He pulled at the long blades of grass beneath him, sucking at the trickle of moisture that clung to the roots and filled the green leaves. He motioned for Moses to do the same.

"This isn't going to be easy, Moses. We're going to have to be strong," Jericho said softly as the boy dampened his lips.

Moses nodded. "My sister needs me," he said. "I have to get back to her."

Jericho smiled. "Tell me when," he said, reaching to stroke the boy's shoulder.

Minutes later, Jericho and Moses were racing through the brush back in the direction they'd come from. Running because their lives depended on it, neither bothered to look back, not even when they heard the burst of gunfire sounding through the afternoon air when one of their captors woke from his nap and realized they were gone.

As the group made camp for the night, Talisa found her frustrations rising. They'd driven most of the day, the militia stopping more times than necessary to search the thick growth of trees for abandoned camps. As time was being wasted and no progress was being made, Talisa had no way of making them understand how they needed to keep on, to get closer to the border to find Jericho. She knew they would think her foolish if she tried to explain how she knew that Jericho was still too far from where they now rested to be found.

Peter looked toward her as she sighed, the heavy gust of air flooding from her body. "Is all well, Talisa?" he asked, concern coating his words.

Talisa shrugged, the gesture missed in the darkness that surrounded them. "It will be well when we reach him, Peter," she finally answered.

The man reached for her hand and squeezed it gently. He settled his back against a large tree that hovered above them, shelter from a faint mist of rain that had begun to drip from the sky. Talisa turned to listen as the man spoke, his words reflecting the warmth of emotion he held for his friend.

"When we were in school, Jericho and I, he was so serious, that one. He wanted to make his father proud and all he could focus on was his studies. We use to tease him because he would not pay the girls any attention. And the girls loved him, they did."

Talisa smiled as the man shared his memories.

"He was dating this one young lady and everyone was so sure that they would marry one day. Even I thought that it would be their destiny to be together. But my Angela, she knew different. This woman came with Jericho to our wedding and when Angela met her, she knew. She told me then that Jericho had not yet met the woman who would be his wife. She said his heart had not yet opened to what was written in the stars. Neither of us paid her any attention. A woman's foolishness, we thought. But she knew. My Angela knew better than Jericho or I did."

Talisa could sense the man nodding his head beside her. She waited for him to continue.

"His heart is wide open, Talisa. You are the love of his life and he is yours. This is but a small storm between you. I can feel it."

Talisa smiled. "Thank you, Peter," she said softly.

"Love him well, Talisa. He is my best friend and I want him to know love like I know love. Be to his heart, what my Angela is to mine."

"I will. I promise."

Peter crossed his arms over his chest. Side by side the two stared up into the dark sky wishing a prayer that their search would soon be over. With her eyes closed, Talisa whispered Jericho's name in her heart, her spirit calling out to his, and some eighty-odd miles away, Jericho answered with his own.

The sky had opened in full force, water pouring down in buckets over the land. Jericho and Moses had sought shelter beneath the thick growth of the trees that bordered the line of dry desert behind them. Both were grateful for the brief reprieve, the onslaught of rain and the ensuing darkness shielding them from the troops trailing too closely behind them.

Onen and his men were relentless, anger fueling their search. The man and the boy had gotten the best of the young leader and he was intent on seeking retribution for the assault on his immature ego.

Jericho cupped his hands beneath his chin, lapping greedily at the moisture that filled his palms. Moses lay on the ground beside him, his back flat against the hard earth. The child lay with his mouth wide open, allowing the flow of rainwater to flood past his lips and down his throat. Both rested cautiously, one ear listening for any sound that indicated the threat of danger might be near by. The other focused on the rapid beat of their own hearts thundering loudly in their chests. Jericho wiped a damp hand across his face.

"We need to keep moving," he said softly, tapping his hand against the boy's leg.

Moses nodded, his small body consumed by exhaustion. Night sounds billowed through the trees around them. The duo lay listening, neither saying anything, relishing the moment of quiet rest. Jericho had never felt so lost in his life. He was concerned more for the child than for himself, the magnitude of his responsibility front and center in his mind. Moses had worked diligently to be strong for both of them but he was still just a small boy wanting to be a child in such a grown-up world.

Moses shifted his body closer to Jericho's, moving to lay his head against the man's leg. "Are you ever afraid in America?" he asked softly, his low tone floating with the cool breeze.

Jericho nodded. "Yes. Sometimes I am," he responded.

"Do they make little boys fight and hurt people there?"

"No. Not like here."

"If I were there I would go to school," Moses professed.

Jericho smiled into the darkness. "You are a very smart boy," he said. 'We will make sure you go to school wherever you are. You promised me you were going to study to be a doctor, remember? I plan to hold you to that promise. I expect great things from you, Moses."

Jericho could feel the boy shaking ever so slightly. Silence reclaimed them as they both fell into their own thoughts. An hour or so later the man and the boy woke from a deep sleep, startled by the sound of voices that resonated much too close for comfort. Jericho had been dreaming of Talisa and for just a brief moment he was totally disoriented, unable to remember where he was. The moment passed quickly as Jericho returned to consciousness, his senses heightened by his own fear. Moses reached for Jericho's hand as they both came to their feet, listening intently to determine just how near to danger they were. The shouting seemed to originate to the west of where they stood, angry voices penetrating the midnight air.

"We must move quickly," Moses whispered.

Jericho nodded as the child pulled at him, urgent for Jericho to stay close beside him.

"This way," Moses prodded.

As his eyes readjusted to the darkness, Jericho focused his gaze up toward the sky. A faint ray of light in the distance captured his attention, the glimmer of brightness shining against the dark sky. A smile of hope flickered across his face as he took in the promises shimmering within the spray of stars above them.

"No," he said firmly, gesturing in the opposite direction. "We'll be safe this way."

The caravan was back on the road just as dawn broke over the horizon. The energy in the air was electric and Talisa found it difficult to be calm. She stared anxiously over the landscape, searching for a sign, just a hint of recognition that Jericho was close. As the morning sun stepped higher in the sky, Talisa could feel her excitement being consumed by disappointment, each stop yielding no sign of his whereabouts.

"Jericho, where are you?" she whispered to herself, fingering the crucifix that hung from her neck. "Please, Lord, show me where he is," she prayed, her eyes still skating over the countryside.

Gunfire suddenly rang in the air and Talisa gripped the car door as the convoy came to a stop. From the vehicles ahead of them, the officers jumped out with their weapons in ready-mode, rushing into the thick growth that lay past the expanse of roadway. The rash of gunfire was followed by waves of shouting, harsh voices ringing angrily through the morning air.

The sky above suddenly went dark as the sun disappeared behind a wave of rain clouds perched precariously overhead, reappearing just as quickly a minute later. Stepping from the vehicle Talisa stared upward, marveling at the sun and moon sitting side by side in the bright blue sky. There was a shift in the temperature, a sudden gust of cool air blowing through her hair. As quickly as it passed, the summer heat regained control. Talisa stood watching as the clouds continued to roll past, spinning off into the distance faster than she could focus on them. When the sun reappeared for a second time, shining just as brightly as it had moments before, an easy calm washed over her. Without a second thought Talisa tore into the woods behind the soldiers, calling Jericho's name as Peter raced behind her, shouting for her to stop.

She sensed his presence before she heard him. She had felt the nearness of him washing over her, flooding through her body like a tidal wave. Then she heard him calling her name, the sound of his voice barely audible over all the commotion. She heard him answering as she continued to shout over the noise of soldiers fighting around her, militia reigning control over an enemy she had no understanding of. As she continued searching, his voice closer with each step, she barely noticed the young men being held at gunpoint as they lay prone on the ground, their hands clasped above their heads. An army captain stepped in her path, upset by her blatant disregard for her own safety. The man stood reprimanding her actions as she pushed past him, ignoring his orders for her to return to the convoy.

As Talisa continued past the turmoil, her eyes darted back and forth searching anxiously for Jericho. Just seconds later Moses stood in the distance, waving his thin arms excitedly over his head. He jumped up and down for her attention, relief flooding his young face as she and Peter raced to the child's side.

Jericho lay on the ground beside him, staring skyward, dazed from dehydration. Delirium danced through his mind as he mumbled her name over and over again. As his gaze met hers, he smiled ever so slightly, his only greeting a quick nod of his head. Dropping to the ground, Talisa leaned her body down over his, pulling him to her. He had lost weight and she could feel his ribs pushing harsh against his skin. His flesh was badly sunburned, charred red and blistered from the intensity of the sun. She whispered his name into his ear, her lips lightly grazing his flesh. "I'm here, Jericho," she whispered softly, "I'm right here, baby and everything is going to be just fine."

It was only when Peter tried to help his friend to his feet that any of them noticed the puddle of blood on the ground beneath Jericho's body. The smile flew from her face as Talisa pressed her hand just beneath his shoulder blades, feeling the warm flow of sanguine fluid spilling over her fingers. "Oh, dear God, no," she whispered, her eyes widening in horror as Peter called for more help. Calling out that Jericho had taken a bullet in his back.

Jericho's breathing was shallow, a slow raspy exchange of air and breath. His head was cradled in Talisa's lap as the car they rode in sped back toward the hospital. A medic had stopped the bleeding enough to stabilize his condition, and Talisa was confident that once they were safely behind the walls of the compound all would be well.

Moses had given them a blow-by-blow description of what had happened, his youthful exuberance enlivening his words. When the child finally drifted off to sleep, the adults could only sit in disbelief, amazed that the two had come back.

Peter sat in the front passenger seat, stealing glances over his shoulder at them. He found Talisa's warm smile and easy tone comforting, and though his friend was slipping in and out of consciousness, he couldn't help but sense that Jericho felt the same way. Peter was almost embarrassed sitting there eavesdropping on them as Talisa whispered words of encouragement in the man's ear. Her assertions held promise of a future any man would have been thrilled to share, and it was at that moment Peter bore witness to the light of love his wife frequently spoke of.

Talisa brushed her fingers through the thick length of Jericho's hair. His braids had come undone and the soft strands fell against her lap and down the side of her leg to puddle against the seat beside them. She hummed softly, leaning over to let her lips brush against his ear.

"I did not come this far to find you, just to have you leave me, Jericho Becton. I need you to stay strong. We're going to get through this together, darling." Talisa brushed her cheek against his. He shivered as if cold and she tucked a wool blanket tighter against his body. "The very first time I saw you, you took my breath away. I was so scared in that operating room, and then I heard your voice and I could just feel that everything was going to be fine." Talisa smiled, brushing her fingers against the profile of his face. "Then, when we were standing together in that hotel suite

I was so excited to be close to you that I couldn't stop shaking. I'm surprised I didn't fall straight to the floor," Talisa continued, chuckling softly. Jericho shifted his head closer in her lap, his forehead resting against her belly button. "You are going to be just fine, sweetheart. I can feel it. Just hold on, baby. You have to hold on."

Talisa closed her eyes, struggling to contain the flow of water that threatened to spill from her eyes. When she opened them again, her gaze met Peter's. He smiled, nodding his head in support before turning back to stare out the front window. Talisa persisted, certain that as long as Jericho heard her voice, knew that she was right there holding on to him, that he would keep fighting to come back to her. "Your mom and dad are waiting for you. Your mom is amazing. I can see what a strong woman she is. You have her strength." Talisa paused, taking a deep breath before she continued. "She wanted me to give this to you," Talisa whispered, fingering the crucifix around her neck. Reaching to unclasp the pendant, she eased the chain beneath Jericho's head and fastened it tight. Talisa ran her fingers gently against the outline of the gold emblem, etching it gently along Jericho's chest. "Everyone is praying for you, Jericho. God will see you through this, baby. You have to believe in that."

Talisa continued murmuring into Jericho's ear for the entire ride, maintaining her hold on him for the duration of the ride. She prayed over him, professed her love for him, whispered promises to him, letting him know that she had every intention of staying right by his side until he was back on his feet and well again.

As they finally pulled into the compound, the car careening through the gates toward the hospital, she reached for his hand and squeezed it. When Jericho squeezed back,

Talisa could feel the pull of energy renewing his spirit. The man opened his eyes for a brief second, blinking them to focus and as Talisa smiled down on him, he moved to bend his lips in response. He motioned as if to speak, his mouth opening and then closing. His tongue slipped past to tap lightly against his lips.

"Shhh," Talisa murmured into his ear.

Jericho squeezed her hand again, then managed to whisper ever so softly, "I love you."

As Peter threw the back door open to help lift him inside, Talisa placed one last kiss against Jericho's lips, one more "I love you" blowing breath into body. As his parents rushed to greet them, both reaching to help pull Jericho from the vehicle, Talisa's gaze locked with his mother's, and as if an unspoken understanding passed between them, both women knew that although the worst had passed, Jericho still wasn't out of the woods and an air of uncertainty hung like a dark cloud above them.

Talisa had grown weary of looking at her watch. Jericho's surgery was lasting longer than any of them had anticipated and although she was confident that he was in good hands, she couldn't help but worry.

The makeshift operating room and lack of medical supplies had been cause for concern, but Dr. Becton had kissed his wife and promised her he would get Jericho through the procedure. As Talisa and the woman sat side by side, both were counting on him to keep that promise.

Irene reached for Talisa's hand, patting it gently as she smiled sweetly. "He's going to be just fine. His father is one of the best surgeons in the world. There is none better. Jericho learned from a master."

Talisa nodded. "He's very proud of his father and you. He loves you both very much."

"He's a wonderful young man and we're the ones who are proud," his mother commented, her head bobbing up and down slowly.

Quiet floated in the air between them, as both women fell back in their own thoughts about Jericho. Irene broke the silence. "I imagine your mother and father are as proud of you, Talisa. It's a wonderful thing you're doing here. Angela and Peter both speak very highly of you. I'm always impressed when I see young women like yourself involved in helping others."

"Thank you. That's very sweet of you."

"What possessed you to volunteer here in Africa?"

"It's just who I am and how I was raised. My father taught me that when you give to others it comes back to you tenfold. Being able to come to Africa was just a dream come true."

"And somewhat fateful, I think. I know you and Jericho weren't able to connect back in Atlanta. Perhaps destiny had her own mission to bring you two together here in Uganda?"

Talisa chuckled. "Perhaps."

"My son's a good catch," Irene said with a wink. "He was raised well, he loves his mother, he's financially responsible, and he's a great dancer."

"Is he now?"

"Oh, yes! I made him take dance lessons when he was a boy. He's very good. Plus he knows how to cook and he can do his own laundry. I highly recommend him."

The two women giggled, ease and comfort wrapping around them as Irene continued.

"When Jericho called to tell us about the two of you, I

couldn't remember the last time I had heard him so happy. You could feel his happiness coming through the telephone lines. I knew then that you had to be very special."

"Jericho makes me feel special, Mrs. Becton."

His mother smiled. "He said the same thing about you."

At that moment, Angela stepped into the room, pulling at the gloves and gown she'd worn in surgery. Dr. Becton followed close on her heels. The smile on her face spoke volumes, the essence of it only surpassed by the glow from the man at her side. Both women jumped to their feet, Peter shuffling in quickly from the other room.

"How is he?" Peter asked, voicing what the other two women couldn't find a voice to ask. "Will he be okay?"

Dr. Becton nodded. "He should be fine. We were able to remove the bullet and thankfully it didn't hit any major organs. He's lost a good deal of blood so he's going to be very weak and we have to watch that he doesn't get an infection. But I'd venture to say he'll be up and about in a few days and we'll probably have to tie him to the bed to keep him still after that."

Irene reached to embrace her husband, wrapping her arms tightly around him as he returned the hug. "Praise Jesus," she exclaimed softly.

Peter jumped with joy, clasping his hands excitedly. He reached to hug his wife, lifting her off her feet as he spun her in a quick circle. "That is good news," he said. "Very good news."

Talisa heaved a sigh of relief, her eyes closing in silent prayer as she gave thanks for the blessings that continued to be bestowed upon them. When she opened them, Irene was staring at her, a warm smile gracing her face. They shared a silent conversation between them as both understood that the future held nothing but promise of brighter tomorrows for them all. Nodding her head slowly, Talisa smiled and Irene Becton's grin widened. Looking up at her husband she tossed him a quick wink as she reached out to Talisa, pulling the young woman into the arms of their embrace.

Chapter 22

Depressing the hook to disconnect her last call, Leila paused for one quick moment before she dialed. Her index finger skated quickly over the numeric pad. Pulling the receiver back to her ear she waited as it rang on the other end. When Mya finally picked up on the fifth ring, Leila sat back against the headboard of her brass bed, pulling her legs comfortably beneath the curve of her behind.

"Hi, Mya. It's me."

"Hi, Leila. Girlfriend, can I call you back later? I'm kind of busy. You caught me right in the middle of something."

Leila shook her head. "No. You were supposed to call me three days ago when you were *busy* with David, Duncan, Daryl, whatever that brother's name was. Who are you *busy* with now?"

"My auction date. He stopped by so we could watch his new commercial together."

"Shouldn't he be asleep or getting ready for work, or something?" Leila asked, glancing at the clock on her nightstand. It was just after eleven o'clock, and she knew the nightly news was well underway.

"He doesn't go in until four a.m. He said he couldn't sleep and that he wanted some company."

Leila groaned. "Mya, do not sleep with that man," she said pointedly.

Mya laughed, cupping her hand around the receiver to whisper into it. Behind her, the man sitting on her sofa was oblivious, his attention focused on the television set. "Sleeping was the last thing we were planning to do tonight, Leila," she said smugly.

"Mya, you really need to slow down before you catch something nasty."

"Don't hate 'cause I get mine and yours, too."

"You've done mine, yours and half the city of Atlanta's. I've lost count with the list being as long and as undistinguished as it is. At the rate you're going, you're sending my condom stock straight through the roof. You are using condoms, aren't you?"

"Yes, I use condoms. Is that all you called me for because I do have better things I need to be doing," Mya responded, attitude rising in her tone. "I sure don't need a lecture from you. You're starting to sound just like Talisa."

"Well, she told me to make sure I kept an eye on you. And that's why I'm calling. I just spoke to Talisa."

Mya blew the newscaster a kiss, holding up her finger to indicate she needed one more minute. "How's she doing? When is she coming home?"

"Our girl flew halfway around the world to get herself into some trouble. Some rebels kidnapped her man. She had to go into the jungle to rescue him, and then he got shot," Leila said, the words spilling quickly out of her mouth.

Mya gasped loudly. "What!"

"But you're busy so we'll talk later. Tell whatever his name is that I apologize for interrupting his good time, and please, don't forget to wrap that thing up good and tight. You don't want anything creepy crawling up your holy temple." Leila hung up the telephone, leaving Mya with her mouth open on the other end.

Barely a minute passed before the phone was ringing. Taking a quick glance at the caller ID, Leila chuckled to herself as she pulled the receiver back into her hand. "Do I have your attention now?" she asked.

"You can be really ugly when you want to be, Leila," Mya answered. "You think you're cute, but I'm telling you, you're not."

"Is your date still there?"

"He can wait. Now tell me about Talisa. Is she okay?"

Leila nodded into the receiver, reaching for a plush flannel blanket that lay across the bed. "Yes," she finally answered as she pulled the throw over her bare legs. "Her nerves are wrecked but she's fine. His parents are there with them and they'll all be coming home next week. She was headed back to the orphanage to be with the Wesley group. Her man had to have surgery but it wasn't as bad as they thought it might be. I think she said his dad did it. His dad's a surgeon, too. Remember?"

"Yeah. You know, you hear about stuff like this on the news but you don't ever think it could happen to someone you know."

Leila nodded as if the other woman could see her.

Mya continued. "So, she and the doctor really hit it off, huh?"

"It would seem that way. She's head over heels in love, Mya. The man sounds like a dream come true for her. I've never heard her sound so happy."

Silence filtered through the telephone line between them as they reflected on their friend and the prospect of dreams coming true. Leila could hear Mya's television playing in the background and then a man's voice breaking through the quiet, calling Mya's name. Mya cupped her palm over the receiver so that Leila couldn't hear the exchange between them. When she returned to the conversation, her moment of reflection had clearly passed.

"Look, girl, let's have dinner tomorrow night. You can give me all the gory details, then. I really do need to take care of some things here."

Leila laughed. "Fine. I'll see you tomorrow."

"Thanks."

"And, Mya?"

"I know. Don't forget the condoms," Mya said mockingly.

Leila smiled. "Be safe, Mya. We love you, girlfriend."

A grin filled Mya's face. "Always," she said, and then the phone went dead on the other end.

Reverend Warren shook his balding head as he hung up the telephone. Stevie and Johanna eyed him curiously, anxious for details on the end of the conversation they were not able to hear. The man looked from one to the other, his head swinging back and forth as he took a seat on the other side of the conference table.

"Stevie, I thought your mission trip to South Africa just

before Mandela was elected had been a challenge. I do believe Talisa has topped that experience."

"Who was hurt, Reverend?" Johanna asked anxiously. "No one from our group was injured, were they?"

"Everyone from our group is safe and well. The doctor volunteering at the orphanage was injured. He was shot, but is recovering nicely. Apparently he and Talisa have become very close since she's been there."

Stevie smiled, an expanse of pearl-white teeth filling her face.

Reverend Warren shook his finger at the woman and grinned back. "Why is it every time I send one of you off on missions you come back married, engaged, or pregnant?" he asked.

Johanna laughed. "I only came back from South America pregnant because I took my husband with me. I told you there was something in that water over there."

"But you met your husband in Costa Rica on the second trip you went on," the man countered. "And you," he said, gesturing with his eyes toward Stevie, "you and Sam met at the airport when you were going to build those houses on the reservation in New Mexico."

Stevie shrugged, a smirk gracing her face. "We've got great memories, don't we?"

Johanna was still giggling. "You really can't say anything, Reverend. Did you forget that you and Cindy did half a dozen mission trips together before you started dating? And twice that many afterwards? I think if we do a little counting, at least one of your children was conceived while you were overseas doing ministry."

The man rolled his eyes, tossing up his hands. He laughed heartily. "Okay. It's like I've said before, great minds think alike and good hearts can't help but share great love."

Johanna leaned up on her elbows, her chin dropping into the palm of her hands. "So, what else did Talisa say? Did it sound like she and the doctor might be serious?"

Stevie piped in. "I do hope so. If anyone deserves to find a nice man, Talisa does. I wonder what he looks like," she said excitedly.

The minister reached for the pile of manila folders on the tabletop as he came to his feet. "I'll be in my office," he said as he headed toward the door. "You two can finish this conversation on your own."

Taking one last look over his shoulder, the man smiled, watching as the two women leaned in giggling, speculating about Talisa's newfound love.

Mary London's hands shook ever so slightly as she twisted the cap off the bottle of Lithium prescribed by her doctor. The past week had been illuminating as her body and mind had adjusted to the medication filtering through her bloodstream.

The doctor had declared her bipolar, announcing that she suffered from a brain disorder that caused the unusual, severe shifts in her mood, energy and her ability to function. The good news was that she could be treated. Things could get better for them all, and with time, she could repair the damage she had caused in her family. The bad news was that like diabetes or heart disease, the bipolar disorder was a long-term illness that she would have to carefully manage for the remainder of her life. Mary understood that if she took her two pills faithfully every day she would better be able to control the raging mood swings and depression that had often consumed her.

As she placed the pills against her tongue, washing them down with a mouthful of water, she could sense her husband watching her. From the corner of her eye she saw him nodding his approval. As she turned to face him, Herman lifted his body from his seat, crossing the room to her side. He pulled her into his arms and hugged her tightly, brushing his thick lips against her forehead. As the two stood holding each other, neither speaking, the telephone rang. Mary met her husband's stare and smiled, pushing him gently away.

"You're in the way, Herman," she said, easing around him to reach for the telephone. "Hello?"

"Mom? Hi, it's me."

"Talisa, baby? Is that you?"

Talisa laughed. "Do you have another daughter named Talisa who calls you Mom that I don't know about?"

Mary chuckled. "Are you okay? When are you coming home?"

"I'll be back in a few days. We leave this Friday but with all the transfers and the flight time I won't get home until Monday."

Mary nodded into the receiver.

"How are you doing, Mom?"

"I'm doing better, baby. That doctor put me on some medicine that's helping to keep me calm. It seems to be working so far. But that's not important. How are you?"

"I'm fine. We had a few problems but things are really good now."

"How's that doctor? Is he still there with you?" Mary asked.

Talisa hesitated before answering and when she finally did speak, she asked for her father, clearly changing the subject. "Why don't I say hello to Dad. Is he home?"

Mary took a deep breath. "It's okay, Talisa. You can talk to me, baby. I won't—"

The words caught in the older woman's throat, emotion cutting off her thoughts. Talisa could hear her mother choking back tears and her own rose to her eyes, threatening to spill past her lashes.

Mary took another breath and spoke slowly. "Baby, I have an illness. I know that now. But for me to really get well I'm going to need your help. I know I've done some bad things but I want to do better. You're my baby, and I love you, and I want to know what's going on with you. Please, Talisa. Talk to me."

Talisa could feel herself nodding. "All right," she said softly, sensing a side of her mother she'd rarely experienced before. As she began to tell her mother about Jericho and all that had happened, Talisa could feel her anxiety being replaced with excitement. It was a new energy that flooded her spirit when she shared the last detail and there had been no angry outburst from the woman. She suddenly wished she were there to give her mother a hug and have her mother hug her back.

Mary shook her head. "Lord, have mercy," she exclaimed. "And you're sure you're okay? You didn't get hurt?"

"No, ma'am. I'm just fine."

"Is Jericho coming back to the States with you?"

"He'll be flying home next week."

"Well, when he's home we should plan a nice Sunday dinner so your daddy and I can meet him."

Talisa smiled. "He'd like that, Mom. Thank you."

Mary tightened her grip on the receiver. "Is he a churchgoing boy, Talisa?" she asked. "He believes in God, doesn't he?"

"Yes. He believes in God."

"Where does his family go to church?"

"I don't know that they have a home church that they attend regularly," Talisa answered, nervousness starting to billow in the pit of her stomach.

"Well, maybe we can get him to go to the Baptist church," Mary said.

Talisa laughed, relaxing ever so slightly. "He might prefer the Methodist church if he wants to go." Talisa could feel her mother rolling her eyes in exasperation.

"I declare, Talisa! Couldn't you find a nice Baptist boy to fall in love with?"

Talisa chuckled softly. "I do love him, Mom. I love him very much," she said, her tone affirming the emotion in her heart.

Mary sighed, a smile crossing her face. "Then I know your daddy and I are going to love him, too."

Talisa swiped at the tear that had rolled down her cheek. Mary glanced up at Herman who had leaned to wrap his arms around her shoulders.

"Well, you need to stop running up this phone bill," Mary said. "This is long distance."

"I'll see you soon."

"Oh, Talisa," Mary said quickly. "Do you get the stories over there in Africa?"

Talisa laughed. "No, ma'am."

"Then you're missing it, baby. JR and Babe are fighting over that boy of theirs again and Miss Erica done started some more mess with Bianca. It's getting good!"

"You'll have to catch me up when I get home," Talisa said with a wide grin. "I love you, Mom. Tell Dad I said hello."

"We love you, too, baby."

As she hung up the receiver, Herman was grinning from ear to ear. "Don't you have something you need to be doing, Herman London?" she asked her husband.

The man shrugged.

"Well, then you need to get out of my kitchen," she said with a smile, her hands falling to rest against her full hips. "Look at the mess you're making on my floor!"

Chapter 23

Jericho sat on the edge of the double bed in his room, testing the strength in his long legs. As he pressed the soles of his bandaged feet against the cold, concrete floor and moved as if to stand upright, a surge of pain shot across his lower back and down the length of his limbs. He winced, the hurt dancing into the lines of his face.

"What are you doing?" Talisa asked, watching him from the doorway, a cup of iced water and a straw in her hand. She rushed to his side, her tone scolding as she dropped the drink onto the nightstand. "Your father told you to rest, Jericho. Resting means you stay in bed."

Jericho heaved a deep sigh as Talisa helped him back into the bed, pulling a thin cotton sheet up and over the length of his body.

"I'm tired of resting," Jericho said, his trademark pout blessing his face. "I need to get back to work."

"No. You need to rest. Your dad is taking care of your patients," Talisa answered, leaning to kiss his lips.

Jericho kissed her back and then smiled. "Fine, I'll rest, but only if you get in bed and lay with me for a while," he said, a mischievous grin filling his face.

Talisa rolled her eyes toward the ceiling, then taking a quick glance at the closed door, she pulled herself up against the mattress, curling her body against his. She leaned her head into his shoulder, one hand resting lightly against his chest. Jericho pressed a moist kiss against her forehead, a sigh of contentment blowing over her flesh as he wrapped his arms around her.

"All I could think about the whole time was getting back to you, Talisa," he said softly, a shiver of cold running up his body as he reached for the straw, tearing at the paper wrapper.

Talisa clasped his hand beneath hers as she moved to help him, easing the cup closer to his lips. "You were right there in my heart, too, Jericho. I couldn't even begin to think about us not finding you."

The man nodded. "So, what now, baby girl? Where do you and I go from here?"

She shrugged her shoulders lightly, lifting her eyes to meet his. "I love you. I can't imagine not being with you, wherever you are."

His gaze was pensive. "There's so much to think about. I know you have to take your group back to the States. And, then you have your family, your job, and your friends to get home to. My parents are insisting I go home to finish recuperating, but I promised Peter and Angela that I would spend at least a year here working with them and the clinic. But I don't even want to think about not being with you ever again."

Talisa lifted her torso up to stare down at him. "I think your parents are right about you going home until you're completely recovered. I know your father is concerned about you getting an infection. You can always come back here when you're better, Jericho. I know Peter and Angela would understand. And, if you decide to come back…" Talisa paused briefly, biting against her bottom lip before continuing "…if you want me to, I will come back here to Uganda with you."

The two sat studying each other with an intensity that seemed to fill the air around them. Silence filled the space between them, filtering easily as they sat in deep reflection. Jericho lifted himself up on his elbows, reaching for the torn straw wrapper. Talisa watched as he twisted it between his fingers, rolling it into a thin paper circle. Easing his body closer to hers, Jericho kissed her gently, brushing his lips easily against hers. "Only if you come back as my wife," he whispered. "I love you, Talisa. I want to spend the rest of my life with you. Will you marry me?" he asked, easing the makeshift ring onto her ring finger.

Joy spilled out of her eyes, flowing in the rise of tears that trickled down the round of her cheeks. She kissed him again, her response blowing in the breath that blessed his lips. "Oh, yes, Jericho! Yes, I'll marry you!"

They cuddled closer, laughing and chatting excitedly at the possibilities their future plans held for them. As they settled comfortably against one another, Jericho took her face in his hands, snaking his fingers into her hair. He stared into her eyes, then leaned in and softly kissed each lid, the brush of her lashes flitting against his lips. Moving his mouth down to one cheek and then the other, he kissed her softly, allowing his mouth to linger for just a brief minute against the warmth of her flesh. When his lips finally met hers, he teased her first, his kisses light, easy pecks before pressing his mouth down firmly against hers. The kiss deepened with intensity, drawing her breath from her body, and then he parted his lips, lightly licking over her mouth with his tongue. Talisa moaned, a sweet murmur urging him on as her own tongue slid out to dance with his.

Jericho shifted his body up and over hers, ignoring a quick pang of hurt to press his bare chest against the fullness of her breasts. Talisa moaned again, ecstasy vibrating against his lips and tongue. He could feel her body softening against his, giving in to the desire that was sweeping through her. He pulled her bottom lip between his teeth, gently nibbling from one side to the other. He couldn't get enough of her mouth, the feel of her skin against his, her tongue lazily licking over his lips and his over hers. The sweet sensations surged from one end of his body to the other, deflecting any pain that may have existed.

His hand eased between them to pull at her shirt, easing the fabric open to give him access to her bare flesh. His fingers slid beneath the edge of her bra, tracing a light line from the cleavage between her breasts to the hook in the back. With apt precision, Jericho snapped the garment open. As his hand snaked back around to fondle one breast and then the other, he was rewarded with a soft shudder as well as another moan.

Talisa was consumed by the rage of emotions sweeping through her. No man had ever been able to reduce her to quivering jelly with just the touch of his mouth against hers like Jericho did. His touch had left her completely breathless, every ounce of decorum lost to the mush he'd made of her mind. Her hand skated across the length of his torso, her fingertips pressing into the firm flesh along his sides, up the length of his arms, over his shoulders, and back again. When her hand met his hand, she pressed her palm to his palm, interlocking his fingers between her own. Jericho pressed his mouth to her breast, easing the candy-hard nipple between his lips. He suckled her gently, his tongue swirling in pleasure. As he moved to ease his pelvis against hers, Talisa knew that if she didn't regain some control, there would be no coming back from the realms of rapture he was pulling them into.

She whispered his name into his ear. "Jericho, baby, we can't," she murmured softly, trying to convince herself more than him. "You'll hurt your back…and some-one…might come in to check…" she muttered, barely able to comprehend her own words.

Jericho chuckled softly, unconcerned as a hand slipped between her thighs, his fingers tapping at the entrance to her secret garden. As he slid his hand up to pull at the zipper of her slacks, Talisa grabbed his wrist to stop him.

"You have to stop," she whispered, her gaze meeting his. "You aren't supposed to be doing this, and you know I can't resist you."

The man smiled down at her and whispered back. His tone was deep with wanting. "Then don't. Let me touch you. I just need to touch you, baby girl. I can't do anything else just yet, but I need to do this. That's all. I swear. Please, Talisa. Don't make me stop." He pressed his mouth back to hers, kissing every ounce of her resistance away.

As Talisa fell into the moment, she barely noticed when Jericho finally eased her pants open, sliding his hand easily beneath the elastic of her panties. Giving in to the pleasure she parted her legs to welcome his exploration, allowing him easy access to her womanhood. His fingers danced against her, taunting and teasing her to bliss. The room was spinning as Talisa gasped out in pleasure. Jericho was as hungry for her as she was for him and the thick line of an erection pressed anxiously against her leg. He whispered into her ear, his voice husky with desire and need as his tongue drew a line against her earlobe and down the side of her face.

"Oh, sweet baby," he said softly, repeating her name over and over. "Oh, yes, Talisa," he cried as he stroked the length of his manhood against her thigh, Talisa grinding herself against him. Her body suddenly tensed and when she did, Jericho could no longer contain himself, his own body convulsing with pleasure. The moment was surreal. They both trembled, orgasmic shivers billowing from one to the other as they lay clinging to each other. As her breathing, and then his, returned to normal, Jericho lay back against the mattress, his energy depleted, but his flesh content. They lay shoulder to shoulder, hip to hip, hand in hand. Talisa smiled, easing her eyes open to stare over at him.

"What am I going to do with you?" she asked, shaking her head slowly.

Jericho smiled back. "Just let me love you," he answered. "That's all I want. I just want to love you."

Leaning over to kiss his cheek, Talisa grinned. "As long as I can love you back, Dr. Becton. As long as I can love you back."

"He's going to give you a hard time, Elijah. You know this, so why are you pushing the issue?"

"He needs to come home for a while, Irene. Not long.

Just a few weeks. If he wants to come back here to the orphanage then he can. I just want him to get well first."

Irene shook her head, smiling over at her husband as they crossed the courtyard to go check on Jericho. Determination was painted on her husband's face, his pale complexion sunburned a bright tinge of red since their arrival. As the couple entered the residence hall, Irene noticed the closed door first, stopping in her tracks as she grabbed at the doctor's arm.

"What?" he asked, giving her a quick glance.

"I think we should come back later."

"Why? What's wrong?"

"Nothing. I think we need to come back later." She pointed toward her son's room. "I think he might have company at the moment and I don't think we should interrupt."

Elijah looked from the closed door, to his wife, and back again. He shook his head and smiled. "As a matter of fact, I haven't seen his young lady for a good while now." His expression became serious. "But he should not be fooling around in there, Irene. He's not strong enough yet and the strain on his back could do him more harm than good," he said, speaking as a doctor.

Irene rolled her eyes, turning to head back outside. "No one said he was fooling around, Elijah. I think they just want some time alone."

The man followed, reaching to wrap an arm around her shoulders. "So, what do you think about her? Your son seems to be very serious."

Irene smiled. "Our son is head over heels in love and I think we might actually get us some grandchildren. I adore her. Talisa's strong, intelligent, compassionate, and there is something very special about their connection. I haven't found anything to dislike about her." The woman rambled excitedly. "Wouldn't it be great to have the wedding in the gardens. I can call the woman who organized the Baxters' oldest son's wedding to come do Jericho's. She was very good. I can't wait to call Talisa's mother so we can start planning."

The man laughed. "No, really," he said. "What do you think and don't hold back."

She punched him lightly in the shoulder, joining in the laughter. "So, what do you think?" she asked.

The man shrugged, stopping to pull his wife into his arms. "I think if our son is half as happy as I am, then we can't ask for any more."

An hour or so later, Elijah returned to check on how his son was doing. Talisa and Irene had joined Angela for a walk around the property, the three women laughing and enjoying a quiet moment of relaxation. When he entered his child's room, Jericho was sitting up in thought, deep furrows carved in his expression. As his father stood watching, Jericho grimaced, pain shooting through his body and peaking at the wound in his back.

"You should be lying down, getting some rest," Elijah said, moving to the man's side. He pressed his hand to Jericho's forehead.

"It was nothing, Dad. And, I don't have a fever."

"That doesn't mean a thing. You should still be resting because what I just saw was definitely something."

"It was just a little pain. It'll go away."

The older man nodded, pulling up a chair to his son's bedside. "So, what were you thinking about? It looked like it might be important."

Jericho shook his head slowly. "I was just thinking about

everything that happened. If it hadn't been for Moses, I'd be dead. That child saved my life." Tears rose in Jericho's eyes.

His father sat watching him, not commenting as Jericho continued.

"We forget how blessed we are, Dad. How incredibly easy our lives are back in the States. No child should be made to endure what these children have had to suffer. No child."

Elijah nodded. "I agree. But all we can do is continue to tell people their story and help wherever and however we can, son. You can't single-handedly shoulder their burdens or fix the world's problems all by yourself."

Jericho pondered his father's comment for a quick minute. He heaved a deep sigh as he rubbed his eyes. "I'm seriously thinking about adopting Moses and his sister. How do you think you'd feel about that?"

The man continued staring at his son, his own gaze pensive. He shrugged, his shoulders jutting toward the ceiling. "I'm not sure, Jericho. That's a good deal of responsibility. Would you want to take that on by yourself?"

"I wouldn't do it alone. I've asked Talisa to marry me, Dad. She and I would do it together."

"My, my, my. This is kind of sudden, isn't it?"

"I love her, Dad. I love her more than I can begin to tell you. When I was captured, all I could think about was getting back to her."

"And Talisa would want to adopt with you? You two have already discussed this?"

Jericho shook his head. "Not yet. But I know she'd support me and she loves them as much I do. They deserve a chance, Dad. I owe Moses that. He wants to be a doctor. I remember when I was his age and I wanted to be a doctor just like you. You gave me that incentive. You helped nurture that drive. I want to do that for Moses. I think I would be a good father to both of them."

Elijah smiled, dropping a hand against his son's leg. "I have no doubts, son, that you will make an excellent father. But I would much rather see you and Talisa, if she's the woman you want in your life, see the two of you have some time to build and grow your relationship before you have to bear the responsibility of children. That time you and your wife are able to share before you bring another life into your world is a very special time. I had that with your mother and I relished every minute of it. I think every couple needs that and I want that for you."

Jericho nodded. "I have to do something, Dad. I'm not going to leave them. I don't know that I could live with myself if I did."

The two men sat quietly together, neither saying a word. The lines deepened across Jericho's brow and so did his father's, the two mulling over the options and possibilities that were available to them both to do something special for someone else. Elijah studied his son for some time, remnants of history wafting through his thoughts. They had shared much together over the years and no father could have been as proud of his child as Elijah Becton was.

He and Irene had wanted more children. They had desperately tried to give Jericho a sibling, but three miscarriages, and many tears later, the couple had accepted that it was God's will that Jericho be their only child. They had adored him, had loved him beyond reason, had given him the world on a platter, and he'd grown into a loving, magnanimous, giving adult both he and his wife had tremendous respect for.

Sitting across from his son, and watching as he struggled to find the answers to do what he felt in his heart was right, could not have caused Elijah more anguish. He would have given anything to ensure Jericho never knew a minute of heartbreak, heartache, frustration or hurt a single day in his life. He would have done anything for his son. Anything. Elijah suddenly sat forward, a light-bulb moment shining from his eyes as the answers for both of them were suddenly illuminated in his mind.

Elijah jumped to his feet, startling Jericho from his own thoughts.

"What's the matter, Dad?"

"I need to find your mother. I need to talk to her about something."

"Is everything okay?"

The man grinned. "It couldn't be more perfect. You take a nap. Now, and that's doctor's orders. You don't have to make any decisions about anything immediately. When I get back, I'd like to talk with you more about Talisa and your plans. Okay?"

Jericho nodded, settling his body down against the bed. "I guess you're right. And I am tired." He sighed.

Elijah patted his son's shoulder. "Don't you worry. I have a feeling things are going to work out just fine."

The children had prepared a special program for their last night at the orphanage. As they sang and danced, Talisa and the other volunteers from Wesley fought back tears, finding it difficult to even imagine saying goodbye.

Jericho sat in the seat beside her, his strong arm wrapped possessively around her shoulders. Talisa smiled to think that just eight and a half weeks earlier she'd been on the fringes of unhappy over having missed his telephone calls. The man squeezed her upper arm as if he'd **sensed** her thinking about him. As she met his gaze she smiled warmly, knowing that the past eight weeks were only the beginning of a lifetime ahead of them.

Clarissa interrupted her thoughts, gesturing for her attention. "Talisa, you have to convince the foundation to let us come back," the young woman whispered loudly. "This has been the best trip."

Talisa smiled, nodding her agreement as Jericho leaned to give her a kiss.

"Have you two thought about a wedding date?" Peter asked, leaning across the table, his elbows propped against the worn wood.

Angela waved her hand. "You two must marry soon. None of this long engagement madness. Time is too short to wait."

Jericho beamed as his parents looked on, anxious to hear their answer. "We'll make plans as soon as we get home and I talk to Talisa's parents," Jericho answered. "We promise that you all will know as soon as we decide."

Talisa was still smiling, happiness radiating through her spirit. The group continued chatting back and forth excitedly, everyone expressing an opinion about the happy couple and reflecting back on the experiences that they'd all shared since they arrived.

From across the room, Moses called out to Jericho to come see what he and a group of boys had accomplished with a box of Lego pieces that had arrived in a recent supply shipment. The young boy was gesturing for the man's attention. As Jericho excused himself, Susie came to take his seat, leaning her frail body against Talisa. Talisa hugged the little girl to her, leaning to press her lips against the child's forehead.

"How's our girl?" Talisa asked softly.

Susie only smiled, her gaze flickering from one adult to another.

Angela beamed. "By the time you and Jericho come back to us, this one and her brother will be cleared for the adoption."

Talisa nodded, turning to Jericho's father. "Are you ready for the challenge, Dr. Becton?" she asked.

The man chuckled, his expression gleaming with pride. "I think we are, Talisa. Irene and I did a pretty good job with that one over there," he said, gesturing toward Jericho. "I don't think we'll do too badly with these two scamps."

Talisa smiled. "It's a wonderful thing you two are doing," she said.

Elijah grinned. "It was the right thing and if it wasn't for Jericho I wouldn't have known it. My son is a very wise man."

The two nodded, both laughing as Susie broke out into a wide grin. Irene laughed with them, opening her arms as Susie reached up to be held. The child wrapped her arms around her new mother's neck, leaning her head into the woman's shoulder. "I have no doubts that we'll probably spoil them silly," she said.

Jericho returned to Talisa's side, Moses holding tight to his hand. "These two should keep them plenty busy," he said, smiling at his parents. "My mother won't be harassing me and Talisa about grandchildren."

"That's what you think," Irene chimed.

Elijah laughed. "Surely you didn't think you were getting off that easy, son!"

"I will have grandchildren, Jericho Becton," Irene said, pointing a finger at her son. "In fact, I expect at least two from you and Talisa, and when Moses and Susie are ready, at least two from each of them. Your father and I plan to grow very old with our grandchildren."

Jericho shook his head. "Hear that, little brother," he said, gazing down to Moses. "That's our mother for you."

Laughter rang joyously around the room.

The next morning Jericho hugged her tightly as the last call for her return flight echoed over the airport sound system. Peter stood behind them waving his goodbyes to the student volunteers who'd begun boarding.

"I'll pick you up at the airport next week," Talisa said, not wanting to release her hold on the man.

Jericho nodded. "Call me the minute you land."

She smiled. "I will, and please, listen to your father, Jericho. You're still not fully recovered. Please, try to get some rest."

Jericho shook his head mockingly. "Yeah, yeah, yeah," he said before kissing her one last time.

Talisa savored the sensation of his mouth atop hers, his tongue gliding lightly alongside her own. When he finally pulled away, breaking the intimate connection, she took a deep breath, willing the influx of air to stall the wave of anxiety that had suddenly come over her. She reached down for the carry bag that sat on the floor at her feet.

"I love you," she whispered, her gaze locking with his.

Jericho pressed his hand to his heart. "I love you, too."

Peter reached to give her a quick hug. "We will not say goodbye, Talisa. Since we will meet again soon, I will say instead, until next time, my new friend."

"Until next time, Peter, and thank you for everything."

As she made her way to the departure gate, Talisa turned

to take one last glance at Jericho. Waving goodbye, she inhaled the beauty of him before he disappeared from her sight, holding on tight to the memory until they could be together again.

Chapter 24

Clouds had billowed like soft puffs of cotton outside the airplane window. Talisa had felt as if she were floating, caught in a dream dimension of air and space. It had been a least an hour since the last bit of sunlight had filtered in from the outside, having been replaced by a cold darkness Talisa was finding difficult to deal with. The airplane cabin was exceptionally quiet, many of her fellow travelers beginning to drift in and out of sleep as they settled down for the lengthy flight back to the United States.

A myriad of thoughts clouded her mind, holding her hostage in a state of unrest: the trip, Jericho, her mother, Jericho. She missed him already, missed the nearness of him, the resonance of his laugh, the glow in his eyes. She missed everything about him, her want of him growing deeper with each passing mile that put distance between them. She took a deep inhale of air, blowing her anxiety out past her full lips. The gesture did not go unnoticed as Clarissa twisted around to face her.

"Is everything all right, Talisa?" Clarissa asked, her voice a soft whisper.

Talisa forced herself to smile. "Everything's fine. I think I'm just feeling a little claustrophobic."

Clarissa smiled back. "We'll be home before you know it. The return trip always feels longer."

Talisa took another deep breath.

"Oh, by the way," Clarissa said. "I have something for you." She leaned down to reach into a canvas bag that rested on the floor between her feet. Rummaging through the contents she pulled a legal-sized envelope from a side compartment.

Talisa looked at her curiously. "What's this?" she asked, bewilderment registered in her voice.

"Dr. Becton asked me to give this to you."

"Jericho?"

The other woman waved her head from side to side. "No, his father," Clarissa responded, shrugging her shoulders. "He told me to give it to you once we were well over the Atlantic Ocean."

Talisa fingered the crisp paper between her fingers, her gaze searching Clarissa's face first, and then her name printed neatly in blue ink on the front of the mailer. "Thank you," she finally muttered, clasping the envelope tightly to her chest.

Clarissa nodded, as she pulled a gray blanket across her legs and she settled back down in her seat.

"Will the light bother you?" Talisa asked, gesturing toward the overhead night-light above them.

Clarissa shook her head no, then closed her eyes as if to drift back into a deep sleep.

Talisa could barely imagine what Jericho's father could have written her as she switched on the overhead light and pulled at the sealed mailer. The letter inside was printed in a man's bold script, the neat penmanship dispelling the myth about a doctor's handwriting being illegible.

As she unfolded the document she took a quick glance toward Clarissa to see if the young woman was watching, but the girl had turned her back to Talisa and seemed to be headed off to dreamland. Focusing back on the letter, Talisa could feel the words pulling at her teardrops as she read the brief paragraphs the man had taken time to write to her.

Dearest Talisa, when our son was born his mother and I would sit together with him in our arms and whisper our dreams for him into his tiny ears. Boy, did we have big dreams for our little boy! Sometimes I think that no child could make his parents half as proud as Jericho has made his mother and I. Jericho has never disappointed us. He has made us proud by making smart decisions. Jericho earned our trust by always being honest and by simply doing what was always right.

When he told us about you we never once questioned his choice. We knew that for him to love you, to even imagine spending the rest of his life with you, then you had to be an exceptional woman. He could not have been more right. I know your parents must be as proud of you as we are. Getting to know you has been such a pleasure. Seeing firsthand how much you love our son gives us great confidence in your future together.

Irene and I have always told Jericho that the

woman he marries should make him a better man. Yesterday, my son told me that not only was he a better man with you, but for the first time he feels fully complete. If I did have any doubts, that testament alone was enough to convince me. Welcome to our hearts, Talisa. May God's blessings continue to be with you both. With much love and affection, your future father-in-law, Elijah.

As Talisa read the letter once again, and then for a third and fourth time, she could barely contain the warm tears that pressed against her eyelids. After reaching to extinguish the light above her head, she wiped her palm across her face, wiping at the moisture that had fallen against the round of her cheeks. Settling back against the cushioned seat, she finally closed her eyes and let sleep ease her into her own dreams.

"Your father and I are very proud of you, Jericho," Irene Becton stated matter-of-factly, the words falling as easily as if she were quoting the time of day. The woman fluffed the thin pillow beneath her child's head. "And, we're very excited!" she gushed.

Jericho smiled drowsily, the injection of pain medication his father had given him beginning to take effect.

"So, what are your plans?" his mother asked, taking a seat on the edge of the bed. "Will you and Talisa marry here or back in the States?"

"We want to speak with her parents first. I think it's important that I have her father's approval. His and her mother's. Don't you agree?" Jericho yawned, wiping a weak hand across his mouth.

Irene beamed down at her son. "I'm sure they'll be as excited as we are." She leaned to kiss his forehead, allowing her lips to linger for just a brief moment.

"Isn't she great, Mom? From the moment I met her, I just knew we were meant to be together."

"Yes, Talisa is a very special woman, Jericho."

The man continued to ramble. "I love her so much. She makes me feel so…so…full. Inside. It's like my heart is overflowing and I just want to bust." A soft chuckle rose from his midsection. "And, she's so beautiful. But being pretty isn't important to her. She doesn't worry about whether or not her hair and makeup are perfect and that just makes her more beautiful. She reminds me of you, Mom. She's strong like you are and she has the biggest heart. I never knew any other woman whose heart was as big as yours was until I met Talisa. And, she loves me. She loves me like you love Dad. I can't begin to tell you how happy I am."

Irene nodded her head slowly. "I am so happy for you, Jericho. I love you, son-shine. I love you very much."

Jericho smiled, the wide gesture pulling from ear to ear. "You haven't called me that since I was in elementary school."

His mother nodded. "You'll always be my son-shine. I don't care how old you are."

Jericho settled comfortably against the mattress, his eyes fluttering open and then closed. "I'm sorry, Mom. The medication has me a little woozy," he whispered into the warm air.

Irene patted his arm, her warm fingers comforting. "That's okay, son-shine. You need your rest." As she watched her oldest child drift off to sleep, her smile was rivaled only by her husband's, who stood watching from the doorway behind them.

Chapter 25

Their lively bantering could be heard down the block, the noise level at a feverish pitch as they welcomed Talisa back home. The four women were gathered in Leila's dining room, salads, French fries, and burgers from McDonald's covering the oak table.

Talisa bit into a Big Mac, relishing the taste of savory beef patties and special sauce. "Mmm," she hummed. "I can't believe how much I missed this."

"There's nothing like fast food to welcome you back home," Benita chimed, her mouth full of ketchup-coated fries. "We even have chocolate fudge sundaes for dessert, girl!"

Talisa laughed, her gaze washing over each of them. "I missed you guys so much," she said, grinning widely.

Leila grinned back. "We missed you, too. So tell us more. What else did you do?"

Her belly full, Talisa leaned back against the dining room chair. "There's nothing else to tell. You've heard it all."

"Well, I'm headed to Africa next week," Mya said jokingly. "You leave not having dated a man for years and come back engaged. If I'm lucky I should be able to find me a husband before I get inside the airport good."

Leila rolled her eyes. "I swear you have a one-track mind, Mya."

"Excuse me for thinking about my future. It wouldn't hurt you two to do the same thing. You're not getting any prettier, you know."

Benita sneered in Mya's direction. "I have a man, thank you. And I'm in no hurry to be married."

"Besides," Leila interjected, "ugly on the inside is uglier on the outside and I don't care how cute you think you are."

"You know, Leila, you get right on my—"

Talisa interrupted her friend. "Don't you two start fighting. Give me one night of peace before I have to go back to refereeing you two."

Talisa shook her head as her two friends eyed each other with disdain, both nodding their heads in agreement.

"Thank you," she said, rising from her seat and gathering the garbage from the table. "So, tell me what you three have been up to since I left."

"Well, I signed on two major accounts this past month. Been too busy with work to do anything else," Benita said, rising to help her.

"How's your quarterback?" Talisa asked, referring to the Atlanta Falcons football player Benita had met at the auction.

Benita smiled. "He's a defensive lineman and he's very sweet. They're away this weekend playing in Boston."

Talisa caught Mya rolling her eyes. "How about you, girlfriend? How's your love life going?"

Mya shrugged. "You know how it is. It's hard to find a good man these days."

"You still seeing old Charlie-newsboy?"

Leila chuckled. "I like that, Charlie-newsboy!"

Mya tossed her a look of annoyance. "He comes in handy every now and then, but brother's cheap. I don't have time for no cheap men."

Talisa leaned to hug her friend's shoulder. "What are we going to do with you?" she asked softly.

Mya smiled and Talisa imagined she saw a faint teardrop rise in her friend's eyes. "Don't worry about me," Mya professed. "I'm getting mine."

"We worry, Mya," Leila said. "We want more than that for you."

Benita moved to change the subject before the moment turned too serious. "So, Talisa, when does Jericho come back so we can meet him? You know there can be no wedding until he passes our approval."

Talisa grinned as the four women moved into Leila's den and settled themselves down against the oversized sectional sofa, ice cream sundaes in hand.

"He's back tomorrow."

"Have you told your mother yet?" Leila asked.

Talisa shook her head no. "We plan on telling them when Jericho gets here."

"Is her medication working?" Benita asked, concern spilling out of her eyes.

"So far, so good. Daddy says she's been doing much better. I'm just going to keep my fingers crossed."

"Let's hope this doesn't send her over the edge," Leila added.

Talisa crossed her fingers together in front of her. "Let's hope *and* say a prayer," she said with a quick smile.

"So, how's the sex?" Mya asked. "Is the brother any good, 'cause he looked like he'd be real good?"

Talisa blushed profusely. "Mya!"

They all laughed. "He was good," Leila chimed, slapping a high-five with Mya. "She's blushing so you know he was good."

Talisa hid her face in her hands, shaking her head. "If you three embarrass me I will never forgive you," she said, looking from one to the other. "No stories about things we did when we were in grade school. Please."

"You mean we can't tell him about the time you fell into the mud pit at the city zoo and all the boys saw your pink panties?" Mya asked.

"They were yellow," Leila interjected.

"No!"

"Well, how about in seventh grade when that boy Tyler pulled your tube top down and showed your breasts to the whole class?"

"That was your tube top and your breasts, Mya," Talisa laughed.

Mya turned to Leila. "Really?"

Leila nodded. "Yeah, that was you. Tyler put that dead garden snake in Talisa's lunch box and she puked on the principal's shoes when she thought she'd bitten into it."

"So, can we tell that story?" Mya asked.

Talisa shook her head. "No, Mya."

Her friend sighed, turning back to Leila. "She really is no fun, is she?"

Leila shrugged. "Sorry."

Benita laughed. "You're all crazy. I swear I'm the only sane one in the bunch."

Their giggles danced around the room as they continued chatting back and forth. A short while later, Leila rose from her seat and exited the room. It was a short wait before she returned with a bottle of Moët Hennessy and four crystal cognac glasses in hand. Mya moved to help her pour, popping the top on the bottle as Leila held the glasses out for her to fill. When they were ready, they each passed a glass to Talisa and Benita, the two women standing up to join them.

"Are you happy, Talisa?" Leila asked.

Talisa nodded. "More than you can ever imagine," she said softly.

"Is he good to you?" Mya asked.

"Better than good. He is my heart and soul."

"Does he love you as much as you love him?" Benita asked.

Talisa grinned. "As much and more."

Her three friends lifted their glasses in salute.

"May this be only the beginning of something greater than any of us can ever imagine for you," Leila whispered, a tear catching in her throat.

"May he stay long, strong, and hard well into old age," Mya added with a quick giggle.

They all shook their heads at the woman.

"We are happy for you, Talisa," Benita added. "May God continue to bless you always."

"To you, Talisa," Leila said. "You are our sister and we love you very much."

"To Talisa and Jericho," the three women chimed, lifting their glasses in salute.

As they each took a quick sip of their drinks, Talisa smiled widely as Leila wrapped her in a warm hug.

"And, no," Leila said, affection coating her words, "we are not wearing anything with ruffles at your wedding!"

Talisa entered the small home humming softly. Her parents were seated in the living room, her father in his favorite recliner with the day's newspaper and her mother on the worn floral sofa flicking the channels on the television remote.

"Hi, Mom, hi, Dad," she said, dropping down onto the seat beside her mother.

Her father grinned. "Hey, pumpkin. Did you have fun?"

Mary patted her daughter's knee. "The girls missed you," Mary said.

"I missed them, too. We had a great time," Talisa said, answering them both. "How was your evening? Did you two have a good night?"

Herman nodded. "It's been fine."

Mary glanced over to the clock on the wall, noting that it was almost time for the late-night news. "Talisa, you really shouldn't stay out so late. You know better than that. What will people think?"

Talisa tossed her father a quick glance. "Sorry," she said, her eyes widening with concern. "But I didn't think ten o'clock was too late."

"You just don't need to be staying out all hours of the night. It ain't right," Mary chastised. The woman's tone raised just half an octave, causing her husband and daughter to eye her with reservation.

Herman laid his newspaper down on the coffee table in front of him. "Mary, did you take your pills today?"

"Leave me alone, Herman," Mary responded, her tone surly.

Talisa reached for her mother's hand. "Mom, you have to take your medicine every day. You know that, right? You know you can't miss any doses."

Talisa could see the bitterness rising in her mother's voice as the woman hissed in her direction.

"Don't tell me what to do, Talisa. I know what to do. I feel fine. If I feel fine I don't need to take anything."

Herman bristled. "Mary, take your pills, now," he demanded.

Like a petulant child, Mary leaned back against the sofa, her arms folded in defiance across her chest. She ignored the man staring at her, her attention focused on the television as she flicked from one channel to another.

Talisa closed her eyes and took a deep breath. When she opened them again, her father had risen from his seat and was heading up the stairs.

Talisa watched him ascend the stairway, his body suddenly consumed by the weight of his burdens. There was no stopping the sudden rush of tears that fell from her eyes. She turned in her seat, her gaze focused on her mother's face.

"So, I come home and you decide to be sick again. Don't you love me enough to want to be well?"

"Don't talk stupid, Talisa. There is nothing wrong with me."

"The doctor said you have to take your medicine, so why aren't you taking it?"

The woman glared in her daughter's direction. "The doctors don't always know what's right," she hissed in response. "I know what's right for me and what isn't. I decide. Not you, and definitely not your daddy."

Talisa nodded her head, rising to her feet. She headed for the stairs, following behind her father.

"We should do something tomorrow," Mary called out to her. "You and me. We should spend the day together, I think."

Talisa turned to face the woman, tears still dripping down her face. "I have other plans. Jericho comes home tomorrow. I'm picking him and his parents up from the airport. We plan on spending the day together."

Mary bristled but said nothing. Talisa watched her for a quick moment before speaking again.

"Mom, if you don't take your medication, you and I are never going to spend another day together. I love you, but I can't do this anymore. I'm sorry but you're going to have to make a choice. If Daddy and I are important to you, then you're going to have to do what the doctor tells you to. If not, then you're going to be very lonely. This isn't fair to me or to Daddy and it's just not right."

Talisa turned, heading up the stairs. Her mother's anguished voice followed her up, rising like the brunt of hot steam.

"It's evil, Talisa. Evil is taking control of you. I can't have that evilness in my house!"

At the top of the stairs, Talisa knocked on her parents' bedroom door. When her father called out for her to come in, she entered the small room and closed the door behind her. The man sat perched on the edge of the queen-sized bed staring out into space. Talisa dropped to the floor beside him, leaning her head against his lap as he swept the hair from out of her eyes and off her face.

"I'm sorry, pumpkin," the man said. "I'm so sorry."

"It's not your fault, Daddy. You can't make her take care of herself. She has to want to do it for herself."

The man nodded as his daughter stared up at him and smiled, an easy bend to her lips that helped to ease some of his unhappiness. He sighed, a deep inhale of breath blowing from his lungs.

"I wanted to wait until Jericho was here and you had some time to get to know him, but I think you should know that he and I are planning on getting married. I love him, Daddy, and he loves me, and he wants me to be his wife."

Herman smiled down on her, pulling her up into his arms to hug her tightly. A moment passed before he was able to say anything, emotion clouding his vision and his voice. "That's great news, pumpkin pie!" he finally gushed. "I'm so happy for you."

"I'm scared she's going to ruin this for me, Daddy. I'm really scared."

Herman nodded, his dark gaze meeting hers. "Don't you be afraid, baby. You have every right to be happy. If this man makes you happy then you marry him. I'll take care of your mother."

Talisa hugged her father tightly. "You're going to love him, Daddy. I just know it."

Her father smiled. "As long as he loves my baby girl and takes care of her, then he and I will be just fine with each other." He gave her a quick wink. "Everything is going to be just fine. Don't you worry yourself."

Downstairs, Mary clicked off the television and headed into the kitchen. The room was quiet, the hum of the refrigerator the only sound. She could hear them upstairs, their voices muffled behind the thin walls, Talisa and her daddy, sharing with each other, not wanting to share with her at all. The reality of that fact was suddenly overwhelming and her body shook, quivering from the hurt.

Reaching for the bottle of medication, she studied it momentarily before pulling at the childproof safety cap. Shaking two pills into her hand, she reached for an empty glass out of the cupboard and filled it with cold water from the sink. Dropping the pills onto her tongue, she swallowed them quickly, washing them down with the drink of water. Dropping the glass into the sink, she headed up the stairs. Perhaps tomorrow would be a better day for them, she thought as she slowly took each step. Tomorrow she would be better and maybe then Talisa and her daddy would want her to be there with them. Maybe tomorrow she wouldn't feel quite as alone as she did that very moment.

Chapter 26

Their flight had arrived on schedule and Talisa stood waiting anxiously in the arrival area for Jericho and his parents. Excitement bubbled tenfold when she saw him slowly easing his way in her direction, his father and mother flanking his sides. Waving excitedly, Talisa felt like a little girl on Christmas morning after opening the one gift she'd yearned most for all year long.

When he saw her, Jericho's face beamed with anticipation as he dropped his carry-on bag to his feet and scooped her up into his arms. Pressing his face into her hair, he hugged her tightly, then dropped his lips to hers, kissing her boldly. The moment took her breath away.

"Welcome home," she whispered as he let her go, his hands still holding tight to hers. She tossed a look toward his parents who stood watching them, smiles pulling at their mouths.

"Hello, Mrs. Becton, Dr. Becton. It's good to see you both."

Irene nodded, reaching to kiss Talisa's cheek. "Hello, darling. It's good to see you, too."

Dr. Becton chuckled. "Jericho, let the poor girl loose. You have plenty of time for that nonsense."

Jericho laughed. "I'm never letting her go ever again, Dad." He kissed her again. "I missed you," he whispered into her ear, his warm breath trickling through her bloodstream.

Talisa glowed with contentment, wrapping her arm around his waist as they headed toward the baggage area.

Irene dropped a hand against her son's arm. "Jericho, your father and I have arranged for a limo to take us home. We'll pick up your luggage and bring it home with us. You and Talisa take off. We'll catch up with you two later."

"Are you sure, Mom?" Jericho asked.

"I can take you home, Mrs. Becton. It's really not a problem," Talisa interjected.

The woman smiled at them. "I know it's not a problem, dear, and I also know you two could use some time alone. Take Jericho home. He needs to eat and he needs to rest. It was a long trip for him."

Jericho rolled his eyes. "You'd think I was three years old," he muttered jokingly.

His father nodded. "Your mother's right. Head on home and get some rest, son." He shook a finger in Jericho's direction. "Easy on the hanky-panky. You're not completely healed yet."

Talisa blushed as Jericho shook his head at his father.

Irene laughed. "Elijah, leave these children alone! Let's go before someone takes my luggage."

"No one wants your luggage, woman!" the man mused as they headed in the opposite direction. "You worry too much!"

When his parents were well out of sight, Jericho pulled Talisa back into a deep embrace, one hand pressed tightly against her back to pull her body tight to his. The sensation of his touch made her quiver, her knees threatening to give out on her. He kissed her again, his lips becoming reaquainted with hers. His tongue tipped past to lick her lips, and she shivered blissfully as he danced inside her mouth. The sensation was wiping all coherent thoughts from Talisa's head, but through the haze of passion, she managed to remember that they were standing in the middle of an airline terminal, spectators eyeing them curiously as they passed them by. Pressing her palms to his chest, Talisa pushed gently, taking a step back. As her gaze met his, both were panting for breath. Jericho grinned unabashedly, taking a step back toward her.

"Are you ready?" Talisa asked, finally able to muster a word as Jericho's mouth danced across her cheek and down the length of her neck.

The man nodded, still kissing a path from her neck to her ear and back again. "I was ready the minute I saw you," he whispered seductively, blowing warm breath against her ear.

A flutter of energy surged through her lower abdomen. Hand in hand they made their way to the parking garage and Talisa's Ford Taurus. They had barely settled themselves inside the car when Jericho reached for her again, pulling her mouth back to his. He had missed the taste of her, had missed touching her, and he was suddenly consumed with making up for lost time. When he'd stepped off the plane, searching her out of the crowd of people traveling from one place to another, she'd been easy to locate. Her intense, sparkling eyes had been inviting. Her luscious, full lips had been waiting to be kissed, calling out for him to oblige. There was no way he could have resisted.

Jericho licked her lips again, opening his mouth to suck them in, allowing his top lip to drift down and take possession of her bottom lip between his teeth, gently biting and pulling. Her palm gently touched his cheek, tracing a slow path along the sides of his face, and when she moaned, the sound of pleasure escaping her, it was all he could do to keep from taking her right there in the front seat of the vehicle. Reluctantly, he pulled back.

Talisa smiled as she noted the faint pout of disappointment that flooded his face. "I don't know if I can drive now," Talisa giggled. "My whole body's on fire."

Jericho laughed. "I know the feeling." He glanced around the parking garage. "If we weren't in a public place I'd make love to you right here, right now," he said, his voice dropping even lower and huskier. "Let's go home," he said, his bright eyes showering his intentions when they got there.

Talisa pressed a palm to his cheek, shaking her head. Searching for the keys that had dropped into her lap, Talisa adjusted her seat belt, started the ignition, and pulled out of the parking space.

"So, were Moses and Susie okay?" Talisa asked in an attempt to stall some of the heat rising between them. Her eyes flicked from the road to Jericho and back again.

The man nodded. "They were fine. They wanted to come this time, but I think they understood why they had to wait until Mom and Dad come back for them next month."

"Will the adoption be final then?"

"It's going to be a few months, but Dad was able to get permission to bring them here until it's completed. We just have to wait for their paperwork to be processed and their visas to be issued."

"Your parents are amazing, Jericho. I was so worried about what would happen to those kids."

"After everything Moses did for me, I was actually thinking of adopting them myself. But when my mother told me she and my dad were interested I knew that was the best thing for them."

Talisa nodded, tossing him a quick glance. "Have you thought about having children, Jericho?"

He waved his head up and down. "I've thought about having children with you," he said, brushing a finger down her cheek.

Talisa smiled. "How many?"

"Dozens."

"No, I'm serious, Jericho."

The man shrugged. "I imagine you and I will have at least two."

"I really would like to have a child, but I'd also like to adopt. There are so many of our children that could use a good home."

Jericho nodded his agreement. "I'd like that, too. In fact," he said, leaning closer to her, his fingers brushing against the length of her arm, "I think we should start practicing making babies right away."

"Dr. Becton!" Talisa exclaimed, feigning shyness.

Jericho palmed a heavy hand against her leg, distracting her as she pulled onto the highway. She choked back a giggle, suddenly feeling like an awkward teenager. When the man leaned to kiss her cheek, easing the tip of his tongue into her ear, she jumped, just missing the rear end of a Lincoln Navigator traveling in front of her.

"You really should pay attention to the road," Jericho teased.

"I could if you weren't doing that," Talisa chuckled softly, her heart beating rapidly.

"Doing what?" the man whispered, his tongue gliding over her lobe.

"Jericho, you're going to make me have an accident," she said, pushing him back against his seat with one palm.

Jericho laughed. "I'm sorry. I couldn't resist."

The ride to Jericho's condo was fairly quick, the flow of traffic moving them quickly to their destination. Although familiar with the North Atlanta area, the gated community where Jericho resided was new to her. The European-style, multilevel unit was larger than her parents' home and only slightly intimidating as Jericho guided her through the security gates to his home's entrance. With a quick code into the security system, the garage door opened, and Talisa eased her vehicle in beside Jericho's Mercedes.

"This is very nice," Talisa said, looking around the expanse of space in the immaculate courtyard.

"You haven't seen it yet," Jericho said as he grabbed her hand and guided her into the interior of the building, leading her from the garage, through his private laundry room, and into the home's kitchen. As they stepped inside, Jericho reached to brush a palm against her breast and Talisa broke out into laughter, swatting his hand away.

"You are so fresh," she giggled.

Jericho laughed with her, pulling her to him. "Yes, I am," he said.

Talisa slipped away from his grasp. "Well, you need to

stop. You need to have some lunch first. Your father said you have to eat and then you have to rest."

Jericho grabbed her again. "Baby girl, the only thing I'm hungry for right now is you," he said, nibbling at the soft spot just beneath her chin.

Both were suddenly surprised by the small, Hispanic woman fussing over a multitude of pots cooking on top of the kitchen stove. When the woman caught sight of them, she waved, lifting a wooden spoon in their direction. "*Hola,*" she called out cheerfully.

Jericho took a quick glance around the room. "Excuse me, but who are you and what are you doing in my home?" he asked.

The woman suddenly seemed nervous, then called out to the other room, calling out to someone in her native language.

The couple cut their eyes toward each other and Jericho suddenly shook his head knowingly. "Well, I'll be damned," he exclaimed, his tone just shy of being harsh.

"What's going on, Jericho?" Talisa whispered as they followed the cook into the living room.

Before he could answer, Shannon Porter came rushing toward them. "Jericho, sweetheart," the woman said cheerfully, "welcome home!" She reached to wrap her arms around him, then stopped short when she saw Talisa.

"Oh, hello," Shannon said, eyeing Talisa with obvious disdain.

"Hello." Talisa smiled, nodding her head in greeting as Jericho tightened the hold on the hand he had been holding. He pulled her closer to his side, the motion possessive.

"What are you doing in my house, Shannon?" Jericho asked brusquely.

Shannon leaned to kiss his lips, her aim falling short

against his chin as Jericho turned his head aside. The woman stepped back, clearly insulted.

"Your mother called my parents when they heard about your trauma. When they spoke with them last week to update them on your condition, your parents said you'd be home today. The minute I heard, I knew I couldn't let you come home to an empty house. There was no way I could let you be alone so I thought I would surprise you."

Jericho nodded his head slowly. "Well, I'm not alone, so you can leave now," he said moving toward the center of the room, pulling Talisa along beside him. Her eyes widened, looking from Shannon, to Jericho, and back.

Shannon eyed her curiously, her gaze gliding from the top of Talisa's head down to her toes. Her face became pinched as if she'd bitten into something sour, her eyes narrowing into thin slits. A rush of red had risen to her cheeks, deeply coloring her milky complexion. She suddenly smiled and extended her hand in greeting. "Hello. I'm Shannon, a very close friend of Jericho's," she said, putting much emphasis on the words close and friend.

Jericho rolled his eyes.

"In fact," the woman continued, "you might say I'm Jericho's girlfriend. But I'm sure he didn't tell you anything about me."

The man shook his head, tension tightening the muscles in his jaw. Talisa dropped the hold he had on her hand, resting her palm against his lower back to calm him. She smiled sweetly, ignoring the outstretched palm. "It's a pleasure to meet you, Shannon. I'm Talisa, Jericho's fiancée, and actually, he's told me everything about you."

The woman's mouth dropped open in surprise and

Jericho fought not to laugh out loud, unable to hide his amusement at her reaction.

"Fiancée? But when…Jericho, how could…" she sputtered as if she were unable to comprehend what she'd just heard. Catching her breath, she inhaled deeply, then regained her tight smile. "Well, when did this happen? Have you two been acquainted long?"

Jericho answered. "I proposed to her when we were in Uganda together. And, we've known each other since she lost her bid at that auction. The minute I saw her I knew that Talisa was the love of my life," he said, leaning to kiss her lips.

An uncomfortable silence descended over the room. Shannon stood awkwardly, her gaze racing between Jericho and Talisa. Jealousy seeped from her pores, causing her bottom lip to quiver with anger. "Well," she said finally, "isn't this special."

Jericho shook his head. "How did you get in here, Shannon?" he asked.

She shrugged, her blond hair swaying ever so slightly. "I still have my key."

"No, you don't. I took that key back months ago."

The woman shrugged. "I forgot I had a spare."

"Well, you need to leave it when you go," he said. "Now, I appreciate your concern, but Talisa and I were looking forward to being alone. I'm sure you understand," he said, his tone balanced between annoyance and amusement.

Shannon swallowed hard, biting against her bottom lip. "Jericho, I think you and I need to talk. Alone. I'm sure Theresa won't mind giving us a quick moment together."

Talisa took a deep breath. "Actually, I do mind. And my name is *Talisa*. Now, I think you've worn out your welcome here. But thank you for stopping by. I'm sure you'll understand that it won't be necessary for you to be stopping by again any time soon."

The woman bristled. "Jericho, you really need to tell her—" she started before the man interrupted her.

Jericho clenched his fists in the air and growled in frustration. "Shannon, why do you do this? It's over between us. Please, go home. Don't make this any more uncomfortable than it already is. Please, I'm trying to ask you nicely."

Shannon's back stiffened, drawing her body up taller on the four-inch Manolo Blahniks she wore. With both hands, she pushed the length of her hair behind her ears, her fingers brushing lightly against the diamond studs in her earlobes. Taking a quick glance around her, she bit down on the inside of her cheek, fighting for control over the anger that was consuming her. A loud sigh blew past her lips as she glared at Talisa, then refocused her gaze on Jericho.

Jericho crossed the room to the front door, opening it widely. "Goodbye, Shannon."

With a slight nod toward Talisa, Shannon stormed out of the house muttering under her breath as she passed Jericho. Behind her, the Hispanic woman followed closely on her heels. As Jericho eased the door closed behind them, he burst out laughing, the sound ringing off the whitewashed walls.

"I can't believe this," Jericho exclaimed, tossing his hands up in the air.

"She's very persistent," Talisa said, her voice quivering ever so slightly.

Noting the change in her tone, Jericho rushed to her side, wrapping his arms around her. "You know how much I love you, don't you, Talisa? You know I don't care anything about that woman?"

Closing her eyes, Talisa nodded. Opening them again, she smiled. Jericho gestured for Talisa to give him a quick minute as he called the security office to insure Shannon and her guest were escorted off the premises, with instructions that the woman was to never be allowed in ever again.

"Aren't you something!" Jericho said, easing back up behind her, wrapping his arms around her waist. "It won't be necessary for you to be stopping by again," he said, mimicking her.

Talisa leaned back against him. "Someone needed to put her in her place," she said, melting into the kisses Jericho was burning against her neck.

"Well, you definitely did that," he said, spinning her around to face him. He kissed her hungrily, his hands wandering brazenly up and down the length of her body.

"Let me show you my home," he said softly, taking a half step away from her. "I should probably check to see what else that woman's been doing since I was gone," he noted.

Talisa followed him back into the kitchen as he turned off the pots and pans simmering over the low flames.

"Do you know what that is?" Talisa asked, peering down into the pot of red sauce.

Jericho shrugged, his shoulders sliding up toward the ceiling. "I don't have a clue. Smells good though."

Looking about the space, Talisa was impressed. The kitchen was very modern, with stainless steel appliances against a backdrop of dark cherrywood cabinets. The counters were clear except for the few utensils the woman had just been using. An intimate dining area had been created just off the kitchen space with a settee covered in raw silk with leopard-print pillows just beneath a large window. A pedestal table with a polished-chrome base and leather-like top sat in the center of the space, with two additional upholstered chairs surrounding it.

From the kitchen, they went back into the living room. Jericho's tastes were very simplistic, Talisa thought, admiring the minimalist design. A black leather sofa, glass coffee table, and two oversized ottomans sat atop a large, abstract carpet in a flaming shade of red. Beneath the carpet, the floors were planked, a dark ebony-stained shade of hardwood that Talisa found appealing. A large fireplace occupied an opposing wall, complemented on the other end by a wall of bookcases packed floor to ceiling with books.

Jericho watched her as she stopped to search the titles.

"Have you read all of these?" Talisa asked, turning to stare at him.

He nodded. "Once or twice. I like to read."

"It's an amazing collection, Jericho. And everything is so beautiful!"

"My mother helped me decorate. I'd still be sitting on cardboard boxes if it wasn't for her." He laughed.

He extended his hand, reaching for hers. From the living room, Jericho guided her down the short length of hallway into the master bedroom. As they opened the door and stepped inside, Talisa was only slightly disconcerted by what they found.

"Well, I think she had plans for you two tonight," she said, her gaze sweeping over the multitude of unlit candles and the grand floral arrangements that had been meticulously placed around the room.

Jericho nodded, scanning her face as he stepped farther inside. He peered into the bathroom and noted the bath beads and rose petals lying in preparation on the edge of the oversized whirlpool tub.

Talisa was silent, standing in the center of the room staring at the king-sized bed draped in black satin bedding. He moved to her side and wrapped his arms around her, leaning to kiss her cheek.

"I'll throw it all away if you want," he said, lifting her chin to look her in her eyes. "If you want me to, just tell me."

"It's kind of creepy, seeing all this stuff here and knowing it was meant for you and another woman," Talisa answered. "I'm not sure how I feel about it, Jericho."

The man nodded as he pointed to the upholstered headboard. "My mother picked out this bed three months ago. No other woman has ever slept with me in this bed. No other woman will ever sleep with me in this bed. This is our bed. Yours and mine. The rest of it, the candles, the flowers, none of it means anything to us if we don't want it to."

As Jericho stared into her eyes, Talisa could feel herself falling into the depths of his gaze. He smiled sweetly and suddenly every thought of Shannon Porter flew right out of her mind. Jericho reached to take her hand in his, lifting her fingers to his lips. The scent of her perfume trailed along her wrist and he inhaled, gently flooding his senses with the sweet aroma.

He raised his eyes to look into hers, then turned her hand, tracing a soft trail over her inner wrist down to her palm with his tongue and lips. Talisa whimpered ever so softly as he kissed each of her fingertips. With slow determination he took each finger into his mouth, sucking and licking them down to the knuckle. When he was done with one hand, he reached for the other. By the time he was finished, Talisa's eyes were closed and her breathing had quickened with anticipation.

Taking a step back, Jericho called her name, whispering it softly into the air-conditioned room. As Talisa opened her eyes to meet his gaze, he began to slowly unbutton his shirt. She watched him as he loosened each button, finally reaching out to help him glide the cotton fabric off his shoulders, letting it fall down to the floor.

Talisa's eyes raked longingly over his chest, bringing a flush of heat to his brown skin when her fingers followed. When she leaned to press her lips to his nipple, capturing it gently between her teeth, Jericho tried to steel himself from the inevitable shiver that surged from one end of his body to the other. Tilting her head upwards, he leaned to kiss her lips, trapping her mouth hungrily beneath his own. Her fingertips brushed against his flesh, scratching at the length of his broad back. She paused for only a quick moment when she touched the scar line that would forever remain a reminder of their experience in Africa.

Pulling at the cotton T-shirt she wore, Jericho motioned for her to lift her arms as he glided the garment up and over her head. A pale pink bra edged in fine lace caressed the lines of her breasts and with one swift motion, Jericho unhooked the clasp, sliding it from her shoulders to fall with his shirt on the floor. Kicking shoes to the floor, he eased her down to the bed, their mouths locked, melded, as if magnetized, lips parted, tongues softly stroking, causing both to murmur in ecstasy, the delightful moans long and deep.

Jericho hovered above her, grinding his pelvis against hers. With his hips pushing against hers, Talisa slowly eased the length of her legs around him, her heels resting just below the cheeks of his buttocks as her thighs clasped tightly around his waist. The sensations were overwhelming, release shuddering through them both. Talisa moaned with pleasure, the sound fueling Jericho's frantic need. Shifting his weight to his side to stare down at her, he gently caressed one breast, kneading it beneath the width of his palm, and then the other, his hands washing attention over every square inch of her.

Jericho's eyes widened at the sight of her, enamored by her reaction to his touch. Her body was fully aroused, her nipples turgid against the soft tissue, eyes clenched tight with desire, heated cheeks, inflamed lips, her mouth open, breath coming in short gasps. She was beyond beautiful and his wanting surged into a towering erection straining to be released.

When Jericho pulled at the snap to her pants, everything except the warmth and feel of him against her was lost. Talisa's desire had puddled moisture in every crevice of her body, her skin glistening with damp anticipation. Opening her eyes, she met his gaze, his desire colliding with her own. As she reached for the waistband of his pants, pulling at his zipper, their motions were almost frantic. Together they were fighting to remove the last of their clothes, jeans and slacks kicked to the bottom of the bed.

A rush of giggles consumed them both as Jericho knocked everything from the nightstand onto the floor as he reached for a condom out of the bedside drawer. With laughter painting her lips, Talisa opened herself to receive him, welcoming him back to her as if he'd been gone a lifetime. Time stopped as Jericho screamed her name and when his cries died away, his body slumping down on top of hers, Talisa could feel the warm tears of mutual joy on his face and on hers.

Jericho didn't have a clue how long he'd slept. When he opened his eyes, the hot rays of an afternoon sun were still shining brightly in a clear sky. Turning to see the digital clock on the nightstand, he noted that it was almost three o'clock. He'd been sleeping for most of the morning and half the afternoon. His bed was empty and he lay alone, a warm blanket wrapped around his naked body. Talisa had lit one of the scented candles on top of his bureau, a fresh floral aroma dancing in the air. Taking a deep breath, Jericho inhaled the fragrance, stretching his body lengthwise against the mattress, before lifting himself upward. There was just a mild twinge of tightness across the muscles in his back, a faint reminder that just weeks earlier he'd had a bullet lodged only inches shy of his spinal cord.

Making his way to the bathroom, he splashed his face with cold water, rinsed his mouth with mouthwash, and then passed a dampened washcloth over his body. Taking note of the candles and rose petals for a second time, he shook his head at the absurdity. He reached for a plush bath towel and wrapped it around his waist, securing one end on his hip.

As he made his way down the hall and into the living room he could hear the radio playing, soft jazz from one of the local college stations playing over the airways. Talisa stood in his kitchen wrapped in his terry bathrobe, shifting items in his refrigerator.

"Hey, you," he said, leaning against the doorframe, his arms clasped across his chest.

Startled, Talisa jumped, dropping a plastic container of margarine to the floor. "Jericho, you scared me! I thought you were still asleep," she said, leaning to pick the dropped item up off the freshly washed tile.

"I can't sleep when you're not there."

Talisa laughed. "Oh, really? I couldn't tell by the way you were snoring in there."

Jericho rolled his eyes. "I'm not the one who snores, remember?"

He moved to her side, wrapping his arms around her. "So, what are you up to?"

"I thought I'd salvage this meal so we can eat something. Aren't you hungry?"

The man shrugged. "I could eat. Did you figure out what it is?"

"It's some kind of chili with sausages and black beans, I think. And," Talisa said pointing to the counter, "all the fixings for chicken fajitas. I take it you like Mexican cuisine or was your friend just taking a chance?"

Jericho smiled. "No, it's my favorite."

Talisa shook her head, her eyes rolling in jest. "I figured as much."

"Why?"

"Because if it were me and I wanted to surprise you, I would do it with all your favorites as well."

Jericho nodded slowly, a grin filling his face. He pushed the terry bathrobe to expose her shoulder and leaned to kiss the soft flesh. "Did I tell you how much I love you?" he asked, reaching up to plant a second kiss on her mouth, gently brushing his flesh over hers.

Talisa smiled. "Yes, you did, but I will never get tired of hearing you say it over and over again."

Jericho moved to take a seat at the table, slowing easing his body into a chair. Talisa noticed the momentary quiver of hurt that registered across his face, concern washing over her as she moved to his side. "Are you feeling okay? Does your back hurt?"

The man shrugged. "It was just a spasm. Nothing for you to be concerned about."

Talisa shook her head. "Your father told us to behave, that you needed to get your rest."

Jericho chuckled. "Making love to you was the best rest I could have gotten."

"But—" Talisa started before Jericho interrupted her.

"But nothing. I know my own body and as a doctor I know what I can and cannot do," he stated, his tone firm.

Talisa's hands fell to her hips. "You're also stubborn and just a touch hardheaded," she said, a smile growing across her face.

Jericho could only shake his head and Talisa leaned to kiss his forehead. He changed the subject. "After we eat I think we should go visit with your parents. I would really like to meet them."

Talisa hesitated, dropping onto the cushioned seat beside him. "I don't know if tonight's a good idea. My mother wasn't feeling well yesterday."

Jericho scrutinized her face, noting the wave of tension that creased the woman's brow. "What happened?" he asked.

Talisa inhaled, a deep breath of air filling her lungs. "She stopped taking her medication. She was in one of her bad moods."

Jericho nodded, reaching to take her hands between his own. "It's going to be rough for a while, Talisa. Patients sometimes have a difficult time adjusting. You're going to have moments when the medication is working well. And then there will be times when her metabolism will be off and the medication will have to be adjusted."

"But she just stopped. For no reason."

"She is learning to understand the difference between

herself on the medication and herself off the medication. When she's on and she's feeling really good, she may convince herself she doesn't need them anymore. It will go back and forth until she settles into a comfortable routine. Having you and your father to support her will definitely help."

Talisa sighed. "I was mean to her. I told her I wasn't going to put up with her ugliness anymore. That if she didn't take her medication I didn't want to be around her."

Jericho nodded. "Baby girl, you have every right to feel that way and you have every right to tell her how you feel."

"But she's my mother."

"And, you love her. But you don't have to be abused if her illness is causing her to be abusive and you don't have to take it without saying something."

The pot on the stove suddenly erupted in a spray of tomato sauce, spewing red down the sides of the container onto the stainless steel stovetop. Talisa jumped from her seat, shutting down the flames beneath the pan to stop the sudden splatter.

Jericho burst out laughing. "Well, I think our dinner is ready," he said, rising to help Talisa clear up the mess.

Talisa laughed with him. "I'm wondering if maybe we should eat some cereal instead."

Chapter 27

The meal was filling, ending with a dessert of pineapple sherbet and angel food cake topped with fresh whipped cream. When Jericho smeared the last of the whipped topping across Talisa's right breast and proceeded to lick the sweet nectar from her skin, dessert moved from the kitchen table, through the living room, and back to the bedroom.

With dinner and dessert behind them, Talisa felt deliriously satiated, every muscle in her body in a relaxed state of bliss. Jericho slowly glided a loofah sponge filled with vanilla-scented body wash over her, which Talisa reciprocated when he was done. As the duo stood beneath the warm spray of water that fell from the showerhead, neither could imagine being any happier than they were at that very moment.

"When are you moving in?" Jericho asked, stepping

out of the shower and into a large towel. He eyed her curiously as he used a second towel to brush the dampness from her flesh.

Talisa chuckled. "Where did that come from?" she questioned.

The man smiled, the warmth of it flooding the entire room. "I have no desire to sleep alone one more night, Talisa. I want you here with me or I can move in with you and your folks. I don't care."

She laughed, shaking her head as she pressed the back of her fingers to his forehead. "You must be running a fever. I can just hear my mother if I even thought about you moving in with us."

"Which is why you need to move in here with me."

They moved from the bathroom back into the bedroom. Searching for her clothes, Talisa was still laughing at him.

"What's so funny? I'm not joking, Talisa. I'm very serious."

"So am I. I'll be moving in with you right after I marry you."

Jericho waved his head up and down. "That's fair." He reached for his personal phone book, a leather-bound directory sitting in the top drawer of the nightstand.

"Who are you calling?" Talisa asked, taking a seat against the edge of the bed as he reached for the telephone.

"I have a friend who's a judge. He can marry us tonight."

"Jericho! You're crazy!" she said, grabbing at the receiver and hanging the unit up.

Jumping onto the bed beside her, Jericho kissed her feverishly, his mouth racing a mile a minute over her lips and cheeks. "I am. I'm crazy about you!"

* * *

After another hour and a second shower, Talisa and Jericho finally made it out the door of his home and back into Talisa's car. Jericho sat quietly in the passenger seat, stealing quick glances in her direction as he replayed the entire day over and over again in his mind. He couldn't begin to express the depth of emotion he had for Talisa. It was overwhelming, like nothing he'd ever experienced in his lifetime. Missing her didn't compare to how much he wanted to be with her, how much he needed her, how totally entrenched she was in his heart now that they were reunited. When he'd told his father he never planned to be apart from her for any length of time ever again, he had not been kidding. As they pulled into the driveway of her family home, he was more than ready to make sure her father and her mother knew that.

When Talisa pushed open the front door, Herman looked up from his newspaper, the expanse of paper unfolded against the coffee table. As Jericho stepped into the living room behind her, the man nodded in greeting, pulling his reading glasses from his face as he rose to his feet. Talisa made the introductions.

"Hello," he said warmly, extending his hand to shake Jericho's. "We've heard a lot about you."

"Hello, Mr. London. Talisa has told me much about you as well. It's a pleasure to meet you, sir."

Herman called up the stairs for his wife. "Mary! Talisa is here and she has company with her!"

Talisa reached up to kiss her father's cheek. "Hi, Daddy. How is she today?"

Her father nodded. "Better. Much better," the man answered, his voice soft. He smiled in Jericho's direction.

"Come on in and have a seat," he said, gesturing in the direction of the sofa. "Talisa's mother should be right down."

"Thank you, sir."

Herman returned to his chair as Jericho took a seat across from him. "So, how are you feeling, son? We hear you had a rough ride there for a while."

"Yes, sir. I'm feeling much better. I'm glad to be home and even happier to be back with your daughter. I don't know what I would have done without her."

Herman smiled, passing a look from Jericho to Talisa, who was smiling widely. Joy filled his daughter's face and he suddenly couldn't remember the last time she had looked so happy.

Talisa glanced up the stairwell. "I should go check on Mom," she said, excusing herself from the room. As she eased her way up to the second floor she could hear her father asking Jericho about his experiences in Africa, listening intently as Jericho responded. At the top of the stairs she knocked on her parents' bedroom door. When there was no answer, she knocked a second time, then eased the door open slowly, peering inside.

"Mommy? May I come in?"

Mary stared up at her from the edge of the bedside. She smiled as Talisa entered the room, coming to take the seat beside her. Neither said a word as Talisa reached for her mother's hand and held it, entwining her fingers between her mother's like she use to do when she'd been a little girl.

"Are you okay?" Talisa finally asked.

Mary cast a quick glance toward her daughter, then hung her head against her chest. A single tear eased past her thick lashes, falling against the brown of her complexion.

"Mommy?"

Taking a deep breath, Mary smiled ever so slightly, then turned back to look her child in the eyes. She nodded her head. "I was just thinking that my little girl isn't a little girl anymore."

"But I'll always be your little girl. Nothing will change that."

"I know. I just..."

Talisa squeezed her mother's hand as the woman choked back a low sob. She waited patiently as the woman struggled to compose herself.

"I'm just feeling a little sentimental is all. I'm sorry, baby. I don't know why I'm acting this way."

"Mom, you have nothing to be sorry for. Nothing." Talisa paused before she continued. "Jericho is downstairs. I would really like for you to come down to meet him."

The woman hesitated. "Are you sure, Talisa?"

"Why wouldn't I be? You're my mother. I love you and Jericho is very important to me. Of course I would want the two of you to meet."

"I'm scared, Talisa. I don't want to do or say anything to embarrass you. Or your daddy," Mary added. "I know I haven't always acted right. Like last night. I wasn't myself."

Talisa nodded her understanding. "Mom, I told Jericho about your illness. He's a doctor. He understands that there are going to be times that you aren't going to be yourself. Especially if you don't take your medication. But that's not important right now. What's important is that you meet him, and he meets you, and you two get to know one another." Talisa grabbed both of her mother's hands between her own, turning so that she was facing the woman. "Mommy, I love this man. I love him very much. I also love you and Daddy with all my heart. You three are the most important people in my life and I want you to know each other and hopefully love each other like I love you all."

Mary heaved a deep sigh. "Is he good to you, Talisa?"

The young woman nodded. "He's very good to me. He loves me very much."

Mary smiled. "My baby's got herself a doctor!" she chuckled softly. "I bet Hazel will just wet her pants when she finds out!"

Talisa rolled her eyes, lifting herself from the edge of the bed. She pulled her mother up along with her. "Well, you can't tell Mrs. Taft until you meet him for yourself."

Adjusting the cotton housedress she wore, Mary passed her hands down the length of her torso, then followed Talisa out of the room and back down the stairs. Jericho came to his feet as the two women entered the room. He smiled sweetly as Mary greeted him, her hands wringing nervously in front of her.

"Mrs. London, it's very nice to meet you."

"It's nice to meet you, too, Jericho. Can I get you something to drink? We've got some dinner left if you're hungry?"

"No, thank you, ma'am. Talisa and I ate a late lunch and I'm still pretty full."

Mary lifted her head in a slow nod. Her husband motioned for her to take a seat on the oversized ottoman beside him.

"So, what were you two talking about while I was gone?" Talisa asked, dropping down onto the sofa beside Jericho. She looked from her father to Jericho and back, giving her mother a wink as well.

"Jericho was telling me about them rebels in Africa." Herman shook his gray head. "That must have been something!" the man exclaimed.

"You young people have more nerve than we ever did," Mary interjected. "I was scared to death for Talisa going off to be in the jungles like that."

Talisa and Jericho laughed.

"Mom, there's just as much city in Africa as over here. I wasn't in the jungles. It wasn't like the Tarzan movies on television."

Mary sucked her teeth. "It was still dangerous. I don't care what you say."

"It was dangerous at times, Mrs. London. You had every right to be worried for Talisa. I was worried about her a few times myself," Jericho said.

Talisa rolled her eyes.

"So, when will you be going back to work, Jericho? Talisa told me you work at the hospital?" Mary asked.

Jericho nodded. "I'm actually in private practice with my father. He's a surgeon as well. But I won't be going back for a while, at least not here. I'm planning to spend a week or two recuperating from my accident, then I have to return to Uganda to finish out the obligations I started there."

Mary nodded as her gaze met Talisa's. The girl gave her half a smile and the matriarch could feel the muscles in her stomach starting to tighten. As if sensing her discomfort, Herman pressed a heavy hand against her shoulder, squeezing it gently beneath his palm. A nervous silence suddenly fell over the room. Both Herman and Mary watched as Jericho reached out for Talisa's hand. His eyes were shining brightly as his gaze met hers. He shifted forward in his seat, edging himself straighter, then cleared his throat before he spoke.

"Mr. London, Mrs. London, I know that Talisa has let you both know how close she and I have become over the last few weeks." Jericho glanced from her parents to her and back again before he continued. "But, I don't know if you're aware of just how much I love your daughter. I'm very much in love with Talisa. She's become the light of my life and I can't imagine spending another minute without her. I know how much Talisa loves you both and it's so important to me that you two feel I'm worthy of her."

Jericho paused, clasping his hands together in front of him. "I want to take care of your daughter. I want to spend the rest of my life making her happy. I know you've just met me and you don't know me very well yet, but I promise you both you won't be disappointed."

Jericho stood up, making his way to stand beside the couple. "Mr. London, Mrs. London, I've asked Talisa to marry me and with your permission, I'd like to marry her this week. Tomorrow, if we can."

Her eyes bulging, Mary turned toward Herman. She clutched the front of her husband's shirt, her body shaking noticeably. He pressed one palm over the back of her hand and the other palm to her cheek. He smiled, his gaze locked on his wife's face, an unspoken conversation flowing between them. When the woman turned back around, her tears had fallen past her lashes, dropping down against her round cheeks.

"My, my, my," she muttered under her breath.

Behind them Talisa sat with her mouth open in surprise, one hand clutched to her heart. Herman came to his feet. He extended his right hand, gripping Jericho's tightly in a firm handshake. His left hand tapped Jericho's shoulder. As he stepped back, Mary lifted herself up and wrapped Jericho in a warm embrace.

"Welcome to our family, Jericho." Herman grinned.

"I'm going to hold you to your word, son. You best take good care of my baby girl. She's the only one I have."

Jericho nodded. He moved back toward Talisa and dropped down onto one knee. As he did, Herman wrapped his wife in a tight hug, holding tight to her as they both stood smiling.

Reaching deep into the pocket of his khaki slacks, Jericho pulled a black velvet box from his pocket. Talisa's eyes widened with shock, speechless as her voice caught in her throat. The tears she'd been fighting suddenly burst forth, flooding her face as they poured from her eyes. Jericho reached for her hand and pulled it to his lips, kissing it gently.

"Talisa, I asked you once in Uganda with a paper ring and you said yes. This time I want to ask you properly." Jericho flipped the lid of the gift box open, exposing an exquisite, three-carat, diamond ring. Talisa's free hand flew from her heart to her mouth. Jericho grinned widely.

"Talisa London, I love you. I love you with every fiber in my body. Will you marry me? Will you be my wife?"

Falling to the floor beside him, Talisa wrapped her arms around his neck, her mouth drawn to his as she kissed him.

When they finally broke the embrace, Jericho chuckled. "I'm going to take that as a yes," he said as he leaned to kiss her tears away.

"Yes, yes, yes," Talisa chimed, staring in awe as Jericho eased the ring onto her ring finger.

When her parents both reached out to embrace them both, Talisa's tears fell for a second time, both her and her mother crying into each other's shoulders.

Herman shook his head. "You two need to stop now," he exclaimed. "You're supposed to be happy."

Talisa waved her head from side to side. "We are happy, Daddy. Very happy," she sobbed softly.

Both men laughed.

Mary wiped the back of her hand across her damp face. "Does this mean you're going back to that jungle with Jericho when he goes?"

Talisa nodded. "Yes, ma'am." She searched her mother's face, searching for some sense of the woman's mood.

Her mother's head bobbed in time with hers as her gaze shifted to Jericho. "I want my daughter married in a church. A Baptist church. And, I don't want my grand-babies to be born in no jungle. So, if Talisa gets pregnant, she will have to come home," the woman said, her tone stern.

Jericho laughed. "Yes, ma'am."

"Mommy!"

"Don't mommy me. I mean it, Talisa."

Talisa rolled her eyes.

"Were you serious about getting married tomorrow, son?" Herman asked.

"Yes, sir. We can get a license first thing in the morning and we can get married immediately after that."

"Jericho—" Talisa started.

The man moved to kiss her lips, stalling any objections she may have had.

Her mother objected for her. "Tomorrow won't work. You can get the license, but I think we need to make some plans. Talisa needs a nice dress. We have to make sure her friends can be there. I need to call the pastor at the church…"

Talisa held up her hand.

"I want to get married at the Wesley Foundation. It's not your church, Mom, but it is a church and it's a place that means a great deal to me. And, if he's available, I know Reverend Warren will marry us."

Both Talisa and her father could see Mary's jaw tighten ever so slightly and both stood ready for an outburst. Their eyes connected for just a brief moment before they turned their attention back to Mary, awaiting her response.

The woman nodded ever so slowly, then suddenly laughed, a deep chuckle that seemed to rise from some-place deep in her midsection. "Lord, have mercy!" she said after taking a quick moment to catch her breath. "It's a good thing I took my pills today!" She reached out to hug her daughter, wrapping her arms tightly around the woman. "Talisa, baby, I love you, and I want you to have whatever kind of wedding you want. Besides, I like the Reverend. He's a good man."

Joining in the hug, Jericho nodded, kissing Talisa and then her mother. "Talisa London, I think it's settled. You're getting married tomorrow!"

Herman London joined in the excitement. "Praise Jesus!" he said, slapping Jericho on the back. "I'm finally marrying off my daughter!"

Chapter 28

The telephone ringing pulled her from a sound sleep. It was still dark outside, the start of a new day barely beginning to peek over the horizon. Still dazed, Talisa struggled to find the telephone receiver. She and Jericho had fallen to sleep talking on the telephone and the receiver lay someplace lost beneath her covers. Finally locating the instrument, she palmed it in her hand and pulled it to her ear.

"Hello?"

"I get up early to exercise, take two minutes to check my e-mails, and find a message that you're getting married today! Is that how you tell your best friend?" Leila shouted into the phone.

Talisa laughed. "I tried to call you but you weren't answering. And a voice mail seemed so…impersonal."

"I cannot believe you. You're kidding me, right? This is a joke."

Talisa shook her head into the receiver. "No joke. Jericho and I are picking up the license this morning, and then we're heading over to Wesley to see if Reverend Warren will marry us this evening. Will you be my maid of honor?"

"I better be!"

"Good. I need you to help me find a dress. Please say you don't have to be in court today."

"I actually have a summary judgment hearing first thing this morning, then I'm canceling everything else. I can meet you at Wesley at lunchtime."

"That's perfect."

"Did you call Benita and Mya?"

"Not yet. I left them e-mail messages like I left you."

"Well, Benita will get hers as soon as she gets to her office. Mya will never get hers. I don't think she's turned her computer on in the last six months."

Talisa laughed. "Will you call them for me?"

"Don't you worry. I promise you we will all be there at noon."

"Thanks, Leila."

"Girl, that man must be some sort of good!"

The two women laughed.

"I'll see you soon."

"Wait until I tell my mother," Leila exclaimed as she hung up the telephone.

Talisa depressed the hook, then waited for a dial tone. When the familiar hum danced in her ear, she dialed quickly, then leaned back against the pillows as she waited for it to be answered on the other end.

Jericho answered on the second ring, seemingly wide-eyed and awake. "Good morning, baby girl," he said, his tone low, a deep growl that caused a shiver to run up her spine.

Talisa giggled. "Good morning to you, too. Did I wake you?"

"I don't think I slept. I told you it's lonely in this bed without you."

"So, Dr. Becton, what do you have planned today?"

"I'm marrying the most incredible woman in the world. She's gorgeous, intelligent and sexy, with a heart of pure gold."

"And she's marrying you?" Talisa said teasingly.

"That's what everyone keeps saying. It must be my devilishly handsome good looks. That and I know my way around a stethoscope. Girls like a nice stethoscope, especially when you warm it up first."

Talisa laughed. "You don't say."

Jericho smiled into the telephone. "I'm excited. How about you?"

"Nervous. A little."

"Why, baby?"

"I don't want to be a disappointment to you."

"That will never happen."

Talisa could feel his confidence spilling over the telephone lines. It warmed her, energized her, made her want the day to hurry by so that tomorrow when she woke up, she would be by Jericho's side, in his arms, Becton her new last name. She knew he felt it as well, the beauty of it shining brightly between them.

Jericho eased his body to the edge of his bed, swinging his legs off the side. "I will be there in an hour to get you," he said. "We'll go get some breakfast, then go get our license. The Fulton County courthouse opens at eight-thirty. I plan on being the first one in line."

Talisa smiled, nodding her head as if he could see her. "I'll be ready."

"I love you, Talisa," Jericho whispered softly.

Her smile widened, a full grin filling her face. "You have my heart, too, Jericho."

As Talisa hung up the telephone, the first shimmer of morning light billowed through the window blinds, shining brightly across the joy painting her expression.

Talisa had been banned from the Wesley Foundation building. Her morning visit with the minister and his staff had incited a rush of activity and excitement that she would not be privy to, having been forbidden to enter the premises until it was time for the ceremony. Reverend Warren had happily cancelled a meeting with the university's campus ministers to officiate over her and Jericho's impromptu wedding. Stevie and Johanna had enlisted the aid of the Wesley students to help prepare the building and the sanctuary, everyone thrilled to be a part of the festivities.

Mary sat anxiously in the front foyer of the student ministry waiting for Jericho's parents. Irene Becton had called her early that morning, overly excited about the impending union between their offspring. The two women had talked at length, making wedding plans and getting to know one another; motherhood and their love for their children, the initial bond between them.

She looked up as her husband sidled up to the seat beside her. He dropped a heavy palm against her knee, his fingers lingering against the hem of her skirt.

"How are you doing, Mama?" Herman asked

Mary shook her head. "This is happening so fast," she said, her voice a loud whisper.

The man nodded his agreement. "He's a good man, and he loves our little girl. Talisa is happy, Mary. That's all that matters."

Mary smiled, changing the subject. "I think it's time you retired, Herman. With Talisa leaving we should try to travel more, do things together. You should retire," she said firmly.

Herman sat in deep contemplation for a quick moment. A group of students had gathered outside the large double doors of the sanctuary, a young blond woman calling out directions. He watched as she checked off a list attached to a clipboard. "Maybe we can go to Africa. We could visit Talisa and Jericho," he finally responded.

Mary chuckled softly. "I don't know about that jungle now!" she exclaimed.

The man laughed with her as he leaned to wrap his arm around her shoulders. The front doors opening drew their attention as the Becton family glided inside, Jericho leading the way.

"Mr. and Mrs. London. Good morning!"

Herman extended his hand in greeting and Mary rose to give the young man a hug. A very attractive black woman and well-dressed white man stood grinning behind him. Mary smiled widely, extending her arms to wrap Jericho's mother in a warm embrace.

Irene hugged her back, laughing gleefully. "Mary, it's a pleasure. This is so exciting!"

The two patriarchs shook hands, introducing themselves. Jericho looked around the room waving to Clarissa and the students as they greeted them. "Is Talisa still here?" he asked.

Mary shook her head. "No, dear. She and her friends just left to go find their dresses."

Jericho nodded his disappointment as his mother laughed.

"She'll be back, son-shine!"

Jericho blushed, color filling his face. Elijah rolled his eyes, patting his son on the back.

Irene glanced down at the gold watch on her wrist. "Goodness," she exclaimed excitedly. "Six o'clock will be here before we know it. You boys need to go home and get your tuxedos pressed and ready for tonight. Mary, we have some things to do here, then I've made appointments for us to get our nails done."

Mary's eyes widened in surprise. "A manicure?"

Irene nodded. "I think you and I need some time to ourselves to just relax and talk. Our babies are getting married, and I don't know about you, but I didn't sleep a wink last night."

Herman gave his wife a quick hug. "Mary was up most of the night, too," he said as he gave the woman another quick squeeze.

"That settles it then," Irene said, taking Mary by the hand. "Jericho, take your fathers and get going. We will meet you men back here by four-thirty."

"Yes, ma'am."

"Mary, let's go check that things are well here and then you and I can take off as well."

"I think we should go shopping, too," Mary said with a wide smile. "This is definitely a good time for a new dress. Then maybe we can meet up with Talisa and the girls at the bridal shop and get a peek at what they're up to?"

Irene smiled back. "Mother, I like your thinking!"

The mood was light and cheery as the two women each picked out a new dress at a small dress shop Irene Becton was a frequent client of. After a quick lunch of Caesar salad and iced tea they headed to Irene's regular beauty salon and their scheduled appointments.

Sitting side by side in two pedicure chairs, both were enjoying the warm water swirling over their bare feet as two young Korean women filed and painted the length of their fingernails. The salon was painted a soothing shade of pale yellow, the walls adorned with framed prints of pretty hands and pretty feet.

"You should be very proud of your daughter," Irene said, glancing toward the other woman. "She's an amazing young woman."

Mary smiled sweetly. "Thank you. Talisa's always been a good girl."

"We spent a good deal of time together in Africa and she always spoke so highly of you and your husband. Your daughter loves you two very much."

Mary gave the woman a shy smile, treading her toes along the surface of the warm bath. A wave of anxiety suddenly flushed the brown of her complexion. Noting the sudden look of reservation that blessed the woman's expression, Irene moved to reassure her. "Talisa had wonderful things to say about you. I think that's why I feel like you and I already know each other so well."

Mary cut an eye toward the woman whose face was filled with a warming smile. She paused, her mouth opening and closing as she struggled to find the right words to share and explain what Talisa might have already revealed. "I wasn't always easy on my girl. Sometimes…" Mary hesitated. Her mind was suddenly like a slide show of images, the ugliness of her behavior playing out in panoramic vision within her mind's eye.

Mary could not even believe how horribly she had

treated her own child over the years, Talisa enduring her abuse without ever complaining. During many of her bouts her daughter had been more of a parent than she herself could have even imagined being. She sighed as she thought about her child and the joy that shimmered across her face since Jericho had come into her life.

Talisa had dated a young man in college who had made her happy and Mary had done everything in her power to destroy her child's joy. The straw that had broken her back had been when she'd discovered that Talisa had been intimate with the boy, giving away her virginity and her heart. Mary had berated her endlessly, had called her names no mother should ever call her child and still Talisa had endured. Talisa had loved her mother unfailingly and Mary hadn't done anything to prove herself worthy of it.

Irene reached her free hand out to tap Mary's forearm. "We do the best we can do, Mary. I know you did as well as any mother possibly could. Talisa is proof of that. It's obvious she grew up with a lot of love. And my son adores her. I have never seen him so happy."

Mary smiled. "He's a sweet boy."

"The two of them will be very good together."

Mary nodded her agreement. "I just don't want my grandbabies born over there in that jungle," she exclaimed.

Irene London laughed, her head bobbing up and down against her shoulders. "Mary, I was just thinking the same thing!"

The four friends were awash with excitement as they headed into Casa Di Moda for Brides, an exclusive bridal shop located in the heart of Buckhead. Between court and cancellations, Leila had managed to arrange a one-on-one consultation for them, negating Talisa's plans to head to their local mall to buy a simple white dress off the rack. A private collection of couture gowns selected especially for Talisa hung on padded satin hangers in wait.

Leila nodded her approval as she shook hands with the stylist who would be assisting them. "And this is Talisa London, our bride," Leila said as she made the introductions.

The petite redhead greeted Talisa warmly. "Congratulations, Ms. London. My name is Brittany, and we're delighted to be a part of your special day. Once you've made your selection, our seamstress will be right out to make any necessary alterations."

"Thank you."

Mya flipped through the row of silk and satin gowns. "I am so jealous," she exclaimed, pulling a strapless, slinky, straight-skirted number with lace and pearl beading from the rack. She held the gown up against her thin body, admiring her reflection in the full-length mirror on the opposite wall.

Benita shook her head, pulling the garment from Mya's hands and returning it back to the rack. "Well, I'm still in shock. Two days ago we were talking about meeting this man and today we get to meet him at your wedding ceremony. Are you sure about this, Talisa?"

Mya rolled her eyes. "Of course she's sure. He's a doctor. A surgeon!"

Talisa's head waved from side to side. "I'm sure because I love him and he loves me," she said, giving her friend a tight hug.

"Yeah, that, too," Mya responded, dropping down onto a padded cushion in the tastefully decorated room.

The women were interrupted as Brittany pushed a silver serving cart into the room. The top was laden with bottles of Evian water, a crystal pitcher of sparkling apple juice, and a platter of assorted cheeses, prosciutto, crackers, breads and fresh fruit. "Refreshments for you, ladies," Brittany chimed, her hands clasped in front of her. She turned to Talisa. "Ms. London, are you ready to get started?"

Excitement gleamed in Talisa's eyes as she nodded.

Three dresses later, Talisa's three friends stood in quiet awe, approval masking each of their faces. Leila smiled, her gaze meeting her best friend's as she nodded her head. "That's the one, Talisa. You look absolutely beautiful."

Talisa could feel the moisture forming behind her eyelids and she fought the sudden desire to cry tears of sheer joy. She turned toward Brittany and smiled. "I'll take this one," she said, stepping down off the pedestal.

The woman smiled back as she watched the four women embrace each other in one group hug. Gesturing behind her, she cleared her throat for their attention. "Ladies, this is our collection of bridesmaids gowns. While I help Ms. London out of her dress, please feel free to search through them until you find something you're ready to try on. Of course, with your time constraint we won't be able to order anything special."

Leila nodded. "Thanks, Brittany. We're not worried about matching."

Mya agreed. "As long as we look cute. That's all that matters," she said as she flipped through the silk and satin fabric swatches.

As Talisa made her way to the dressing room door, she turned back around to face her friends. They had each claimed her happiness as if it were their own and it shone on each of their faces, gleaming from their eyes into the room. Leila met her stare and held it, the two grinning broadly at each other. When Leila winked, her smile widening even more, Talisa could no longer hold back the tears she'd been trying to hold on to.

At precisely five-fifteen, the women finally came through the back door of the foundation, heads newly coiffed, nails freshly painted, the beginnings of their makeup applied. Talisa's mother greeted each of them as they entered. Mary kissed her daughter's cheek, then spun in a circle to show off her brand-new dress.

"How does the mother of the bride look?" she asked, her gaze sweeping over her surrogate daughters.

"Very nice, Mrs. London," Benita answered.

"I love your dress. You look gorgeous," Mya responded, admiring the silk dress and lace jacket the woman wore. The pale green color was flattering to her complexion and her hair and makeup were meticulous.

Mary leaned to kiss Talisa's cheek. "Is it okay, baby?"

Her daughter nodded. "You're beautiful, Mom!"

Mary grabbed the young woman's hand and guided them down the narrow hallway.

"You girls are getting dressed in Talisa's office," she said as they entered the room, closing the door behind them.

"Can't we go look at the sanctuary?" Talisa asked.

"No. They can go, but you can't. It's a surprise."

"Why?"

"We wanted it to be special. For you to see it as you're walking down the aisle. Irene and I have been working on this all afternoon. I can't wait for you to see what Jericho's mother was able to arrange. That woman is something else!"

There was a knock on the door and Irene Becton peeked her head inside. "Hello, ladies. May I join you?"

"Speak of the devil!" Mary said, gesturing for her to enter. "Irene, I just called your name."

Irene gave Mary a quick hug, then introduced herself to Talisa's friends. When the formalities were complete, she reached to kiss Talisa. "Talisa, we tried to catch up with you girls but you ladies were just too fast for us."

Mary grinned. "The nice woman at the bridal shop said you picked a beautiful gown."

Leila moved to give the woman a warm hug. "She did, Mrs. London, and I'm sure it's exactly what you would have picked for her."

Talisa squeezed her mother's hand. "Mom, you're not upset that you weren't with me, are you?"

Mary shook her head no. "Not at all, Talisa. You sure can't plan a wedding in one day and be everywhere at the same time. I know you girls did good. Irene and I had our mother responsibilities to take care of. Didn't we, Irene?"

Irene smiled. "Yes, we did, and we had a wonderful time together this afternoon getting ready. This is so exciting!"

"I'm so nervous," Talisa responded, dropping down into an upholstered chair. "I'm shaking."

"No time for that now, dear. You need to get dressed. Your mother and I can't wait to see the dresses you girls found. Can we, Mary?"

Mary nodded in agreement. "You girls get dressed now. Irene and I need to check on a few more things, then we'll be ready to start the ceremony."

Talisa shook her head as the two women kissed them each and then rushed from the room chattering excitedly.

"Well, I guess they're getting along just fine. And I was worried," Talisa laughed as Leila laughed with her.

"It's good to see your mother so happy, Talisa," Leila said, Mya and Benita echoing the sentiments.

Minutes later, when both matriarchs knocked for the second time, they were all dressed, Mya putting the finishing touches on Talisa's makeup. As her mother entered Talisa stood up and turned around to face her. The two women smiled broadly at each other.

Mary clasped her hands together in front of her, fighting the rush of tears that suddenly wanted to spill from her eyes. Irene reached a warm hand out, pressing it against the woman's back, her own tears teasing the inside of her eyelids.

Talisa's dress was white satin. A simple sheath cut that fell to an empire waist and stopped just above her ankle. The bodice was embroidered with pearl beads, a quiet accent that added just a hint of shimmer. A simple white satin pump with a moderate heel completed her attire. The woman was stunning.

Her freshly manicured hands reached up to finger the pearl earrings that adorned her ears, a gift from her maid of honor. "How do I look?" Talisa asked, looking from one mother to the other.

Mary nodded, unable to find her voice for fear she would burst out crying. Irene smiled. "Beautiful, Talisa. Absolutely beautiful," she said softly. "All of you girls look incredible," she said, smiling upon the three women standing beside the bride.

Mya and Benita grinned as Leila wrapped them each in a warm embrace. Their dresses were similar in color, varying shades of a gorgeous cobalt hue in three different designs and lengths that flattered and complemented their individual figures.

A knock against the wooden door interrupted the moment and Talisa's father called to them from the other side.

"Are you girls ready yet? I'm ready to walk my daughter down the aisle now!"

Talisa laughed as her mother pulled the door open. Making his way inside, Herman grinned, clasping his wife's hand beneath his own. "Well, I'll be…" he said, his head bobbing up and down. He wiped at a tear that had fallen against his cheek.

"We're all ready, Daddy," Mary said.

Herman leaned to kiss Talisa's cheek, holding her tightly as if he were not ready to let her go. Talisa fell into the warmth of the embrace, very much her father's daughter as memories of their time together flooded through her.

"I love you, Daddy," she whispered into his ear.

The man nodded. "I love you, too, pumpkin."

As the group made their way into the sanctuary, the pipe organ was playing softly. Talisa could smell the flowers before she saw them and when they threw open the sanctuary doors to welcome her, she was in awe. She gripped her father's hand tightly, suddenly overcome with a wealth of emotion. Leila smiled widely, reaching to kiss her best friend's cheek as the processional began.

Irene Becton had filled the room with every available flower that existed in the town of Atlanta. Between her contacts and the footwork of the Wesley students, they'd scavenged every floral shop, supermarket and sidewalk vendor. Even a few gardens hadn't survived their ravage as they'd plucked every stem they could. The room was overflowing with arrangements, flowers in every imaginable shade in the color spectrum. The flowers were complemented by a multitude of candles that flickered light and warmth around the altar behind Reverend Warren who stood with his Bible in hand, dressed in his white covenant robe and embroidered stole. Against the backdrop of the stained glassed windows the room was breathtaking.

Jericho stood in wait at the minister's side, dressed handsomely in a black tuxedo suit, white dress shirt and silver satin tie. Jericho's father, similarly attired, waited beside him, hands clasped behind his back, his pride-filled expression beaming around the room. The Wesley students filled the pews and they rose to their feet when the organist stopped playing and three flutists began to play "The Wedding March."

The moment he saw her headed in his direction, it took every ounce of composure Jericho had to keep from rushing down the aisle to pull her into his arms. Talisa was breathtaking, he thought, as he wiped at the tears blinding his view. She embodied everything he could have ever wished for in a wife and the expression across his face and hers spoke volumes. If there had been any doubts, any single moment of questioning whether they were doing the right thing or not, all was suddenly gone. Both knew as they reached for the other's hand, Reverend Warren asking who gave the woman to be wed, that their union was as right as rain against a summer drought.

Second chance for romance...

When
Valentines
Collide

Award-winning author
ADRIANNE
BYRD

Therapists Chante and Michael Valentine agree to a "sex-therapy" retreat to save their marriage. At first the seminar revives their passion—but their second chance at love is threatened when a devastating secret is revealed.

"Byrd proves again that she's a wonderful storyteller."
—*Romantic Times BOOKreviews* on *The Beautiful Ones*

*Available the first week of February,
wherever books are sold.*

KIMANI™
ROMANCE

www.kimanipress.com

Essence **bestselling author**

DONNA HILL

If I Were Your
Woman

The second story in the Pause for Men *miniseries*.

A messy affair left Stephanie Moore determined
to never again mix business with pleasure. But her
powerful attraction to Tony Washington has her
reconsidering—even though she suspects Tony may be
married. She'll need the advice of her Pause for Men
partners to help her sort out her dilemma.

Pause for Men—four fabulously fortysomething divas
rewrite the book on romance.

*Available the first week of February,
wherever books are sold.*

**KIMANI
ROMANCE**

www.kimanipress.com

Where had all the magic gone?

FOREVER, FOR ALWAYS, FOR LOVE

Award-winning author

KIM SHAW

Determined to rekindle the passion in her failing marriage, Josette Crawford undergoes a major makeover. But when life changes threaten to derail her love train, she and hubby, Seth, wonder whether their love is strong enough to keep them together forever.

*Available the first week of February,
wherever books are sold.*

KIMANI™
ROMANCE

www.kimanipress.com

USA TODAY bestselling author

BRENDA JACKSON

The third title in the Forged of Steele miniseries...

Beyond Temptation

Sexy millionaire Morgan Steele will settle for nothing less than the perfect woman. And when his arrogant eyes settle on sultry Lena Spears, he believes he's found her. There's only one problem—the lady in question seems totally immune to his charm!

Only a special woman can win
the heart of a brother—
Forged of Steele

**Available the first week of January
wherever books are sold.**

KIMANI™
ROMANCE

A brand-new story of love
and drama from...

national bestselling author

MARCIA
KING-GAMBLE

All
ABOUT
ME

Big-boned beauty Chere Adams
plunges into an extreme makeover
to capture the eye of fitness fanatic
Quentin Abraham—but the more
she changes, the less he seems to
notice her. Is it possible Quentin's
more interested in the old Chere?

*Available the first week of January
wherever books are sold.*

KIMANI™
ROMANCE

www.kimanipress.com   KPMKG0010107

Winning her love wouldn't be so easy
the second time around…

HERE
and
NOW

Favorite author
Michelle Monkou

When Chase Dillard left Laura Masterson years ago to pursue
his Olympic dreams, he broke her heart. Now that they're
working together, Chase has lots of ground to make up if he
wants to win her back.

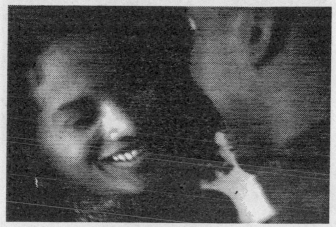

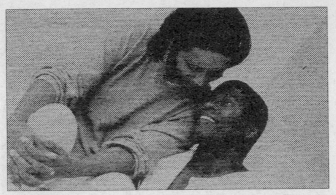

Celebrate Valentine's Day with this collection of heart-stirring stories…

Love in Bloom

"These three authors have banded together to create some excellent reading."
—*Romantic Times BOOKreviews*

FRANCINE CRAFT,
LINDA HUDSON-SMITH,
JANICE SIMS

Three beloved Arabesque authors bring romance alive in these captivating Valentine tales of first love, second chances and promises fulfilled.

Available the first week of January wherever books are sold.

ARABESQUE®

www.kimanipress.com

KPLIB0620107